UNEASY IN
NEW ORLEANS

CAROL CARSON

Cover Design and Interior format by The Killion Group
http://thekilliongroupinc.com

ACKNOWLEDGEMENTS

Thanks to my fellow MORWA writers who have kept me propped up all these years, with a special shout-out to Julie Beard, Eileen Dreyer, Angie Fox, Shirl Henke, Jeannie Lin, Shawntelle Madison, Karyn Witmer-Gow and Pat Rice, in absentia.

Thank you to Nicole Norris for a superb beta read, Nam Nguyen for the excellent developmental editing advice and Dana Waganer for perfect proofreading. Thanks to Kim and Jenn at the Killion Group for the spectacular cover.

A special thank you and a big hug to my long-suffering critique partner, Megan Kelly. Thanks for great friendship, great input and the great big fat red pen.

As always, to Darl. I love you more than I can say. I couldn't do this without you.

To Corey and Patrick, just for being you.

Nothing is impossible with God. Luke 1:37

PROLOGUE

That impossible girl, Finnigan Jones, paid absolutely no attention to him. He sparkled. He glimmered. He shimmered. He even swayed in front of her, waving his arms above his head like a traffic cop. Nothing. She didn't blink an eye.

Finn, uber-focused while concocting an original barbecue sauce in her culinary class couldn't see a perfectly good apparition right in front of her. Even in the high-ceilinged room with dazzling sunshine bouncing off the gleaming fixtures through the tall windows.

Mon Dieu. What was a ghost supposed to do?

John Michael Winters, once-upon-a-time New Orleans chef extraordinaire, groaned. Out of all the people in this class, he selected Finn to mentor because she was going to be a special chef. He knew these things. She was the best student, of course, but if she couldn't see him...?

From a stainless steel food shelf, he plucked a tamarind pod, drifted back in front of her and nudged it against her selected pile of ingredients.

Her eyes fluttered and she frowned. She pried open the brown pod and sniffed. Wrinkling her cute little nose, she retrieved a bit of the pulp from inside and took a tiny taste. "Hmm...Distinctive flavor," she murmured. "Sweet and sour, but, um, I really, *really* don't remember picking it up for my sauce."

She stole a quick peek around the class, as if anyone else besides him would have put the unusual spice in front of her. Taking one more shot at grabbing her notice, John Michael did his best dance step, one he'd been well known for in his alive days—two shuffles left, two shuffles right, then a complete swirl and a deep bow. After his magnificent performance, he launched away and disappeared from her view.

"Oh, my God," she whispered, her eyes wide. She placed a shaking hand over her heart. "I'm seeing ghosts. I knew I shouldn't have had that second Peach Bellini daiquiri last night."

He had her attention now.

When the class finished, Finn, both figuratively and literally, exchanged her perfectly wonderful chef hat for a perfectly awful neon pink cap sporting the logo *Explore NOLA Tours*. She dashed from the classroom. She could at least have thanked him for the tamarind. It would earn her barbecue sauce an A plus in *Soups, Starches and Sauces*. Oh, well. Kids these days. He'd have to catch her on the flipside.

CHAPTER ONE

Was that a dead body?

Drawing a ragged breath, Finn Jones blinked hard to clear her vision.

She wanted to blame her eyesight, the harsh sunlight or the glare off the asphalt pavement. She even wanted to blame her cheap, lousy-ass sunglasses. None of it worked.

She could still see *it.*

Her heart sped up. Perspiration trickled between her boobs. Gulping, she swallowed her dread. In the midst of conducting a walking tour through the French Quarter with eight, honest-to-God paying customers, she didn't dare let them know panic was about to take her away like an alien abduction.

She darted a glance in their direction. Busy talking about how hungry they were and whether the hotdogs from the Lucky Dog vendor nearby were any good, they didn't notice.

How could they be so clueless? How could they not see it?

She'd seen dead bodies before—in Uncle Ed's funeral home. Until now, she'd never seen one in its natural state. Those other earthly remains had been dead for several days and embalmed. They were laid out nice and neat, appropriate wax-like figures, in a satin-lined coffin at Big Ed Finnigan's Funeral Parlor and House of Rest.

Corralling her meandering thoughts, Finn moved her sunglasses to the top of her head. She closed her eyes, took a deep breath and then opened them again. Her throat narrowed and she swallowed around a huge lump. From her position next to the two-story building, he—and she was sure it was a man—looked pale, stiff and decidedly dead. The body slumped across the gallery railing on the second story of the converted apartment building, one arm dangling over the side. *Dear. God.* And this, after seeing a ghost in class earlier.

On a muggy summer day when dead bodies had no business scaring the bejesus out of her, the corpse draped above her head like Spanish moss looked nothing like any she'd seen at a funeral.

She took another covert look, and then peeked at her tourists. Their interest was no longer on lunch. They were staring at her, no doubt wondering why she was sweating like a teenage boy on his first date.

Finn diverted their attention away from her by pointing across the alley to a fountain, hoping the words coming out of her mouth made sense. Pray God they noticed nothing out of the ordinary.

Cadavers weren't on her itinerary of historical, interesting sights in New Orleans. Although the French Quarter boasted plenty of bars and great restaurants, intriguing characters and architecture unseen anywhere else, tourists didn't generally come to see dead people. At least she hoped not. Her mind raced with what to do next.

"What is that up there?"

Finn groaned. The slender young woman, half of a honeymooning couple from Atlanta, had her gaze fixed on the gallery where the body drooped, horrifyingly dead to anyone with half a brain. It appeared the bride had all of hers.

"A lovely example of cast iron, isn't it?" Finn lied, unwilling to drag her customers into something dreadful. Simple wooden dowels made up the railing but who could tell the difference from where they stood. After all, everyone recognized the French Quarter by its beautiful ironwork.

The newlywed pointed, shading her eyes against the early afternoon sun. "No, that wasn't what I meant, although it is pretty. Up there, doesn't that look like a body to you?"

Her husband, a tall gangly guy who reminded Finn of a younger version of the actor Jeff Goldblum said, "Sure does, Sugar."

With difficulty, Finn managed not to curse out loud.

One of the three women whose undertaker husbands—what were the odds?—were here attending a conference said, "My stars, it surely does look like a man."

The honeymooning husband turned to Finn, disbelief on his face. "Is it a prop or something? To make New Orleans look more authentic?"

Authentic? Did he think this was normal? Finn was many things, but slow on the uptake she wasn't. She jumped on his farfetched idea. "Right! That's exactly what it is. Making sure you're paying attention."

"It looks so real," one of the undertaker's wives murmured, blinking over her bifocals as she stared upward.

"Quite right," agreed another, turning toward her friends.

"Doesn't it?" Finn said as she began backing up Toulouse Street. "I'm afraid it's time to move on. Over here is what they used to call a *garconniere*." She continued her story. As a guide with Explore NOLA Tours, she'd described this area hundreds of times; she didn't need to look at the sights while her mind sputtered with ideas of what she should do about the corpse.

She spoke a few more minutes and hoped they didn't notice how she cut her talk short. She herded them across the street to a small grocery where they could buy soda or ice cream. When they disappeared inside, she whipped out her cell phone.

"Jack? It's Finn."

"Hey, *chere,* what can I do you for?"

"Jack," she whispered, "I saw a body, a real, honest-to-God dead body."

"Uh-huh. Hey, Cordry, you got that warrant ready?" Papers shuffled in her ear as he continued, "Finn, what was that again?"

"I just saw a dead body during my walking tour," she said raising her voice. No one near her even looked her way. New Orleans. Go figure.

"Come on. You sure?"

"Sure what? That it was a dead body?" This was so typical of Jack. He never took her seriously, never had in twenty years and never would in twenty more.

"This is New Orleans. You know we got all kinds here. Sure it wasn't a mannequin or a blow-up doll or even someone passed out after one too many frozen daiquiris? Remember when you called me last Halloween about another dead body?"

"Jack."

"And it turned out to be a damned fool's idea of a joke on his brother? And how about during Mardi Gras? I seem to recall a naked tattooed woman sleeping in some lucky guy's lap who you thought was being strangled."

"Jack."

"Yeah, *chere*?" he said, obviously distracted and not paying the least attention to what she was saying because, okay, she admitted it, she did sort of, maybe, have a history with him.

"Listen to me." She paused. "Are you listening?"

"Yeah, I'm listenin'."

"You've known me my whole life. Do I sound like a hysterical female right now? This time it's real." She didn't give him time to reply. "My tour is almost over and then I'm going back. Meet me at the northwest corner of Dauphine and Toulouse. I'll be the live one." She punched her phone disconnecting the call. Men.

Okay, she'd done her civic duty by letting the police know. If hardheaded Jack wasn't listening, it was his problem. She hoped he got in trouble. Damn him. On a good day, she raced to get home, clean up and get to culinary class on time. Check out dead bodies? No time.

Was it wrong to wait? Too bad. She couldn't help it. She needed to get rid of her tour group first. After all, *he* wasn't going anywhere.

She wished it could be easily explained so Jack could have his usual fit when he found out she tried to bring him out for no reason. Nevertheless, a reason beckoned—a cold, dead reason.

When Jack arrived, he could call *CSI: New Orleans* or whoever needed to be contacted besides his obnoxious self.

Rushing like a lunatic, Finn finished her tour, collected her tips and left her tourists in front of the praline shop to venture through the rest of the streets of the Quarter on their own. Ordinarily, before she released them she walked them over to The One and Only Voodoo Shop, owned by her bachelor uncles, Neville and Finis Bettencourt, who appreciated the business. Today, not only did she not want to delay her investigation, she didn't want the tour group to mention the body to her aging uncles. She loved them dearly but they would waste no time dashing around and bringing voodoo medicine to chase away evil or help the deceased find his way unimpeded to heaven, which would inevitably draw a crowd of gawking people.

Instead, she headed back to Toulouse where her *new best friend* awaited.

She ran, her mind telling her to slow down. When she turned the corner of Dauphine, she looked up out of breath. *Still there.* She stared at the nearly eight-foot high brick wall separating the courtyard from where she stood. Thick rampant vines clambered over the jagged edges. Leaning on the hood of a car to get a better look, she yanked her hand away when the heated metal burned her palm.

"Damn," she murmured. She didn't want to investigate. She didn't want to wait here on the street for Jack to show up either. If it turned out to be a mannequin or a blow-up doll as he suggested, she'd look ridiculous. Yet again. She could imagine the wicked hand of practical joker, Pete Lamb, in this. He worked for a competing tour company and wasn't above this sort of prank for his own amusement. She should have considered this earlier, but her scrambled mind refused to cooperate.

Heaving a sigh, she walked to the alley-side of the property, and then stepped up onto the bumper of a VW van parked next to the wall, and with some effort boosted herself over the top. She stumbled into the grassy courtyard scraping her knee on the way down and dropping her over-stuffed backpack. From her prone position, she appeared to be alone. Traffic on the other side of the wall resounded, muted voices called from the street but otherwise all remained quiet.

Finn climbed to her feet expecting to be caught, but

no one came running out to harass her. She tiptoed across the grass to the wooden stairs then started up. With each creak of the rickety steps, she waited for someone to holler at her. Or worse.

When she got to the top, she hesitated. She ran her sweaty palms down the thighs of her blue jean shorts. God, what was she doing? Every instinct she possessed told her to wait for Jack, but she continued on, unwilling to admit she needed his assistance. After all the body was dead. It couldn't hurt her now, and if she'd learned nothing else from TV cop shows, she wouldn't touch him or anything around him.

She clutched her backpack against her chest and advanced along the gallery past three apartment doors. She stopped cold when she got close enough to the body to stare at his pale, un-moving face. She frowned and leaned closer. He looked familiar.

A quick shuffle of feet sounded behind her. She turned around.

A man stood above her holding a gigantic gun in his raised hand, the light blocking his face. It was the last thing she saw.

Finn woke with her face pressed into the splintered wooden floor of the gallery, the pungent scent of frying onions prickling her nose. A throbbing headache pierced the back of her skull. She sat up, woozy and confused. Fingering the goose egg rising on her head, she looked both ways down the length of the gallery. No dead body. No live body. No body at all. She was alone. Her backpack lay beside her, undisturbed.

Climbing to her feet on shaky legs, she grabbed her fallen cap and backpack and took herself down the stairs and out into the courtyard. She pulled a metal lawn chair over to the wall and climbed over, every bone in her body complaining.

Reluctantly, Finn headed for the police station two

blocks away on Royal. She was going to kill Jack. Why hadn't he shown up? What would he think when she told him her story? She cringed. To him Finn was Emmy's scrawny little sister, making her way through life telling ghost stories to the tourists. Even at the ripe old age of twenty-five, the recently skinned knee proved him right.

Finn walked past the iron fence surrounding the Eighth District police headquarters, her heart thudding. *All she had to do was walk inside and tell Jack what happened.* An unknown assailant knocked her unconscious, her so-called dead body disappeared, and bad guys might want to silence her. How difficult could that be?

She pulled open the door. Guilt rolled over her, even though she'd done nothing wrong. It was either the suspicious looks she received from the officers milling around, or the rank odor of stale coffee and nervous energy. Either way, they stared at her as if she'd committed a major crime.

A stiff smile plastered on her face, she lifted her head and marched into the detectives' arena.

She spied Jack Boyle standing with one lean hip angled against his cluttered desk munching on a Po Boy sandwich. He'd taken off his suit coat and stood with the sleeves of his white dress shirt rolled up and his tie loosened. His dark blonde hair brushed the tops of his ears, and appeared as if he'd run his hands through the thick strands more than once. As usual, he looked good enough to eat.

"Hey, boys, look what the cat dragged in," he said between bites. "Finnigan Jones, New Orleans' most infamous ghost hunter tracking down spirits for the tourists."

Yep, that's where she stood with this particular New Orleans homicide detective. If the look Jack gave Finn when she crept into his male dominated space was any indication, she was in for a long day. Longer than it had been already.

"Where the hell were you?"

"I got tied up." He grinned at his partner, Cordry, who chuckled good-naturedly. "Not literally, unfortunately. A guy can dream though, can't he?"

"Have at it, Boyle. Whatever floats your boat." Sitting at a desk across from Jack, the forty-something Cordry gave Finn a thumbs up. His face crinkled with a grin. She had no idea what his first name was—Jack never used one.

"I need a minute, Jack." She put her hands on her hips. "This is important."

"Sure thing. What is it?" He set his sandwich on his desk and turned to face the other men in the room, wiping his hands on a napkin. He winked at the lanky sloe-eyed detective he called partner. "You've misplaced one of your tourists? Or found a ghost you can add to your Quarter itinerary?"

A snicker erupted from the corner of the room.

"Don't be such an ass."

His eyes widened in mock horror. "Who? *Moi?*"

Jack was as honest as anyone she'd ever met. Brutally honest. He was also too darn good-looking and too big a smart ass for his own damn good. And he knew it. She wanted to slap the smirk off his face. If her head didn't hurt so much, she would have.

She and her older sister Emmy, Jack and his younger brother, Tommy, had all played together in the same Irish Channel neighborhood as kids. Two houses apart, they practically lived at each other's homes. Jack had bedeviled Finn since he'd learned how to string a sentence together. Once, she'd harbored feelings of lust toward him. It passed abruptly at the naïve age of fifteen when she discovered him with Emmy, on the same bed she shared with her sister. The vivid image of Jack's pale, muscular rump bouncing on the bedsprings stayed with her for several years. It was a fine backside, but her future vision of a white house, picket fence and miniature Jack Boyles playing in the yard faded forever.

"What's the problem?"

"Do you remember our phone conversation of, oh, half an hour ago?" Finn ground her back teeth in frustration.

He nodded, squinting at her, as if she might disappear in front of his eyes. Maybe he was hoping. He picked up his sandwich, took a bite and stared at her over the paper wrapping.

"I need to speak with you," she said. "Privately."

Jack dropped the sandwich on his desk, took Finn by the elbow and walked her into an interrogation room. He closed the door behind him and leaning against it, folded his arms over his chest. "Shoot."

She, too, crossed her arms. She'd heard somewhere mimicking another person's body language showed interest. Hopefully, he didn't know that so-called fact and misinterpret it as sexual interest. Finn merely wanted to grab the upper hand. As if she could ever do it with him. "Remember? I said I saw a dead body."

"I thought you were kidding."

"Did it sound like I was kidding? It was real and I expected you to do something about it."

Jack's mouth quirked into a slight grin. One eyebrow arched in question. "Oh? Like what, *chere*?"

Could he be more insufferable? She barely refrained from rolling her eyes. "I was giving my usual tour. We stopped on the banquette so I could show them the gallery on the back of an apartment building. You know, the gallery, the courtyard, a little local architectural history."

Jack rubbed his chin with the side of his index finger, then nodded. "Okay, go on."

"Anyway the courtyard was empty, but this odd shadow appeared above. It looked like someone bent over the rail on the gallery. When I studied it closer, I thought it was a body, a very dead body. Even though I was scared spitless, seeing a dead body is kinda unsettling, you know, I got my tourists' attention back to the building on the other side of the courtyard. With ten minutes of the tour left I finished up, after I called you."

His face sobered. "Okay, so maybe I should have paid closer attention."

"Thank you." She continued, her voice shaking. "I went back to the scene of the crime-"

"Scene of the crime?" He shook his head. "You've been watching too much TV."

"—thinking you'd be there to help me investigate. I figured the body wasn't going anywhere."

"You shouldn't be *investigating* anything."

Now was probably not the right time to tell him she'd taken a part-time job with Tommy, a private investigator, for late night surveillance. Tourism had been off since Hurricane Katrina emptied the streets of people, particularly the tourists, and she needed the cash. "I've seen dead bodies before."

"Yeah, at Big Ed's. All dressed up in their fancy clothes, and laying in a casket. Not the same thing." He snorted but his gaze remained serious.

Recalling the scene, she grimaced. "No, it wasn't the same thing."

"Whatever. I ask again, how can you be sure it was a dead body?"

"Well, I can't now, it's gone."

"Gone?" He frowned. "What do you mean gone?"

"I went back after my tour. I thought you'd be there,

but you weren't, so I climbed over the wall to take a closer look and it wasn't there anymore." She tapped her foot in agitation.

He slapped his forehead. "Did you even stop to think a bad guy might still be around?"

"No."

"And can we add trespassing to your other offenses? What the hell do you want me to do about all this now?" He threw his hands up.

"Investigate. Isn't that what they pay you for?"

"Yeah. Real homicides. Not some crazy story about a dead body which isn't anywhere to be found." He slanted a look at her skinned knee, then up at her cap with Explore NOLA Tours printed in neon pink, and the wavy red curls escaping from beneath. He shook his head and blew out a slow breath.

"Couldn't you look for blood or some other forensic evidence?" she asked.

"Did you see blood?"

"Maybe, Detective Boyle. I was a little rattled."

"Now don't go all snippy on me, Finn." He pointed to the shadowed inside window in the room, then took her by the elbow and steered her out the door away from prying ears. From the gesture, she figured he meant they might be alone in an interrogation room, but it didn't mean someone wasn't listening on the other side of the wall. She appreciated the gesture, but she would never say so. After all, he humiliated her by letting the entire squad room think he thought she was a nut job.

Without another word, they walked outside into the hot sunshine where he sat her down on the concrete ledge, which held in place the wrought iron fence surrounding the building. When he looked around and saw they were alone, he stood over her, leaned down and said, "I'll take a look as soon as I can get away, I promise. You're right. It's my job."

"Thanks, Jack. I'd feel better about it." She winced before telling him the other news about her foray into police detection. "There is one part, though, I kinda left out."

"Damn. I knew it." He rubbed his palms down his face. He stared at her, his clear, blue-eyed gaze focused and intense. "What is it?"

"When I went back to check on the body, somebody clobbered me over the head."

He sat down beside her, never taking his gaze from hers. "What? Are you kidding me? Are you okay?"

Finn tugged on his shirtsleeve. "Shush. Someone will hear."

"Who? Well, damn, Finn." Concern etched lines on his familiar face. "Are you okay?" he asked again.

"Other than a roaring headache and a lump on the back of my head, I think I'll live." She swept a finger over the goose egg beneath the edge of her cap. Still there and growing.

"This changes everything," Jack said, frowning. He took her chin in his hand and turned her head studying her eyes. Gingerly he brushed the fingers of his other hand over the lump. He grimaced.

Finn slumped back against the fence. "Finally you take me seriously."

"*Chere*, you're in way over your head here."

"I know," she murmured. "I know."

"Could you identify your assailant?"

"Probably not but the dead guy kinda looked familiar."

"Familiar how?"

"I don't know exactly, except it's how when you see someone out of context, like the druggist is eating at the same restaurant, and he looks familiar but you can't place him. That's kind of how it feels."

"I don't like the sound of any of this. Whoever hit you can probably identify you, probably knows you saw something. You could identify the body, at least."

"I suppose you're right."

"You might be in danger now." He gave her a pointed stare with those cool blue eyes of his.

"I don't want to admit it, but I know." Actually, she didn't feel like thinking about it, much less talking about it. Each word pierced her head like an ice pick to the brain. All she wanted to do was go home, swallow a handful of aspirin and soak in a hot tub. "I know."

"I'll investigate but first you have to promise me something."

Uh-oh. "Oh, boy."

"Don't worry. It doesn't involve sex, unless, of course," he gave her a devilish grin, "it's what you want. I've been known to cure many problems, even worse than a little bump on the head."

Finn punched him on the arm. "That's so not what I want. What happened to Bitsy?"

He sighed, releasing her chin. "She left me for greener pastures."

"You mean for a man who could commit?"

He clutched his hand to his chest. "You sure know how to wound a guy."

"Not you. You've got a tough hide."

"That's me. Those good Catholic nuns beat it into me. Too bad you didn't get the same treatment. Maybe your head wouldn't be hurting like a bitch right now."

"How true."

He grinned. "Bitsy wasn't much good in the sack anyway."

Finn groaned. "I could have gone my whole life without knowing that, Detective. She was pretty, though."

"You thought so?" He pursed his lips. "Tell you

what? I'll come over for a drink when I get off."

"Why? And do you really think I should be drinking."

"So we can compare notes and I can make sure you're okay, but no, you're right. You shouldn't be drinking."

"Ha. What do you want?"

His right brow rose in disbelief. "Now, why would you say such a thing?"

"I know you, Jack. You always want something."

"Not with you, I don't."

"No, never with me." Sad to admit but undeniably true. She hadn't fantasized about the two of them more than, oh, a thousand times since she'd seen him in the altogether. But she was safe—he knew she wouldn't take his flirting seriously or expect anything from him.

"Tonight all I want is the pleasure of your company."

"Yeah. Right."

"I'll give you a break since your head hurts. We'll meet in a neutral place; say six-thirty in the upstairs bar at the Riverside on Bourbon. We'll laugh at the tourists trying to sneak peeks into the strip clubs."

Finn shook her throbbing head. "I don't know."

"Take two aspirin and lay down 'til then. I'll buy."

"Aren't you the generous one."

Jack whispered in her ear, "I make it a practice. See you at six-thirty, *chere*."

He started to turn away, then said, "I'm writing up an official report. Whatever else happened, you were assaulted."

He wrapped an arm around her shoulder and kissed her cheek. She reached up and tugged on his ear.

"Ow."

"You can be such a jerk, Jack. You should have been there."

"Yeah," he said, ducking his head but keeping one eye on her. "I feel bad about it, I do, but how'd I know you'd go and get yourself hurt? I was caught up in an ongoing murder investigation, Cordry went mental on me, and in all the confusion I forgot about your call."

"This is your idea of an apology?"

He held out his hands, palms up. "Best I got. Doesn't mean I don't love you."

"Jack."

"I can't help teasing. You make it so easy."

Feeling a bit wounded she asked, "Teasing me?"

"Especially you."

"What do you mean?"

"I'm no shrink. I think it's called flirting."

"You need to work on your technique."

"You're probably right." He winked as he turned to go.

Finn stood up and trudged down the street, the cacophony of the riverboat calliope slamming her eardrums. She waved as she rounded Royal and headed toward the river to catch her streetcar. "See you at six-thirty."

"I'll be there, Nancy Drew."

"Butthead," she muttered beneath her breath. Still, through the agony of her aching head, she couldn't help but smile.

Finn lived in the maid's quarters, a tiny doll-like cottage, behind her aunt's elegant, white Greek Revival style antebellum Garden District home. Hers was not the most spacious place, but the price was right. Rent-free. Aunt Gert liked having Finn close by and she figured having another person around would keep away intruders. Why? Finn didn't have a clue. Living in the quiet, genteel neighborhood was more than worth a few nights spent in the company of Gert and her multitude of cats. And her massive Garfield memorabilia collection.

Because Carnival Cruise ships sailed from the New Orleans riverfront, Aunt Gert cruised once a month searching for suitors and Finn did cat-sitting duties free.

With a waterproof pillow propped behind her neck, Finn closed her eyes and let the heat of the bath water soothe her aching head and tense body. Unfortunately, even the pop and crackle of the fragrant orange sherbet bath bubbles couldn't keep terrifying thoughts of her mortality from her stricken mind. *My God. I could have been killed.*

She tried to think of other things, things she loved—chocolate layer cake, Oreo cookies, her mom's shrimp gumbo. She must be hungry. She tried thinking of sex but it had been so long since she'd actually made love with a man, food seemed like a more realistic fantasy.

She reached over the side of the tub for her towel. When she couldn't locate it by feel, she scanned the floor. Where was the damn thing? Leaning over she saw it. How did it get behind the leg of the old-fashioned claw foot tub?

Before she could get to the towel, the squeaky doorknob turned. Finn yelped. Anticipating more mayhem against her already beleaguered body, she frantically searched the bathroom for a weapon as the door inched open. Her fingers latched onto the plunger behind the toilet. If nothing else, the ick factor might keep her tormenter at bay.

"Why are you taking a bubble bath in the middle of the afternoon?"

Surprised to see her sister, Debbie, Finn released a long sigh. She hadn't seen her in six months, but was thankful it was someone she knew. Finn dropped the plunger. "It's not the middle of the afternoon."

"Is so."

"Are you alone, or should I be grabbing my towel?"

"Just little ol' me."

So, what did the little hellion look like today? Debbie, her seventeen-year-old younger sister, was supposed to be in Florida living with their retired parents. She was an "oops baby" coming along when their parents were closing in on fifty. Needless to say, she was spoiled rotten. "Hello, Debs. Good to see you. Where's Mom and Dad?"

"Home. In Florida."

"How'd you get here? Steal Dad's car?"

"Greyhound." Debbie dropped the toilet lid and sat down, her elbows on her knees, her chin in her hand. Finn couldn't take her eyes off her hair, shockingly lovely shades of purple and grass green. With Debbie's gold-flecked caramel brown eyes, she sported all the de rigueur Mardi Gras colors. She wore blue jeans with a ragged tear in the left knee, a black Harry Potter tee showing an ample amount of flat tummy—and a pierced belly button?

Finn looked closer. Definitely a new addition. "It's great to see you, but a phone call would have been nice."

"No time. Bad news on the home front." She chipped at the purple fingernail polish on her index finger.

Finn sighed, leaned her head carefully against the back of the tub and closed her eyes. "Something new?"

"Finn, it totally is this time."

"Oh, yeah? What?"

"Not real bad news. You're going to have company."

Finn lifted her head to stare at Debbie. "Please don't tell me it's Mom and Dad. They were just here."

Finn loved her parents, in a single dose, sort of like a flu shot. Once a year took care of the possible side effects—strained patience, angry tirades and suggestions for lifestyle changes. Hers. Finn loved her job as a tour guide but it was supposed to be temporary. After five years, her mother didn't think it was a good career choice.

Dorie thought a teacher or a nurse was a more respectable profession and, of course, grandchildren would be nice. Her father never failed to harangue her about the unsavory characters one found in the French Quarter. Little did her father realize many of those unsavory characters were tourists who were not only her livelihood but New Orleans' as well. How was that her fault anyway?

"Nope, not Dorie and Dan." Debbie never called their parents Mom and Dad. Maybe it was the late-in-life baby thing. They treated Debbie as an equal. A spoiled rotten equal who pretty much got everything she asked for. Debbie lifted her head and grinned, giving Finn an uncomfortable feeling in the pit of her stomach—the one you get when the pilot comes over the intercom to say, "We're having a *slight* problem with one of the engines."

"Me," Debbie continued with a broad smile. "I'm your company."

"You've come for a visit?" asked Finn, hopefully.

"Kind of."

Finn sighed. "What happened this time?"

"They kind of kicked me out."

"Kind of?"

"We-ell, it had something to do with Freddy."

"The skater boyfriend?"

"Yeah."

"What did Freddy do? Drugs? Trouble at school?" Finn groaned. "Don't tell me he got arrested."

Debbie shook her head. "Nothing so stupid. Freddy's, like, way cool. He and I were fooling around after school. Dorie came home earlier than I expected and she, like, you know, found us."

"Fooling around? I take it you mean sex."

"Yeah. I think she, you know, probably heard us before she saw us. Freddy is a moaner. I was letting him—"

"Too much information, Debs. And you shouldn't be having sex anyway. A moaner. Please."

"Sorry," she muttered, not sounding the least bit repentant. She grinned and went back to chipping her nail polish.

"I hope you were at least using protection."

"Yeah."

"What did Mom say?"

"She, like, went totally ballistic on me. Said I was exactly like Emmy, and how come I couldn't be more like you?"

"Me?" She stared at Debbie. No way. "She held me up as a good example?"

"Yeah, you don't have sex."

"With sound effects." Finn closed her eyes. "And *not* at the parents' house."

Debbie rolled her big, brown eyes. "You know what I mean."

Unfortunately, she did. Finn didn't have sex. At least not in the last couple of months, or maybe more honestly, the last year. But who was counting? Why did Debbie have to bring it up on a day Finn would as soon forget? "Thanks, Debs. I so appreciate my little sister pointing out my lack of a sex life. Anything I can do for you, just say so."

Debbie got down on her knees and rested her arms on the side of the tub. "Let me stay? Please."

"Sure. What are sisters for?"

CHAPTER TWO

Jack waited until Finn disappeared into the crowded streets, and then took off at a jog. He couldn't believe how stupid he'd been about not helping when she called.

Most of the time he still considered her a kid. It was a lousy excuse. As he careened around pedestrians, pin-balling against lamp posts and newspaper dispensers, he remembered the rambunctious tomboy she'd been. All elbows, knees and coltish long legs with a riot of red out-of-control hair.

He loved her, though not in the way most men did—hot and sweaty hours spent between the sheets. He loved Finn like a sister. Always had. He'd be heartbroken if anything happened to her because he'd been a stubborn idiot. The blow to her head could have killed her.

After running hard several blocks, he wound down to a fast walk to catch his breath. Then as it returned to normal, he had an epiphany—as Cordry called his own well-known moments of clarity. He pulled up to a complete stop, one hand on his hip. Staring at his feet, he wiped the sweat from his brow.

For Jack, things were black or they were white, but this thought came to him in a gray, sex-induced, fog. A brother didn't ogle a sister's rounded ass when she walked away or wonder how her breasts would feel cupped in his palms. He sure as hell didn't notice how she smelled—clean and lemony, a scent that rocked him to the core. Damn. What he felt was most definitely not brotherly love. It was desire, plain and, though anything but, simple. He was trying to sell himself a bill of goods if he didn't admit he lusted after Finn.

"Jack," he muttered, "she's a grown woman. You really are a moron."

He was thinking about her as he did all women he found attractive, but this was Finn. He wasn't fixin' to get in the sack with her for a few months and then walk away. And he wasn't a commitment type guy.

He deliberately switched his mind away from Finn's body, to the supposed dead body she'd claimed she saw. When he got to the corner of Dauphine and Toulouse, he cupped his eyes against the glare and stared at the brick structure Finn described, then up at the gallery. He studied the second-story line of doors in the L shape of the building but no body, dead or otherwise, hung on the railing.

Shaking his head, he looked both ways then climbed over the wall. No one peeked out a window at him or pointed a gun through an open doorway as he crossed the courtyard. He prayed no idiot would shoot first and ask questions later. Acting as if he belonged there, he climbed the stairs. He hoped he wouldn't be sorry he refused to wait for backup. Either you broke the rules and paid the consequences, or you looked like a damned fool. Sometimes both.

He wasn't sure where Finn saw the body, but it was nowhere in sight now. Crouching, he found what looked like blood smeared over several inches of the floor. He pulled a latex glove from his back pocket and snapped it on. Lightly touching it with one finger he found it still sticky to the touch, then he sniffed it. Oh, yeah, definitely blood, and too much to have come from Finn's skinned knee. He stood up, rubbing his finger down his pants leg. He studied the closed apartment doors.

He turned then and spotted a bundle on the railing. As he bent to inspect it, he jerked back. His throat hitched. It was a voodoo doll. Stepping closer to study it, the hair on the back of his neck rose.

A six-inch doll hung from the rail with a string around its neck and three straight pins poking out of the chest. Beneath a miniature baseball cap with New Orleans printed across the front, short corkscrews of cherry red yarn hair stuck out at all angles. Dressed in a pink tee shirt, denim shorts and Mardi Gras beads, even down to the tiny mole below the right eye, the doll was an exact duplicate of how Finn looked today, minus the pins in her chest, the taut rope around her neck and the fake evil grin.

Jack took a deep breath, and then let it out slowly. He refused to believe in the bad mojo of a voodoo doll, but he couldn't discount the threat. Rubbing his forehead, he searched for more clues.

Birds chirped in the trees, children played below in the alley, the sun shone bright as ever. All appeared normal. Finding dead bodies or creepy voodoo dolls wasn't. Finn, of course, had no idea how much trouble she was in. Neither did he, to be perfectly honest. Still, the doll, an in-your-face message, couldn't be discounted. How serious the threat he didn't yet know, but he would find out.

Since he was supposed to be the professional, he yanked out his cell phone and called the Eighth. He asked Cordry to meet him with a forensic team. Body or no body, Finn had been assaulted here. He feared for her safety, and he hated the entire crummy situation. Damn her meddling butt.

When the phone rang, Debbie jumped up off the floor of the bathroom to retrieve it for Finn. She handed her the cordless, then whispered, "I'm gonna get a Coke," and scampered from the room as if she knew who was on the other end.

"Hello?"

"Finn, honey, glad I caught you at home."

Mom. How convenient. How fitting. As Debbie would say, how, like, totally ironic.

Finn took the phone from her ear and stared at it. How did the woman always know the worst possible time to call? Could you see a listening device from the outside? She frowned. And why did Finn think her mother would bug her own daughter's phone? Paranoid much? It had been a bitch of a day.

"Finn? You still there?"

She brought the phone back to her ear. "Sorry, Mom. I'm in the bathtub."

"Why are you taking a bath at, what time is it, four?"

"It's a long story. Were you calling to say hello, 'cause I can call you back as soon as I get—"

"No, no, this is important and can't wait."

Finn sighed. It never could. Why had Dorie and Dan, the esteemed Jones parental unit, moved to Florida two years ago to retire? It wasn't as if the weather was better than in New Orleans. Hurricanes blew through Florida, too. They didn't golf or play tennis, bridge or pinochle. Her dad loved maneuvering his golf cart—bought the first week they arrived—on the neighborhood streets. So, it was either to get away from Finn and Emmy, which neither chose to believe, or to be around other folks their own age, except teen-aged Debbie still needed to be raised.

"It's Debbie," Mom continued, irritation obvious in her strained voice. "I don't understand how any child of mine would allow a man to take advantage of her, especially with a ninny, Freddy what's-his-name."

"Uh-huh, Debbie who?" she asked, kidding.

"Your sister, Debbie. Who else?"

As if Finn could ever forget the irrepressible teen, eavesdropping on her every word from the other room. "I'm sure Debbie wouldn't let anyone take advantage of her. She's strong, independent-minded. Maybe she's experimenting. What happened?"

"Experimenting? My God, Finn, you didn't see them. In her bed. Well, let me tell you, it doesn't bear repeating but you can guess what they were doing. Just last week they were out in the backyard in the hammock, during the daytime, mind you. Silly me. I thought they were doing homework and school isn't even in session. How stupid could I be?"

"Mom, you're not stupid," Finn said, trying to placate her.

"Thanks, hon, but I should have been paying closer attention. I was making your dad's favorite meat loaf when I get this call from Lorraine MacManus next door, she was nearly hysterical, telling me to do something about Debbie's fornicating—"

"Fornicating?" Finn asked, with a laugh.

"Fornicating. Don't you dare laugh. It was Lorraine's word, not mine. She said I'd better do something about Debbie before she called the police. I stepped out into the yard and there they were, right in plain sight for God and anyone else to see, including Lorraine MacManus. Debbie's top was off and he had his mouth on her bare breasts. Finn, it's embarrassing to even say this but his pants were unzipped and down around his thighs and Debbie had her hand on his—"

"I get the picture, Mom. I don't want to hear about my little sister's sex life."

"Freddy, even with his skinny little butt, is quite well endowed."

"Mom!" Finn laughed out loud.

Her mom giggled like a little girl causing Finn to laugh all the harder. "I should have been stricter with her long ago. I was more than willing to ground her, but your father, when he found out, you know how he gets."

Oh, yeah. Dan Jones, former dockworker and Gold Gloves boxer, put up with no nonsense from his daughters while they were living beneath his roof. And, if he'd been the one who caught Debbie and her boyfriend instead of Mom, the boy would have been lucky to come out of the confrontation with those same unmentionable parts intact.

"I'm calling to tell you she's coming to New Orleans. I expect she'll want to stay with Emmy, poor girl."

Finn wasn't sure if her mom pitied Emmy or Debbie. "Emmy's out of town. Vacationing in the south of France with a rock star."

"Really?"

"I have no idea," Finn admitted. She must have heard it from someone.

"It's probably better anyway because I want you to take her under your wing. I'm sure it'll only be for a short while. School starts in a month and she won't want to miss out. She'll probably be calling Freddy, as well. With his package, he could be in the movies. And you know what kind of movie I'm talking about."

Package? Finn groaned, slapping her free hand into the cooling bath water. Her mother knew the correct slang?

"And, believe me, I've seen my share of porn."

"Mom!" Appalled, Finn wondered if her mother was having a hormonal imbalance or simply reliving her younger years. Finn had no earthly desire to picture Dorie and Dan watching porn together, but now she couldn't get it out of her head. What she didn't know and all that. Yuck.

Wanting to change the subject, she leaned her head back and stared at the peeling paint on the ceiling. Innocently, she said, "I'm tempted to say, when should I expect her? But she's here already."

"Well. That was fast. I'll stick a check in the mail for her expenses. It's actually good that Emmy's gone. She'd just give her more crazy notions about sex. Do you know what that girl told me the last time we talked?"

"No." Knowing Emmy, she couldn't even guess.

"Both those girls get their sex drive from their father."

"Mom! Please. I don't want to hear about it." She wished she could give her own sex drive a chance to roar down the asphalt highway of her life. She'd love to give Debbie and Emmy a run for their money. However, she wasn't discussing it with her mother.

"I'm sorry but it's true. Dan always enjoyed sex."

"Mom. Enough already." Argh. She'd always been frank and open about sex with all the girls while they were growing up, but this was most definitely in the category of too much information. "Tell me what Emmy said to you and keep your and Dad's sex life out of it. My bath water's getting cold."

"Oh, all right, I have to go to the market myself to pick up bologna for your father's lunch tomorrow. She told me she's seeing three men at the same time. Three! I don't think she meant, at the same time literally—"

"God, I hope not."

"—but she's dating three men. How does a woman juggle three men and keep a job and everything else she's got going on in her crazy life? Emmy's always been able to get by with very little sleep. She's amazing."

"Amazing isn't the word I would have used."

"Anywho, Finn, you take care and let me know what I can do to help you with Debbie. She thinks she's an adult but she still needs guidance. Perhaps it's good she's getting away from Freddy. They're much too young to be serious."

"Did she say they were serious?"

"If you'd seen what I've seen in the last two weeks, you'd say they were serious, serious as a heart attack. Thank God she's on birth control."

"You put her on birth control?" She'd never offered Finn or Emmy any options. Finn, of course, hadn't needed any, but she would have liked the opportunity.

"Oh, heaven's no, she did it all on her own. They have medical clinics on every corner in Florida. It's wonderful. This state is quite liberal considering all the stuffy old folks who live here."

"Okay, Mom. Got to go, I'm shriveling up like a prune. Will let you know how Debbie's doing. Love you."

"Love you, too, honey. You take care of our baby girl."

"Will do, Mom." Baby girl? Finn rang off. Picking up her washcloth, she draped it over the top of her head, allowing the water to run down her face. She leaned back and heaved a sigh.

Debbie, holding a bag of potato chips in one hand and a Coke can in the other, stuck her head in the doorway.

When she didn't immediately say anything, Finn turned her head and found Debbie studying her. "What?"

"You've got way bigger boobs than I do."

"Thanks for noticing. Maybe you haven't grown into yours yet."

"Hope you're right. By the way, when am I arriving?"

Finn stuck her tongue out, then pulled the washcloth over her face. Yanking the drain plug, she said, "Very funny."

Finn got dressed and downed four ibuprofen. She found Debbie plopped in front of the TV watching the news. *The news?* Refusing to get drawn into a one-sided conversation about the current political situation, Finn picked up her keys off the end table.

"I'm sorry, I have to go. I have leftover Citrus Ginger Chicken in the refrigerator if you want something to eat besides potato chips."

"Did you make it?"

Finn nodded. "I was experimenting with a new recipe."

"How was it? Did anyone else have any?"

"It was good. Outstanding actually." Finn planted her hands on her hips. "Why all the questions?"

"Well, uh..." She refused to meet Finn's gaze.

Finn rolled her eyes and sighed. "I admit I've had problems in the kitchen in the past but I'm better. I'm learning." *Oh, how she was learning.* Only one other person knew Finn attended culinary school. Finn had no intention of telling Debbie, who would blab it to Mom, Emmy and half of the civilized world. Some things were best left a secret, especially when it came to her family. "I've also got Lean Cuisine in the freezer."

Debbie turned back to the TV. "Where you going?"

"I made dinner plans. Before I knew you were gonna be here." Of course, they were two and a half hours from now but Debbie didn't need to know.

"A date?"

"Sort of." *Please don't ask any questions I can't answer without lying.*

"Okay. Can I watch this?" she asked, holding up the DVD of *Pretty Woman*.

"Sure."

It wouldn't hurt for her to see how a person's life could derail. Then again, maybe Debbie wanted to catch that runaway train. The Julia Roberts' character turned out okay. She ended up with Richard Gere and a boatload of cash. Maybe Debbie would see it as a motivational video. Career training.

Finn left the house, locking the door behind her. She fired up her ten-year-old faded yellow Bug, then scrambled across town, through the CBD and the French Quarter and, at last, to the three story brick building which once had been a hotel and now housed the Culinary Arts School of Louisiana.

She luckily found a parking space on the street and trudged up to the second floor classroom, making it to class with minutes to spare. But with her head pounding.

They were supposed to make a ham and broccoli quiche. While preparing the dish, Finn got the feeling someone was watching her. A chill shimmied up her spine. Distracted and a bit unnerved, she eyed the other students, but no one was watching her.

The quiche refused to set, and it came out looking like the green slime covering the surface of the bayou. "I have a headache," Finn explained to the chef instructor, sounding whiny even to herself, "and a concussion."

"No excuse." *Great. Just great.*

Her name was Wanda Westrom but her students called her the Wicked Witch of the South behind her back. With stiff grey hair hidden beneath her chef hat, beady black eyes, a skinny body that would look perfect beneath a long black dress and attached to a broom, she bore a striking resemblance to a certain memorable witch.

Finn's life was hectic working two jobs, but *this* was what she wanted. Cooking calmed her, soothed her, refreshed her, made her seem like a normal human being capable of kicking food's butt and taking names. Yeah, Finn Jones, one-of-a-kind chef! She sighed. She'd better put more effort into these culinary classes. Between giving tours and taking pictures at night for Tommy, exhaustion overwhelmed her. She wondered if this was how Emeril got his start.

Two hours later, she rushed from class to meet Jack for dinner in the French Quarter.

In spite of the rowdy crowds searching for fun on Bourbon Street she actually found a parking space around the corner on the not-much-quieter street of Iberville.

She took a deep breath and walked into the frenetic pace of Bourbon, the spicy food smells and raucous noise invading her head. She gave a hard stare to every man she passed, even turning around to see if anyone followed her, her heart thudding in time to her fast pace. Each time she expected to see her assailant. She couldn't get to the restaurant fast enough.

She spotted Jack, looking as yummy as anything would on the menu, standing in front of the restaurant eyeing the bug-eyed, happy tourists. Dressed in snug faded black jeans and a Margarita-colored polo, he exuded confident masculinity. His five o'clock shadow and overlong hair merely added to his appeal. One older woman actually stopped and turned around to ogle his posterior.

He grinned when he spotted Finn but it instantly faded as he stared at her face. "Feeling all right, *chere*?"

She nodded. She'd tossed off her double-breasted chef's jacket and left it in the car. Wearing dark indigo jeans, a vee-neck white cotton sweater, silver hoop earrings and strappy four-inch sandals, she looked darned cute if she did say so herself. She'd even corralled her curly hair into a semblance of respectability. Maybe a little cleavage wouldn't have hurt. She should have worn her Victoria's Secret push-up bra, which gave her the look of double Ds instead of her C. It didn't matter to Jack, but just once she'd like him to see her as a woman.

The man wasn't even looking at her figure, only her face. She knew dark circles hovered beneath her eyes, which no amount of concealer could hide.

She forced a smile. "A leftover headache, nothing to write home about. Did you go to the scene of the crime after I left you? Do you know what happened? Did you find the body?"

"Whoa." He grabbed her elbow and steered her inside the dim, noisy restaurant. "Slow down. One thing at a time."

They followed the hostess through the restaurant and then traversed the narrow stairs to the second floor where she seated them on the gallery overlooking Bourbon and handed them menus. They ordered drinks—his, a Corona, and hers, iced tea.

Finn looked down, never failing to be amused by the view—the ogling tourists, the tacky shops and strip clubs, the overall infectious vibe. In spite of its eccentricities and slowly returning crowds of tourists, she loved this city with all her heart and never, ever thought of leaving.

When their drinks arrived, she lifted her glass. "*Laissez les bon temps roulez.*"

"You bet." He lifted his beer, then emptied a good portion of it in one swallow. "Not that I've been having all that many good times lately."

"One can hope."

"I'll drink to that." He finished his beer and motioned for the waitress to bring him another.

Finn leaned forward. "What did you find out, Jack? I'm dying to hear."

He winced. "Poor choice of words, *chere*."

"Whatever," she muttered. God, this man could be downright irritating. "Is a big wart sprouting on my nose? Broccoli in my teeth? Hair standing on end?"

"No." He studied the menu. "No. You're fine. It's something else."

"What?"

He looked up, his features placid and unreadable. "It's just you've grown up and, though it took long enough, I finally noticed. I'm a man. We have urges. Not that it's gonna happen between us."

"Is that all?" At least it explained why he was acting so weird. Nice to be noticed even if nothing happened between them.

"I was kinda wondering about the dark circles under your eyes."

And, with that compliment every good thing she wanted to say to him flew out the window. "Thank you so very much for mentioning them."

"Anytime." He ran his finger around the water ring on the tabletop, then leaned back in his chair, folding his arms over his chest. "You were right. We're pretty sure a body had been there. We found blood evidence. The forensics guys are going over it, but without remains, it's impossible to make a case or say an actual crime took place. Other than your assault which I am proceeding with, by the way."

"Okay. And no probably about it, I saw a body."

The waitress appeared with Jack's second beer and they ordered. He ogled her butt when she left proving, that, yes indeed, he was a man. They made desultory conversation about Debbie's visit, a difficult case he was working on, even the weather.

When the conversation waned and their meals finished, Finn managed to walk away without saying something stupid, even going so far as to let Jack pay for both of them.

He walked her up Bourbon and around the corner to her car, then kissed her cheek and told her to take care. She watched him wade through the stumbling, drunk tourists and disappear in the crowd.

She wanted to go home and collapse, but her other job called. Jack didn't know about it and he would never approve of her working for Tommy. The brothers were so combative it was as if they were Olympic competitors contending for the same gold medal. She could hear it now. Jack would give her grief about not being licensed, not knowing what she was doing, getting hurt, blah, blah, blah. If she needed unwanted advice, she'd call her mom.

The Crescent City Detective Agency, located across Canal in the Central Business District, was a single room on the second floor of a furniture warehouse. To get to Tommy's office Finn had to climb an outside staircase. Since it was dark, and Finn didn't know the neighborhood well, particularly at night, she drove her car up the alley and parked next to the stairs where she could run up and be back down in a matter of minutes.

Finn looked both ways before climbing out of her Beetle. She grabbed her backpack, locked the doors and plodded up the rickety metal stairs, sorry by the time she got to the top, out of breath, her head pounding. The owner kept the door locked, but Tommy had given her a key in case she ever needed to return for an extra camera, listening device or a pair of binoculars when he wasn't available. She fumbled the key into the lock. The door slammed shut behind her. She flipped on a light then walked down the carpeted hall to Tommy's office, the last door on the left.

Light shone beneath the door. She turned the knob and walked inside. Tommy stood with his back to her in front of his desk, a Diet Coke in one hand, a cell phone in the other. He tossed the phone onto the desk when he heard her. He turned and smiled, then beckoned her to one of two mismatched, mahogany dining chairs.

He looked a bit like Jack—light brown hair cut short, with blue-gray, deep set eyes and always a broad smile. He was a few inches shorter than Jack, but as lean and muscled. Both oozed the same masculine self-confidence. Tommy was friendly, always optimistic and outgoing. Like his brother, he'd never met a person, particularly a woman, he couldn't charm. While Jack tended toward a more introspective personality, neither man took their personal life seriously.

Tommy strode around his huge scarred walnut desk, bought at a deep discount from his landlord, and sat. He propped his black sneakers on the desk blotter. "Hey, it's my favorite snoop. How's it doing?"

"I've had better days." She flopped into the chair opposite him and dropped her backpack onto the floor. She gestured to his drink. "Got another one of those?"

Behind his desk, he kept a miniature refrigerator. He dropped his feet to the floor, pulled the frig door open and handed her a can.

She pulled the tab, took a big swig and settled into her seat with a sigh, the bubbles tickling her nose.

"Tourists?" he asked.

"Among other things."

"Least you got work."

"Yeah, guess I shouldn't complain. Keeps me in school."

Tommy was the only person who knew about her culinary classes. She hadn't wanted to tell anyone, but he often needed her in the evenings, so she told him to avoid lying. She'd reluctantly confided in him, then threatened death or dismemberment if he told anyone else.

He rubbed his eyes, then smiled at her, his face

hopeful. "Did ya get any juicy pictures the other night of Clarissa Franco's wandering husband, Johnny? I came up blank the night before when I tried. Instead of meeting up with his girlfriend, the miserable excuse-for-a-husband tried to gamble away the rent money."

Finn grinned. "Lucky me. Mister Franco most certainly does have a little something-something on the side. The two of them are quite photogenic, and I have the pictures to prove it." She dug in her backpack for the digital camera. No professional photographer, she still managed to get more than a few shots of them kissing, groping and more. One of him grabbing her ass was particularly provocative. Finn felt like a crass voyeur but it paid the rent. Or in her case, school tuition.

Tommy reached for a folder and flipped it open. Rubbing his hand over his head as he looked through it, he said, "Simple case of wife suspicious of the hubby. She wants the pictures to prove he's out screwing around on her so she can take him to the cleaners at the divorce proceedings."

"Well, he is and she can." She handed over the camera.

He grinned as he clicked through several shots. His eyebrows rose, a slight smirk twisted his lips. "Nice. A carriage ride through Jackson Square. What a romantic guy."

Finn nodded. "I got a few on the carriage but they didn't do much more than talk, hug and kiss a little. Afterward they found a more private spot and got down to business."

His grin widened as he handed it back to her. "I see that. Good job."

Without thinking that Tommy needed copies of the pictures on the camera, she stuck it back in her pack. "Okay, onward and upward. Where do I find the next one?"

"Brenda Sue Washington's husband, Delbert." He lifted another folder and waved it at her. "She says he goes to his second job at the casino every Tuesday and Thursday night at eleven. At least he says he's going. She has yet to see a paycheck, so she has her doubts."

He handed her a photo from inside the folder. She tucked it into her backpack after taking a quick look-see. The man seemed innocent enough. With the studious, metal-framed glasses, he could be an accountant or a bank teller. Or a serial killer, for all she knew. You could never tell by a person's looks.

"Home address and a description of his car are written on the back."

"Okay, so I follow him and see where he's really going? And take pictures, of course."

"You bet. Exactly like the last one." He ran his gaze over her. "You won't want to wear that white sweater tonight taking those pix. You'll stand out like a billboard."

"Okay. These couples. Jeez."

"Ain't love grand?" He shook his head. "Makes me want to rush right out and get hitched. Again."

"Aren't you the romantic?"

"That's me all over." He grinned. "Got a problem with it?"

She shook her head, returning his grin. "No, your business, not mine. So, how come you're not doing this other job tonight? I'm not complaining, mind you, I need the money."

"I've got something else on the docket." He leaned back in his chair and folded his arms over his chest. He winked. "It's clandestine."

"Clandestine? Ooh. Is that why you're dressed like a funeral director?"

He laughed, then tugged his black and gray striped

tie into place. "I thought I looked damned good."

"You look, uh, professional."

He cocked his head and struck a Napoleonic pose, sliding his hand inside his jacket. "Thanks. I think."

"You ought to lose the sneakers, though." She laughed. "I never see you in a suit. Honestly? You kinda look like a serious case of indigestion."

She caught him as he was taking a drink of his Coke. He coughed and laughed at the same time, spewing soda all over his desktop. He jumped to his feet. "Jonesy, Jonesy, hell, that's about all the encouragement I can take."

She grabbed a bunch of tissues from the corner of his desk and helped him mop up the mess. He was still wiping tears from his eyes when he sat back down.

"So, have you seen Emmy? I heard she was out of town. In the south of France with a movie star."

She pursed her lips. "You know we don't talk much."

"I didn't ask if you talked, I asked if you'd seen her."

"Either way, no. Why? Have you?"

"Yeah, we had lunch together day before yesterday. She looks good. I think she's working out."

"I didn't know you two ever met for lunch. Do you do it often?" And why were they meeting for lunch? Emmy only did things that benefited Emmy. What did she want from Tommy? Was he one of her three men?

"Whenever we can arrange our schedules." He smiled. "I like her company."

"So why are you asking me about Emmy? And doesn't she always look good?" As if Finn needed any reminders about how they compared in the looks department. Finn had unruly red hair. She kept it a medium length to try to tame it; Her older sister had long, wavy auburn locks that would look beautiful even if she were standing outside during a hurricane. They were both tall, but Finn was lean and athletic with freckles everywhere, while Emmy's size six curvy figure drew envious looks from women and lustful looks from men. No way would Emmy allow freckles anywhere on her perfect body. Finn often wondered if they were honestly related.

"Oh, yeah, she looked as bodacious as ever but acting kinda mysterious. She was evasive about what she's been up to and where she was going on vacation." He rocked back in his chair with an avid gleam in his eye. "I think I kinda like the mysterious vibe she's got going."

Of course he did. All men did. Emmy was catnip to their libido. Disgusted, Finn got up to leave. She grabbed another camera, then lugged her backpack over her shoulder. "I'll stop by tomorrow after I get the next batch of shots."

"See you then. Take care. You're looking kinda tired."

"Thanks." Exactly what a girl wanted to hear from a hunk like Tommy. She'd like one of the Boyle brothers to notice her when she was at her best. She, too, was a woman.

Finn ignored her desire to slam the door behind her like a child. She shut it quietly and stepped out with her thoughts elsewhere.

She heard a faint noise. She wasn't alone. A tall stranger whose face looked familiar came toward her, his strides long and deliberate. "You the one takin' pictures of me?"

"No," she automatically lied.

His tone left little doubt about how he felt about her. 'Dislike' would be too kind. 'Outraged and highly motivated to harm her' seemed more likely. Which was when she remembered why he looked familiar. Franco, the wandering husband she'd photographed last night in all his pants-around-his-ankles glory. It took a nano-second to register the thought that he shouldn't have known where to find her before extreme terror kicked in.

Closer to the stairs than Tommy's office, Finn managed to dash past him in her rarely-worn heels.

He grabbed at her but she ducked. She reached the outer door and twisted the doorknob. He yanked her from behind, and pulled her toward him. A nasty blast of stale breath hit her in the face. The knob slipped from her sweaty hand. She wrenched her backpack off and screamed. She swung it and connected with his head. He grunted and lost his grasp on her.

Finn took advantage of the moment and wrenched open the door. She scrambled out to the landing. With one foot on the first step, he jerked her by the back of her sweater. She screamed bloody murder again and swung around to hit him.

Tommy appeared and yanked Franco up, smashing him in the jaw. The man stood in the tiny space swaying. Finn took advantage. She swung her backpack. This time, Franco sidestepped. And she hit Tommy full force.

He lost his balance, arms cartwheeling in the air as he reached for the rail. He missed and tumbled down the steps, crashing against each riser with a horrible thump until he lay crumpled at the bottom. Franco raced down the stairs, hurtled over Tommy's prone body, then disappeared up the dark alley.

Finn flew down the steps, her backpack forgotten. Tommy lay at the bottom, his eyes closed, his jaw clenched.

She knelt by his side, her breath jerking in and out. She patted his cheek, and prayed he wasn't dead. She couldn't take two dead bodies in one day, no matter how insensitive it sounded.

He opened one eye and squinted at her, his face pinched. "Hell, I, I broke my...damn it all to hell...my damned leg."

She pressed a hand to her quaking stomach. "Oh, my God. I'm so sorry. It's all my fault. I'm an idiot. How could I miss him and hit you?"

"Not your fault. Who the hell was he? You recognize him?"

She nodded. "Johnny Franco."

"Damn. I wasn't looking at his face in those pictures."

"What were you looking at?" she asked dumbfounded.

"The woman, Finn, the woman. Franco's wife, my stupid client, must have told him she hired me. I guess he looked up my office location or the bitch actually told him. Damn it all, this hurts like hell." He swallowed hard. "I think I'm gonna puke."

Finn jumped to her feet. "My cell phone is up in my backpack. I'll go call an ambulance."

He stopped her by grabbing her hand, then managed a lopsided grimace. "What have you got in there anyway? It weighs a ton."

She wiped perspiration from his forehead with the hem of her sweater. "Oh, you know. Leaflets and maps to hand out to tourists, extra Mardi Gras beads and caps, bottled water, camera, wallet, pepper spray, police whistle, the usual. Girl stuff."

"Girl stuff? Since when did girl stuff become an arsenal?"

Her pulse still racing, she ignored his question for fear of bursting into tears at her relief that he was going to be fine. She ran up the stairs, found her backpack, and pulled out her phone. She called 9-1-1, explained the situation then trotted down the stairs.

"Are the troops on the way?" he asked in a raspy,

panting voice.

"Yep." She knelt again, then caressed his cheek. "Can I do anything to make you more comfortable?"

"Kiss me."

Her heart lurched. "What?"

"Kiss me. It'll take my mind off the pain."

Without even thinking about it, she leaned over and pressed her lips to his. He reached one arm around her neck, pulled her close and kissed her in return. Using his tongue and lips with proficiency, he didn't kiss like a man in pain. He kissed like a man looking for more. He massaged her neck with one hand, his other came around to hold her waist. He smelled clean, tasted of Coke and kissed like a champion.

She quivered from her girly parts all the way down to her toes. Wow. Who knew? She couldn't have been more surprised if he'd gotten up and performed the River Dance.

When the sound of sirens echoed in the distance, he dropped his hand from her neck and whispered in her ear, "Finn, honey, I feel like I could run a marathon."

She sat back on her heels, her lips tingling, her breath catching in her throat. "Glad I could help."

He chuckled, struggling to sit up. She put her arm around his shoulder and helped him. "Better?"

"This is embarrassing." He slanted an eye at her, his mouth quirking in a crooked smile. "What'll the paramedics say?"

She patted his back, attempting to regain her equilibrium after a kiss that left her reeling. "Hey, it could have happened to anyone and besides, it was all my fault. Falling down those steps, you're lucky you didn't break your neck, both legs, and half a dozen other bones. You've got nothing to be embarrassed about."

He grinned, then spread both hands over the bulge in his lap. "I wasn't talking about my damned leg."

CHAPTER THREE

Exhausted and alone, Finn sat in the hospital waiting room. She stared as the hands on the generic round clock on the wall slowly ticked by. Puke-green walls, cracked orange plastic chairs, the signs pointing to the various ways you could get lost in the maze of meandering halls, all highlighted by harsh fluorescent lighting. It made her feel lonely and dismal, with not another soul in sight to share her misery. Even the air felt thin and lonely. Stupid, really.

People said hospitals smelled funky but she smelled nothing but herself—a nasty combination of motor oil and rotting food, and other horrible substances she'd picked up in the alley when she knelt to help Tommy.

She hated hospitals. Of course, no one ever said they liked them. It seemed everyone she'd ever met had a memory, invariably a bad one. Hers were two-fold. At twelve, she broke her arm and four-year-old Debbie suffered a mild concussion in a car accident on their way to feed the ducks on a sunny spring day in City Park. Dorie, who'd been driving, came away unscathed but shook up.

Without warning, they'd been sideswiped by an underage kid taking his dad's LeBaron out joyriding. With all the enormous moss-draped live oak trees in the park, it was a wonder he didn't hit one of those first.

The abruptness of the accident rather than the actual pain of the injury Finn recalled the most. The nightmare played over and over in her head—the crunch of metal on metal, Debbie's sad whimpering, the hysterical teenager, the screech of the ambulance siren on the ride to the hospital.

After getting a cast put on her arm, she'd sat close by Debbie's crib, her arm propped up on a pillow, drifting in and out of sleep. Dorie and Dan sat beside her on borrowed folding chairs, Emmy asleep on the floor. Finn refused to leave her baby sister's side.

She remembered waking long enough to hear the medical staff shuffle in and out, speaking in low, muffled tones. Everyone, including the nurses, wanted her to go home but she wouldn't leave until Debbie woke up. That head injury explained a lot about Debbie's mental state these days. Little joke, Finn thought. Very little.

She checked the clock again. Half past midnight. Her most recent weapon of choice, her backpack, lay at her feet. She had called Jack on her quick drive to the hospital as she followed the ambulance. He was supposedly on his way but, for now, all she had for company was her lousy self. How had this happened? How had she managed to knock a full-grown man down a flight of stairs? Wonder Woman she wasn't.

She'd confessed to Tommy she was an idiot. She was, of course. She felt awful. The only way she could have felt worse was if one of Aunt Gert's cats choked on a hair-ball and died while Gert was away cruising, courting her gentlemen friends. Still, the hot, hot, unexpected kiss had been wonderful.

God. What a mess. And Tommy had looked so great in his suit tonight, boyish yet sexy, a lethal combination. Now his suit sported a rip in one pants leg and a torn shoulder. Greasy oil soaked the back of the jacket. In other words, she'd ruined it. She wondered how much he'd paid for it and then chastised herself for thinking of the cost instead of Tommy's welfare.

"Well, what have we here?" Jack sounded tired, yet calm. "You look like your dog died."

She didn't have to look up from her perusal of the green tiled floor to recognize that particular voice. Meeting his eyes, she said, "Hey." She then went back to studying the floor tiles.

"Hey yourself." He sat down beside her, patted her knee, then left his hand on her leg. Reassuring warmth penetrated her jeans. "How's Tommy?"

He smelled clean and fresh like he'd recently gotten out of the shower. On the other hand, she stank like Bourbon Street at five in the morning before the garbage trucks swept up the trash. "They're setting his leg now. Tommy didn't want me in there. He said, and I quote, 'in case I scream like a little girl.'"

Jack snorted. "What happened? On the phone you said you knocked him down the stairs?"

She lifted her head and met his gaze. "I did."

He laughed, then squeezed her knee in a comforting way. "What'd he do? Make a move on you?"

"No. *No!*" She shot him a disgusted look. "Actually, he tried coming to my rescue."

"And why did you need rescuing? I thought girls nowadays rescued themselves."

"Very funny."

"Sorry." He squeezed her knee again. "He'll be fine. Please don't tell me this had anything to do with your dead body."

"No. I don't see how. I was at Tommy's office when this guy, all fired up about having his picture taken, took off after me. Tommy tried to help but when I swung my backpack at the guy, I accidentally hit Tommy and knocked him down the steps."

"What were you doing at Tommy's in the middle of the night anyway? And if it has anything to do with sex, I don't want to know."

"It doesn't." Finn sighed, then leaned back in her chair and stared at the ceiling. "You're not going to like it but I've been working for Tommy."

"Oh." Jack's fingers tightened on her thigh. "In what capacity?"

"Photographer." Jack's jaw tightened. She scratched her temple where motor oil clung to a few strands of her hair. Gross. "I'm not doing actual PI work."

"Taking pictures *is* PI work. Last time I checked you didn't have a license."

"I'm taking pictures." She sat up straight and eyed Jack. "I'm not doing anything else. I give them to Tommy. He does the real investigative stuff."

"Tommy knows better. You ever heard of the Louisiana State Board of Private Investigators?"

"No," she admitted.

"A PI license requires training, testing...dammit, Tommy knows all that."

"He's busy, and I needed the money."

Jack jumped to his feet and began pacing.

"Aren't you going to go see Tommy?" she asked, hoping he'd forget her and concentrate on his brother.

"In a minute." He stopped in front of her, with his hands on his hips, his steel blue gaze intent on her. "Tommy could lose his license."

"Oh?"

"Don't play the innocent with me, *chere*. I'm onto every ploy known to womankind. None of them works."

Angered, Finn jumped to her feet as well, forgetting her headache. Why did he always have to be so obnoxious? Jack's eyes widened but he didn't step away. They stood nose to nose, or rather her nose to his chest, but she gave her best imitation of a glare. "I don't know anything about ploys. Tommy said what I was doing wasn't illegal. Technically."

"Technically," he repeated. He threw up his arms. "Why me?"

"Could you shut up and listen a minute. I'm only taking pictures. I hand the camera over to Tommy. I never even look at the shots." True, it was a little white lie but she didn't think it could hurt and it might actually help her cause. "I'm barely scraping by with the tours. You know tourists."

"I know." His gaze didn't waver, but she saw something else in his eyes that surprised her. He seemed to be sympathizing with her. God—would wonders never cease. "Go on."

"That's it. I take pictures."

Jack sat back down, then blew out a slow breath. "I'm not absolutely certain of the law here, but you seem to be cutting a very fine line. I'll talk to Tommy."

"Thanks, I think."

He stood up and held out his hand. "Let's go see the clumsy idiot. Letting a girl knock him down a flight of stairs. Wait until that little story gets around."

"It was an accident."

"Ha. At least with a cast on his leg, if I browbeat him about you working for him, he can't chase me."

"Good to know," Finn admitted. She took his hand and they sauntered down the hall together.

Two hours later, Finn left Jack at the hospital to go home and finally put her aching head and body to bed. It had been one hell of a long day.

In all the excitement of Tommy's accident, she forgot to ask Jack if he'd learned any more about her missing body.

As she reached for her car keys, she remembered

something else.

Damn.

She'd left her notebook at school. She couldn't function without her class notes, recipes, ideas. If anyone else found it, she'd be history to say nothing short of a laughingstock. And, this afternoon's instructor would not find it humorous.

From the hospital, she followed the darkened back streets to the school on tree-lined Esplanade with its eclectic mix of large beautiful nineteenth century mansions and businesses, raised neutral ground running down the center of the boulevard. Surprisingly quite a bit of traffic, both pedestrian and vehicle, moved about. Maybe things were picking up for New Orleans' tourism. She said a little prayer in hopes it was true.

When she explained her situation to the security guard at the school, he let her in. She paced across the shadowed lobby, then plodded up the stairs. The second story housed the Culinary Arts School of Louisiana. With few lights on, the old building seemed sinister at night. Of course, sinister didn't realistically describe the school. Even if the instructors were downright scary at times.

She made her way up the dimly lit stairs, careful of her every step. She walked down the hall to the classroom, her footsteps echoing softly. She pushed opened the door. Her notebook lay right where she'd left it on the floor by her seat. She tiptoed across the room, which still smelled of cooked broccoli. And something else. Perfume? Cologne? A man's tantalizing, spicy cologne? How odd.

She turned for the door and gasped, stopping dead in her tracks.

In front of the door stood a man.

Sort of.

Kind of.

His body looked, well, she hated to even think it, but ghost-like. In point of fact, she could see right through it to the small window in the door. Shivering, she stood her ground and stared, unable to move.

The apparition hovered with one hand on his hip, the other clutching what looked like an old-fashioned, tarnished brass fry pan, his face a mask of masculine indifference. Finn would've sworn his coal-black eyes weren't moving at all. He looked exactly like old photos she'd seen of chefs, right down to the large white toque on his head, the heavy black brogues on his feet.

His body wavered, as if Finn saw him under water. Did stress bring on hallucinations? Apparently drinking Peach Bellini dacquiris wasn't the only thing to make you see apparitions. Next she'd be seeing pink elephants, for God's sake.

"You are not real," she stated. "Are you? Please say no."

"Mademoiselle." He bowed. "*Comment allez-vous?*"

How are you? Was he kidding? After seeing a translucent French-speaking ghost? She'd have fainted if she had less breath in her lungs.

He stared at Finn with large eyes, his gaze fierce.

Suddenly, the door opened behind him and the security guard stepped in, right through him. The ghost shimmered into nothingness.

"Did you find what you were looking for?" He twisted his head back and forth. "Thought I heard voices but it looks like you're alone. Who else would be here anyway?"

"Who else," she echoed, her voice trembling like a leaf. Her unearthly companion had disappeared when the door opened like, well, like an apparition. "Talking to myself. I do it late at night when I'm exhausted. Long day, you know."

"Tell me about it," he muttered, ushering her out the

door. With a last peek over her shoulder, she shook her head. She was tired and seeing things that weren't there. Obviously. There was no such thing as ghosts.

      ∾

Gertrude Finnigan Westfield Pantera Charboneau rapped on Finn's back door the next morning and noisily stepped inside the kitchen, calling her name.

Half asleep, in bed with the door closed, Finn peered at her alarm clock, groaned when she saw it read a little after six, then rolled over and pulled a pillow over her head. Light wasn't even peeking under the closed shades. It had been exceedingly late when she'd made her way to bed last night, or more accurately, early this morning.

She had made sure Tommy would live to dance another day with Jack there to take care of him. She retrieved her notebook from school, and fed and watered Gert's brood. She'd gotten home, bleary-eyed and exhausted, around three. The congested streets of New Orleans in the middle of the night shocked her, someone who seldom ventured out past midnight these days. New York wasn't the only city that never slept.

"Debbie, darlin', what a lovely surprise. What are you doing here?" Gert said in her husky, whiskey-inflected voice. "Don't tell me Dorie and Dan are here, too."

Muttering and mumbling, Finn crawled out of bed and slouched into the front room in her pink tee and pink plaid pajama pants. She flipped on a table lamp and spotted Debbie on the couch, a fleece blanket bunched around her legs, her multi-colored hair standing on end, her eyes alight with joy at the sight of her aunt.

Gert was Dorie's older sister by five years. Like all of the Finnigan women, she was tall. Unlike Finn, Gert was willowy, model thin and sexy. Even into her seventies, Gert was a knockout. Plastic surgery helped.

Today she wore a hot pink velour tracksuit with a sequined purple tank beneath. The tank read RED HOT MAMA. The breasts beneath were round, perky and silicone filled.

Gert had been married three times, to wealthy men who worshiped at her stiletto-covered feet. They'd left her so well off, she'd already paid off the mortgage on her pricey Garden District home, socked away a small fortune and had enough cash left over to give Donald Trump a run for his money.

Oddly enough, all three ex-husbands were still enamored of Gert and would marry her again with a mere come-hither nod from her direction.

She was now on the lookout for husband number four. She and Carnival Cruise Lines had an ongoing love affair. She cruised once a month searching for Mister Right. Finn was certain the cruise line gave her a deep discount, if for no other reason than Gert charmed it out of them. And, of course, if nothing else, for the men who cruised with her. They followed her around like she was the Pied Piper. Little did they know most of them were too old for Gert. She was looking for a younger man, wealthy, of course, preferably in his forties or fifties.

Today her thick wavy red-gold, shoulder-length hair desperately needed a touching up. Her gray roots showed. Undoubtedly, in the near future she would be seeing the biggest gossip in the Quarter, Mary Frances O'Shea of *M.F.'s Hair to Dye For*, for her color touch-up and all the latest dirt from the New Orleans' ever-entwining grapevine.

She came in and sat on the second-hand beige corduroy-covered couch, pushing Debbie's feet aside to make room. Leaning over she pulled Debbie into a warm embrace then kissed her cheek. Holding her at arm's length, she studied her face. "Debbie, honey, you are a sight for sore eyes. And, I love your hair. Did you do it yourself?"

"Yep."

"This child doesn't have a single, solitary wrinkle on her face. Will you look at her? She's as fresh as a newborn babe."

Debbie giggled like the teenager she was.

"Gert," Finn said, settling herself in the only other chair left in the room, also second-hand. She pulled her bare feet beneath her. "She's seventeen."

"Aunt Gert, you don't, like, have any wrinkles either."

"Botox," Gert maintained, winking at Finn.

Debbie continued, after nodding her understanding. "I'm here all by myself. The parents are, like, still wallowing in sunny Florida."

"Sorry to hear that," Gert murmured. "Maybe on my next cruise I'll go to Florida and see them. It's been an age since I saw your mother. And how's Emmy?"

"Same ol', same ol'. She's out of town," Finn said. She hadn't spoken to her in a good two weeks but Emmy seldom changed. She stifled a yawn. "Good to have you home. Any prospects this time?"

"Nope. Not a damn keeper on the entire ship except the captain and though I tried, he claimed he's a happily married man. Can you imagine? And he's Italian. Very mysterious, with a lovely accent." She shook her head. "It's good to be home, though, Finnigan. How are my little darlings?"

Her little darlings were the six cats Finn took care of while Gert cruised. Archie and Drew were five-year-old orange tabbies named after two New Orleans Saints football players. Angelina and Scarlett were sisters of the heart, one black Abyssinian and one white Mohair, named after beautiful Hollywood actresses. They had yet to be fixed. According to Gert she didn't want to spoil their femininity and since they weren't in any imminent danger of getting pregnant from the boys there was no rush. The two latest additions were kittens—literally alley cats picked up behind Gert's house—brother and sister, Jake and Maggie. An avid pop culture junkie, Gert drank it up, never missing her favorite TV show, *Entertainment Tonight*. According to Gert, Mary Hart was still the only reliable host, even if she hadn't been on the show in years.

"Jake lost a tooth," Finn announced. "He's been chewing on your garden shoes, the ones you leave by the back door. Otherwise, all is good. They are playing well together. The kittens, particularly, have been fun."

"Good, good. I had time to say hello and give them each a kiss before I crashed late last night," she said, clapping her hands together, giving the two of them a cherubic grin. "Despite not finding true love on board ship, I did make a date with the cab driver who brought me home."

Debbie's eyes widened. "Awesome. You work fast, Aunt Gert. I could use lessons."

Finn grinned. "No, you couldn't. According to Mom you could give them."

"That Dorie," Debbie moaned. "She's, like, living in the dark ages."

Gert leaned back against the couch and sighed. "If she's living in the dark ages, where does that put me, the Pleistocene era?"

Debbie leaned over and hugged Gert. "Never. You're da bomb, Aunt Gert."

"And then some," agreed Gert, patting Debbie's bed head.

"Finn, tell her about Tommy." Still awake when Finn came in, she had told Debbie the sanitized version of the sordid tale. Finn did not, however, relate her experience with the dead man and the subsequent bump on her head, afraid Debbie might decide to stick around longer if she figured Finn led this TV-like exciting, thrilling life every day.

"Tommy Boyle, what a scrumptious man he is," Gert raved. "Those blue eyes, the Robert Redford hair, that tight little butt. If I were a few years younger, I'd eat him up with a spoon."

Debbie giggled. "I always thought Jack was fine."

Finn listened with avid attention.

"Oh, he's good-looking all right, and smart as a New Orleans banker," admitted Gert, "but Tommy, he's as beautiful as a Greek god. Yum-yum. And so lively and obvious, boyish even, it's all in his delicious, expressive face."

"He falls in love at the drop of a hat," Finn added.

Gert grinned. "That's so incredibly romantic."

Finn laughed. "And, like you, that's exactly why he's been married and divorced three times."

"I didn't know he'd been married," Debbie murmured, her eyes wide, her mouth a perfect O.

"Yep. He can't seem to help himself." Finn shook her head. "He's gullible when it comes to a beautiful woman."

"So, what happened to Tommy?" Gert asked.

Finn explained how he broke his leg. After Gert commiserated with her, she clapped her hands and said, "At least he's on the mend and no permanent damage. Let's go out for breakfast. My treat. Do you have a tour this morning, Finn?"

"Not until ten."

"Good." Debbie grinned and got to her feet. "Sounds like a plan."

"Before we leave, though," Finn said, "tell us about this guy, the cab driver you made a date with."

"He's tall, dark and handsome, with thick hair beginning to gray at the temples. Still in good shape for a man his age."

Finn managed not to laugh. If she knew Gert, the man in question was probably a good twenty years *younger* than Gert herself.

"He told me, in secret of course, the cab driving gig was a front. He's actually writing a tell-all book about some big undercover operation for a three initialed government agency."

"For who, do you think?"

"You know, one of those government agencies— CIA, FBI, DEA, NBC. Who cares? It's exciting to know a man like that."

"Like, in a get yourself shot kind of way," Debbie said. "I watch TV, you know."

"Bah," Gert scoffed. "Throw some clothes on, ladies, let's go get us some Belgian waffles. I know the best place in the city and," she winked over her shoulder as she left the room, "I know the chef intimately."

"Intimately?" Finn grinned as she stood up.

"A lady never tells." Gert winked. "Does she, Debbie?"

"Maybe not ladies, but news flash! Us girls give it up all the time."

"So I'm led to believe," Finn muttered on her way to the bedroom.

"I heard that," Debbie called after her retreating back. "At least I'm getting some."

Gert burst into peals of contagious laughter.

Finn swallowed another bite of syrup-soaked Belgian waffle, a thread of uneasiness unraveling around her head over her decision not to tell Debbie and Gert about her recent misadventures.

What if her head injury was more serious than a mere headache? What if she keeled over in a faint right here in the restaurant? What if she ended up in the hospital? Shouldn't someone other than the Boyle brothers know what had happened to her, like her own family? Could she be more melodramatic?

Surely Debbie wouldn't get crazy ideas about staying forever. She had to go home eventually. Once Dorie got over her pique she'd want Debbie back home in time to go to school in a couple of weeks.

"What's up, Finn?" Gert asked, putting her fork down and wiping her mouth with her napkin. "I can see the gears churning."

"Wow," Debbie said, her own fork halfway to her mouth. Maple syrup dribbled off it and onto her plate. "Are you psychotic or something?"

"The word would be psychic, Debbie darling, and no, I'm not. I know when someone's mind is elsewhere. Is it more than worry about Tommy?"

"Tommy's going to be okay. Something happened to me and I'm debating whether I should tell you two or not."

With a pointed look at Debbie, she continued, "I'm not sure Debbie is adult enough to understand."

"Aww, come on," the object of their discussion whined. She licked syrup off her bottom lip. "Isn't it bad enough I get that kind of crap from Dorie, like, all the time?"

"I wasn't talking about sex," Finn said.

Debbie stuck out her tongue at Finn. "It's not always about sex, you know."

"But don't we wish it was?" Gert said with a wistful look on her serene face, pushing her hair behind her ear with one hand and waving with the other.

"Gert, you're not helping," Finn said, choking back a laugh.

"Sorry," she said, sounding not the least bit repentant. "You were saying?"

"Oh, okay, you two," Finn began, "but promise me you won't go all crazy on me. Both of you."

"Promise," Gert said with her hand over her heart.

"Scout's honor," Debbie intoned, raising three fingers on her right hand.

Finn frowned at her. Debbie was most definitely not a Girl Scout. "Okay, yesterday on my morning walking tour I spotted what I thought was a dead body on the second story gallery of a house in the Quarter."

"Whoa," Debbie whispered.

"Whoa is the word, all right. When I went to investigate, which I know I shouldn't have done alone," she said when Gert opened her mouth to say something. "If I called Jack and it turned out to be something else, I'd look like an idiot. Again."

"It's, like, happened before?" Debbie asked in all innocence.

Gert smiled. "It could happen to anyone. Finn meant well. Didn't you?"

"Of course I did, but Jack thinks I'm like the little boy who cried wolf one too many times. But this time I was pretty sure so I called him and the butthead had the nerve to brush me off. I went to take a closer look anyway in case I was wrong."

"You did?" Debbie said, eyes wide.

"I wasn't wrong this time."

"There was, like, a real, dead body?"

"I thought so," Finn said, remembering the horror she felt when she saw him. "I leaned down to take a closer look and got conked on the head. When I came to, the body was gone and I was all alone with a bitch of a headache."

"Wow," Debbie repeated awestruck, her eyes even wider if such a thing was possible, her mouth open in a perfect O.

"Finn, honey." Gert reached across the table and

took her hand. "Are you okay?"

She nodded. "Other than a headache, I'm fine but I thought you two should know."

"And then you had the run-in with this guy at Tommy's office," Gert said. "You lead quite the exciting life."

"A lot more excitement than I want, believe me." Finn studied Debbie to see how she was taking all of this. If the look on her face, one of utter stupefaction, was any indication Debbie was more shocked and appalled than interested in following in her sister's shaky footsteps.

"Did you tell Jack?" Gert asked.

"Yeah. As soon as I pulled myself together, I walked over to the Eighth and chewed him out." She grinned. "I think he might have even felt a little guilty about it."

"As well he should," Gert said, her mouth a thin line of disapproval. "The man wasn't doing his job."

"Though I was initially pissed off with him I did understand," Finn said. "Sort of. I've called before when I thought something was going on and it wasn't. He thinks I'm an idiot."

Debbie sighed, her eyes glazed. "Your life is like an episode of 'CSI': Finding bodies, and getting chased by bad guys. And I thought your being a tour guide was kinda, like, boring." She gave Finn a sheepish grin. "No offense."

"None taken, Debs. It can be boring sometimes, but most of the time I like it. I get to meet people from all over the world and walk the streets of not only the best city in the world, but the one I love. Hey, I don't generally see dead people. I'm not the kid from the *Sixth Sense*."

"By the way, sweetheart," Gert said, "I'm leaving on another cruise in the morning."

"Nice, safe cat duty sounds like just what I need,"

Finn said, then they all went back to finishing their breakfasts and talked of other, more familiar and commonplace, things.

Finn, for her part, relaxed. It felt like she'd been keeping a huge secret, something she hated to do and wasn't even good at. Keeping the secret of culinary school was hard enough without adding more lies to her repertoire.

"Whatever you do, don't tell Dorie," Finn said. "She'll have a cow. She already thinks I'd be better off as a nurse or a teacher, even though I'm not qualified as either. Even worse, she'd probably want me to come to Florida and live with her and Dad."

"A fate worse than death," Debbie intoned, with an elfin grin. "How do you think I feel?"

"You're a kid," Finn said. "You belong at home. Not that I don't want you visiting. I love seeing you."

"Yeah, but I can't stay, can I?"

Gert patted both their hands, ever the conciliator. "Now, girls, there's nothing wrong with Florida. It's simply not New Orleans. And nothing compares. And Debbie, much as you're almost grown-up, you still need your mother. Every girl needs her mother."

"Got that right," Finn said. "Now, ladies, I hate to interrupt this love fest but some of us have to go to work."

After a wonderful, relaxing and oh, so fattening, breakfast Finn stepped out into the humidity and the sunshine, waved good-bye to Debbie and Gert and hopped the St. Charles streetcar. Within minutes she arrived in the French Quarter where she walked to the post office to buy stamps and mail off a few bills before her first tour began at ten.

She traipsed inside and groaned at the long lines in front of her. She yanked off her sunglasses and let the door fall shut behind her. As she adjusted to the difference in lighting, she peered around. Irritated people stood in long lines. Distracted, angry workers waiting to go postal frowned at them. Photos of America's Most Wanted graced the wall. A typical day inside any post office in the U.S.

She started to take her place in line when one of the photos caught her immediate attention.

Finn knew this woman.

She'd seen her up close and personal through the camera lens not two nights ago. The waffles in her stomach churned like they were still in the mixer.

She peered closer, her feet seemingly taking her across the room of their own volition.

The same dark eyes—brown and wide-set, the same thick, unnaturally brassy blonde hair. She couldn't see all of her since the picture was a head shot, but she knew Margaret Jane Barron as a wide-hipped, full-breasted woman with a colorful butterfly tattooed above her left nipple. Amazing how Tommy's digital camera's zoom function worked.

According to the FBI's stats she stood five-six and weighed one hundred fifty pounds. Wanted for embezzlement. Sheesh. It listed her description—sex, race, even nationality, even down to scars and birthmarks, although it failed to mention the butterfly tattoo. It listed the date and place of her birth—Tacoma, Washington, the same city where she'd committed her crime.

It did not explain what she was doing in New Orleans.

Or why she was getting it on with Johnny Franco in Finn's viewfinder.

CHAPTER FOUR

Shocked, Finn stared at the photo on the flyer.

If the feds wanted Margaret Jane Barron on embezzling charges in Tacoma, Washington, what the heck was she doing carousing with Franco in New Orleans? Finn studied the other wanted photos again but Franco was not one of them. Not that she expected him to be. Surely, Tommy would have known that much about him. Or would he have even checked? This was supposed to be a simple case of infidelity, not a federal case.

Finn smiled to herself. Knowing a little something, very little in actuality, about the way men's brains worked, it was no wonder Tommy hadn't recognized Johnny Franco when he'd accosted them the previous evening. She would have bet her next paycheck that Tommy could ID Margaret Jane Barron in a New York minute with or without her clothes on. Yet if he was standing right beside the amorous Johnny Franco, Tommy wouldn't recognize her gentleman friend.

Finn plopped down on one of plastic chairs lined up against the wall, her thoughts whirling. She fished her cell phone out of her backpack debating whom to call first—Jack or Tommy. When she went to punch in Jack's number, a woman standing in line not five feet from Finn cleared her throat. Loudly. She pointed to the wall. Finn saw a sign that detailed no cell phone usage with no words but an overly-dramatic, yet obvious, drawing. If she wasn't mistaken using a cell phone inside this building would cause your head to explode. Talk about going postal.

Finn grabbed her backpack and marched outside into the heat of the day. As she pushed through the doorway, she glared over her shoulder at the nosy woman who smiled back and waggled her fingers good-bye.

Leaning against the building, Finn tapped in Jack's cell phone number. She cursed when it immediately went to voicemail. She left him a convoluted message about a woman on a wanted poster in the post office being involved in one of Tommy's PI cases. She hoped he could figure out what she was trying to say. Then she called Tommy at home figuring he was probably there since it was unlikely he'd make it into his office today.

"Yo, wassup?" he answered, surprisingly upbeat.

"Tommy?"

"The one and only." She could hear the smile in his chipper voice.

"It's Finn. Is something wrong?"

"Jonesy, sweetcakes, what could possibly be wrong? I'm feeling super-duper. Did you know I broke my leg?"

Pain meds. "How is the leg?"

"What leg?"

Oh, boy. "Tommy, can you talk to me about your business?"

"I'd rather not," he stated with what Finn thought sounded like a giggle. Tommy? Sexy, masculine Tommy? Giggling? She had an insane urge to giggle herself.

"I'd rather talk about Emmy, speshif—spesift—spec-if-i-cal-ly," he said slowly enunciating each syllable. "Damn that's a hard word—" He drifted off into more laughter.

Under any other circumstances, this conversation would have been funny. This time, however, Finn was more concerned that either Margaret Jane Barron or her lover, Franco, would come after her—again—and break her leg or some other essential body part. And then, go looking for Tommy and start in on another body part of his.

"...about her boobs," he concluded.

"I'd rather not," Finn said, shaking her head.

As if he hadn't heard her, he continued, "Do you know if they're real or not? Not that it matters to me persh-onally, of course. Just curious. I don't remember them being so, so, well, damn, so out there before."

What was it with men? They could be drugged to the gills and still fantasize about breasts? Good God. She should have gone to work for a female private investigator.

If she knew one.

If she knew one who would hire someone with no experience and no license.

If she knew one who would hire someone with no experience and no license who managed to get their boss's leg broken. Okay, Tommy was her only option.

Unable to keep from goading Tommy about his breast fixation, Finn said, "Emmy knows Victoria's Secret. Intimately. Have you heard of her?"

"Nope. Don't know her or her secret. What's her last name?" After a long pause, he continued, "Wait a minute. I think I saw her on TV."

Finn swallowed her laughter. She was enjoying this—sort of. Discussing her sister's boobs wasn't high on her list of topics she wanted to discuss with anyone, including Tommy. Jack was going to be a lot more helpful. It was time to wrap it up. "Queen Victoria, I believe is her name, and her secret is how she kept it up for so long."

"Wow. I'd like to meet this woman when I get back on my feet."

"And off the pain meds."

"Yeah, that, too."

"I'll make the introductions myself. I'm going to let you go now. You rest your leg."

"Jonesy, I am resting my leg. I'm on the couch with the TV on. I've got ESPN going and I've got a pile of Sports Illustrated and—"

"Swimsuit Edition?" she interrupted. That might explain the boob fascination.

"Yup, that one, too, and some other magazines Jack found at the market."

"Good for you." Nice to know Jack had taken care of him. "Please go easy and don't overdose."

"Not a chance. That damned Jack took the bottle with him. He said he'd come back to dishpens- dispensh, ah, hell, give them to me."

"Good thing," she muttered as she stood and shaded her eyes against the sun, sweat pooling between her breasts. "Love you. Take care."

"Back at ya, sweetcakes."

Sweetcakes? Twice in one convoluted conversation? What the what? He'd never called her that in her entire life. Finn went back inside the post office, copied the pertinent information about the Barron woman on a notepad she fished from the bottom of her backpack and went to stand in line for the stamps she'd originally come in for. She had a tour in ten minutes. As much as she wanted to help the FBI find one of their Ten Most Wanted, she did have a living to make. However pitiful it was. Still, there was one line she couldn't get out of her mind. *Reward leading to arrest.*

Yikes. How much? She could sure use the cash for

tuition.

She switched back to thoughts of Tommy and prayed he didn't hurt himself reaching for the remote or the latest sex-charged copy of *Playboy*. Her thoughts zoomed right off the track with a mental picture of Tommy and a Playboy Playmate doing the dirty deed. She almost proposed something indecent to the doddering eighty-something old man standing behind her in line.

It had been too long for Finn. She reached into her backpack, pulled out a candy bar, un-wrapped it and took a big healthy bite. Chocolate never hurt, even after a huge breakfast of Belgian waffles. But, it ran a long second behind actual sex. With an actual man.

When Debbie got home from breakfast with Gert and Finn, she made cookies—oatmeal raisin, her favorite—to get her mind off Freddy and how much she missed him.

One hour later, as she munched on a cookie, Debbie knew it hadn't helped. The little dark raisins merely reminded her of his beautiful brown eyes. She thought about calling or even sexting him but then she remembered why she was in New Orleans in the first place. Oh, well.

She could send him some photos on her cell phone of herself making cookies in her bra and panties so he wouldn't forget her while she was gone. Only she wasn't *in* her bra and panties but she could undress for the money shot. Maybe holding a spoon and a bowl strategically placed and forgetting the underwear altogether. Ha. That would get to Freddy.

For some reason sex was on her mind. It was on Freddy's mind *all* the time. They were teenagers. They were supposed to experiment according to *Seventeen Magazine*. It was natural and normal. And, naturally, she was nothing if not normal.

She gazed out the window at the back of the enormous house next door. A beautiful boy—a beautiful, studly, teenage boy—was stretching his legs to get out of a steel gray Corvette convertible parked in the alley. He was a good six feet tall and as he stood there, the breeze caught his long, wavy, sun-streaked surfer brown hair. Oh, wow. He slammed the car door and strode up the walkway to the back of the house. Debbie grabbed up a handful of cookies. She couldn't get out the door fast enough. Freddy Who?

∞

Finn's regular two o'clock tour that afternoon was the most difficult of her illustrious career. And quite possibly, the worst she'd ever given. She wasn't expecting any tips since she couldn't keep her mind on her job, forgetting her story about St. Louis Cemetery No.1 and who was buried there. The name Marie Laveau escaped her entirely. Someone had to remind her.

She couldn't remember the script she'd memorized years ago. She couldn't remember the names of streets she'd loved and walked on her entire life. If pressed she undoubtedly couldn't even remember whom Jackson Square was named for.

The hot sun bore down on her five customers, radiant young adults from Seattle with intricately knotted scarves around their necks, even the guys. They wore expensive, designer jeans and Doc Martens on their feet. They should have been fun and memorable, asking intelligent, inquisitive questions. Your typical coffee swilling college students. From the same slightly green complexions to the red-rimmed eyes, they were simply hung over. There was no other explanation for their quiet reticence. Ordinarily, everyone loved Finn but then, she wasn't herself today either.

Not fifteen minutes into her tour as they walked down Royal past expensive antique shops and elite jewelry boutiques, Finn struggling to recall even one interesting French Quarter anecdote, one of the young men winked at her. She frowned in return. God. Was he hitting on her? That never happened. She looked closer at his wan face, bloodshot hazel eyes, and sparse beard stubble. He appeared to be ogling her breasts. She swiveled around to point out something interesting. Anything. Interesting. Anything. New Orleans. Anything she could think of.

When they turned the corner onto Dauphine Finn tried ineffectually to ignore his grinning face. She came to an abrupt halt when she spotted the apartment building where she'd found the body the day before. The woman behind her stumbled into her back. Finn apologized, then unable to help herself, she looked up and was sorry she did. She blinked her eyes. There, draped over the rail, was another body.

Please God. Not another one. This one, she finally noticed, didn't look like the last one. It didn't look the least bit real. Straw tumbled out around its head and feet.

Hangovers notwithstanding, her group seemed more concerned with enduring the tour than enjoying it. Finn couldn't agree more. With one last look and a shake of her head, she walked them over to her uncles' voodoo store. For the first time in the tour, they seemed delighted. Neville and Finis were equally delighted to see her arrive with possible customers.

After exchanging pleasant inanities with her uncles and agreeing to bring Debbie and meet for brunch at The Commander's Palace next Sunday she departed. The boy who winked at her gave her a fifty-dollar tip, whispered his name in her ear—Todd—and his room number at the Meridian Hotel. If she actually showed up, she'd feel like a hooker. Not that she would. She kept the fifty dollars, thank you very much, and smiled her appreciation.

Should she call Jack about the straw man? No. It wasn't even a body. Would he give her grief? Yes. Would he call her the girl who cried wolf one too many times? Probably. Even if the killer was taunting her, and how odd would that be, why call Jack?

The mind boggled.

She shrugged her shoulders, then left the voodoo store and trekked back to the corner of Hell and Purgatory. She knew it was crazy, that she was undoubtedly certifiable but she needed to see the scarecrow for herself up close and personal. It was probably an early Halloween decoration. In August? She might be the stupidest person in the entire French Quarter but she needed to satisfy her curiosity.

This time she went to the front of the building, stole a quick peek around and seeing no one, pushed against the front gate. It wasn't even locked. She tiptoed through the narrow walkway back to the courtyard, Mace in one hand and a bottle of water in the other.

She stared up at the railing, and could now see the figure much more clearly. There was no doubt. It was a scarecrow.

Her cell phone chimed. She jumped, her heart racing, then dropped her Mace. She rummaged around in her backpack until she snagged the darn thing. She tapped the screen, then gave a tentative, "Hello?"

"Finn, is that you?"

She didn't immediately recognize the voice but the petulant tone she recognized with no problem. Argh. "This is Finn."

"Darling girl, it's Wes."

Oh. Dear. God. Wesley Ellis St. Clare III. If she wanted more grief in her life, she couldn't have asked for anyone more perfectly obnoxious to handle the job. She stared at the phone as if it were a snake come to life. "Wes, what the hell do you want?"

"Is that any way to speak to me? You used to love me."

She thought it was love two years ago, until he abandoned her on their wedding day. Time and meaningful therapy twice a week for several months showed her the difference between true love and infatuation. The dartboard on her bedroom wall with his photo stuck to it and hundreds of darts thrown at his well-fed face helped, too.

"I repeat, what do you want?"

"What makes you think I want anything?" he grumbled, as he always did whenever things didn't go his way. He still set Finn's teeth on edge. He wanted something. Why else would he call her now?

"I know you, Wes," she said, "and I don't like you. I think I told you I never wanted to speak to you or see you ever again."

He sighed. "That was two years ago. I figured you'd changed your mind after all this time. I don't hold any grudges."

He didn't hold any grudges? He left her at the altar in a white, sequined, strapless wedding dress she'd saved months and months for, holding a bouquet of baby's breath, pale blue carnations and purple asters, and a church full of friends and family. Who blubbered for a solid week afterward? Who, after months of seeing a therapist, still wanted to strangle the man with her bare hands? Why would he hold any grudges?

"What do you want?" she asked, struggling to sound civilized. "I have things to do."

"I thought you might like to go with me to—"

"Go with you?" She gritted her teeth, fighting the urge to scream hate-filled obscenities at him. "I want to do absolutely nothing with you. I don't care if you invite me to the governor's inaugural ball, hell, even the

President's inaugural ball. All eight balls or however many there are. I don't care if you invite me to be King of Carnival at Mardi Gras, I won't go."

"Okay, I think I'm getting the picture. I thought you might like to see a concert or something."

"You couldn't possibly get the picture, you, you..." Fuming, she took the steps two at a time up to the second landing and stared down at the scarecrow propped against the rail. "*You* left me. *You* deserted me. *You* are a good-for-nothing, scum-sucking, overbearing, self-centered, damned-for-hell, uh, uh, toad."

Silence met her rant. Maybe that was a bit much. Fine by her. She punched END. Fisting her hands at her side, she took several deep breaths to calm her nerves. She hadn't spoken to the man in two years. Two whole years! And he still had the power to make her mad enough to spit nails. She practiced several more deep breathing exercises she'd learned from her therapist, and bit by bit calmed down.

Under control again, sort of, she squatted by the dummy. It looked like the kind they used to demonstrate life saving techniques. Only this one was dressed like a scarecrow. Sort of. There was definitely straw sticking out of the plaid shirt and the denim overalls were ragged at the hem. The whole thing defied logic. Why a scarecrow? Why here? Why now? Did it matter? No. At least, not to her it didn't. She was trespassing, again, and she had no reason to be there aside from her damnable curiosity. Which killed the cat, if she remembered correctly.

She left the same way she came and marched to the streetcar stop, ignoring the tourists and the traffic, her head high, her heart settling into a more normal rhythm.

As she stood in the neutral ground in the center of the street waiting for the streetcar, an older man in a tan trench coat and fifty's style brown plaid hat jostled her.

He looked like something out of a black and white movie come to life in living color. When Finn inspected his face, he scowled at her, every line in his face creasing. He pointed a finger at her chest. "Watch where you're going."

"Sorry," she muttered. She was so not in the mood.

"You better be. Or else you will be."

"What's that supposed to mean?" The woman who stood next to her shrugged her shoulders. "I don't even know you."

"It don't matter. You watch your step, missy, or you'll be a dead woman."

"Bite me," Finn snarled as the streetcar arrived. He pushed ahead, elbowing his way around her and the other woman to get on. "Jerk."

The woman nodded her head in agreement. "It takes all kinds."

"Don't I know it." Finn got on board ignoring the rude man as she made her way down the aisle. She had two free hours before her culinary class so she was going to go see Tommy at his apartment. Visiting him was a surefire guarantee to make her forget the idiocy her life had become.

Finn rang the buzzer. When no one answered, she tried the door and found it unlocked. She entered the apartment and found Tommy lying immobile on his couch, his synthetically encased leg reclining on a foot stool. He had the TV remote in one hand, a can of soda in the other. He'd tuned the TV to a football game. Strewn all around him were magazines, newspapers, discarded fast food wrappers and half empty cans of soda.

"Jonesy," he murmured, grinning. His eyes twinkled with manufactured, drug-induced, good will. "How ya doin'? Don't mind the mess, the cleaning lady hasn't come by yet."

"You don't have a cleaning lady."

He winked. "True, but I'm gonna need one after this."

"At least you sound more coherent than the last time we talked." She gently pushed his leg aside and sat on the footstool facing him.

"Jack cut my pain meds in half. He said I was beginning to sound like Paris Hilton. Not sure what that means but it must have been bad."

Finn laughed. "You weren't making much sense."

"I always make sense. At least to myself." He dropped the remote and set his soda on the floor. He crossed his arms over his chest and gave her a mock frown. He needed a shave, his hair stood at attention in several places and the red and green striped rugby shirt he wore was stained with something red. Gert was right. Even like this, he looked boyish, yet sexy. And in dire need of some female TLC.

"I have something to tell you," she began. "Are you sure you're coherent? I'd hate to have to tell you again."

"Ha. I'm as coherent as ever. Honest. Hit me."

"You know those shots I took of the philandering Johnny Franco and his lady love?"

"How could I forget? She of the lovely breasts and neon butterfly tattoo."

"That's the one. I saw her photo up on the wall in the post office."

Tommy jerked as if he'd been touched with an electric cattle prod. "What?"

"FBI's Ten Most Wanted."

"No kidding. What for?"

"Something big. I can't remember. Hold on." She dug out her notebook and took a look. "Embezzlement in Tacoma, Washington."

"Wow. She's a long way from home." He unfolded his arms and placed them on top of his head. Staring at the ceiling, he continued, "Embezzlement. That covers a multitude of sins, none good. She must have taken a boatload of cash from someone important. If I remember my PI training at all, you have to have stolen hundreds of thousands to get on their list."

"What does it mean to us?"

He squirmed, moved his leg and winced. "Good question. I doubt she wants photos of herself floating around. I sure as hell wouldn't. That could be why Franco was so upset. On the other hand, one might not have anything to do with the other."

"Meaning," Finn said, picking up the thread of his thoughts, "Franco might simply be mad that we caught him cheating on his wife. He might not know what his girlfriend has been up to or even who she really is."

"Anything is possible," he agreed. "Finn, not to change the subject but I really need to take a leak."

"Oh-kay." What exactly did he want her to do about it?

He grinned. "And, no, you don't have to hold my equipment while I go. I need you to help me get to my feet, then walk me to the bathroom. The last time I tried to get to the bathroom by myself I fell and walloped the shin on my good leg."

She put her arm around his waist, then helped him to rise. Together they hobbled across the room, through the bedroom and to the bathroom on the other side. He put one hand on the door and turned to look at her. "If you hear me fall, come in and help a grown, humiliated, half-naked man to his feet. Otherwise just stay here, then get me back to the couch. If you don't mind."

"Not a problem. Are you sure you can do it by yourself?"

He grinned, then reached out his free hand to mess

up her hair. "I've managed to piss by myself for thirty years. It would be embarrassing to admit I can't do it now because I broke my damned leg. Of course, if you really want to come in and hold it for me, I won't complain."

"Sorry, big guy, but you're going to have to take things in hand yourself."

"Not things," he said, closing the door behind him. "One big thing."

While he was in the bathroom, his cell phone rang with the theme from *Jaws*. "I'll get it for you," she hollered. "Be right back."

She found his phone on the end table beneath the September Playboy. "'Lo?"

"Is this Tommy Boyle's phone?"

"Yes, it is. Can I take a message?"

"Yeah, tell him Roy Windom called. I own the furniture store below Tommy's office."

"Okay."

"His office was broken into early this morning before we even opened the warehouse at five. There are papers and files and stuff all over the floor. I don't know if anything was taken. I called the cops and they said they'd make a report but they said Tommy needed to take a look and see if anything's missing. They tried calling him but didn't get an answer. They told me they'd try to reach him again later today. That early in the morning there really was no need to track him down at his apartment and wake him up for a simple burglary. I think the computer's hard drive is missing. I don't know what else."

"God." Not what Tommy needed on top of his broken leg.

"Why isn't Tommy here? I know he keeps peculiar hours but he's usually around by mid-day."

"He had an accident. He broke his leg last night

falling down those outside stairs."

"Damn. Sorry to hear that. That didn't have anything to do with the break-in?"

"I don't know."

"Please let Tommy know and give him my best for a speedy recovery. I broke my shoulder once. It was hell on wheels and hurt like the dickens."

Several hours and several Advils later, Finn stared at today's chef instructor, Chef Westrom. The woman stood with her hands on her narrow, white chef's coat-covered hips, her chef's hat tilting off the left side of her head. Her beady eyes, black as her cold heart, stared at the quaking young man beside Finn. Even seated, Finn could feel his knees shaking. His head bobbed in agreement with each word the instructor spewed in his direction.

Finn listened, cringing, her own heart in her throat, as the woman upbraided the poor guy, a fellow student. For his misdeeds, which were miniscule in Finn's mind, he was taking a beat-down the likes of which she'd never heard. He hadn't whipped his cream properly. He hadn't cooled his bowl properly. According to the chef, he hadn't done anything properly since he dragged himself out of bed this morning.

Days like this made Finn ponder the wisdom of her career choice. In spite of it all, she thanked God she wasn't the one on the receiving end today. She had been the brunt of this particular instructor's wrath on two other days she'd not soon forget. She didn't care to repeat the terror she'd felt with the spotlight shining on her. The humiliation lasted long after the actual day, several weeks, truth be told.

As the sound of the old bat's vitriolic rant slowed, then stopped altogether Finn mustered the courage to lift her head. She found herself eye to eye with the woman herself.

"Surprisingly, Miss Jones, your dish was perfectly adequate."

High praise indeed. Finn released the breath she'd been holding. "Thank you, Chef."

"That doesn't mean there isn't room for improvement."

"Of course," Finn agreed, nodding her head. A thick red curl escaped from her chef hat and bobbed in agreement next to her nose.

The instructor's eyes narrowed as Finn quickly stuffed the renegade hair back up under her hat. Luckily, the woman moved on to her next poor victim.

Was she cut out to be a chef? She loved to cook and try new recipes out on her friends. Was it enough? Could she put off her animosity of the Wicked Witch and look past this class to see a brighter, and hopefully, better paying, future as a real honest-to-God chef?

Every day she reminded herself this was what she truly wanted.

Damn. Could she grow a pair? She gave herself a mental butt-kicking. This *was* what she wanted. And nothing was going to stop her from reaching her goal. Get over yourself, Finn.

She seriously did not want to spend the rest of her life traipsing through the streets of the French Quarter, especially in the overbearingly hot, humid days of summer, repeating the same tired, boring stories of its historical past to paying tourists. No matter how much she loved the French Quarter she could give her talk in her sleep but, admittedly, some days she bored herself.

More importantly, did she want to be the one sister who waltzed through life never accomplishing anything of importance? She knew the answer to that one.

No way. Make that a resounding *N. O. Way.*

She removed her white coat and striped chef hat, stuffed them into her backpack and started for the door with the rest of her forlorn fellow students. She saw movement out of the corner of her eye near the bank of windows on her right. She blinked several times. It looked like the same person—er, ghost—she saw last night.

She stared, a bark of laughter caught in her throat. He saluted her with a serious expression on his face and a tip of his tall white chef hat, then his form shimmered, wavered and disappeared altogether. She bit the inside of her lip. She refused to acknowledge, even to herself, that she was seeing ghosts. Again. And a chef? What was that all about? Lack of sleep? Lack of oxygen? Lack of common sense?

She was exhausted, sleep-deprived or going crazy but she was most definitely not seeing ghosts.

Finn didn't believe in ghosts. Not Casper, not Blackbeard, not even the Ghost Whisperer. Sheesh.

Even ever intrepid Debbie would be having a coronary if she saw this ghost and she believed in everything supernatural. Including her favorite TV show, *Supernatural*.

Finn was drained. After all, she'd been bashed in the head after seeing a dead man, accosted by a deranged, angry man, then spent half the night in a hospital waiting room worrying about Tommy. She'd even been threatened today by a perfectly horrible stranger at the streetcar stop.

Any normal person could have a hallucination or two. Any normal person, even, might think they'd seen a ghost. It could happen. She'd be fine once she got a good night's sleep. It was one too many shocks in too few hours.

When she got home, exhausted and irritable, she found Jack sitting on her stoop drinking iced tea from one of her own glasses. In his snug black jeans, tight black tee shirt, he exuded his usual take-me-to-bed charm. He gifted her with a disarming smile. She knew that look. She was in trouble. And it wasn't because she'd recently seen a ghost.

"Where you been? Debbie didn't know. She was nice enough to get me a glass of tea, though, before she galloped over to Gert's to play with the cats."

"D'you want to come in?" she asked, refusing to answer his question and lie about her whereabouts.

"After you," he said, standing up and stepping aside. "I've got good news and I've got bad news."

"And I have news for you."

He grinned. "Let's share."

CHAPTER FIVE

Jack refused to talk until they sat at her kitchen table. Glasses of iced tea dripping condensation and a plate of Debbie's homemade oatmeal cookies lay between them. The sweet scent of cinnamon and nutmeg made Finn's mouth water. She broke one in half and stuffed it into her mouth.

"How was your day?" he began pleasantly enough. "I got your voice mail, and Tommy kinda sorted it out for me. Not only is the woman you saw on the poster in the post office wanted by the FBI and on their Ten Most Wanted List, but you snapped her photo while she was adulterating. The kicker being the guy who came after you at Tommy's last night was also in the shot. Have I got it right?"

"Yeah, pretty much. She's the one I photographed and she's definitely wanted by the FBI for embezzling. She also has a lovely butterfly tattoo on her left breast."

He hooted. "Good to know if I ever get close enough to her to check it out."

Finn took a sip of her tea and munched on her cookie. She wasn't going to say a word about the scarecrow or the fact she'd been back to the apartment building again. All best left unsaid.

"You're a font of information," Jack said, eyeing her over the rim of his glass. He grabbed a cookie, gave it a sniff and stuffed it whole into his mouth.

Finn raised her brows. "Wow. Font. Kind of a big word for a dumb cop."

He flashed a quick grin, still chewing. "You'd be surprised what I know."

"I always am."

"I have no idea what's going on with this FBI fugitive, though," he admitted with a shake of his head. He wiped a crumb off his lower lip. "What the hell have you and Tommy got yourself into?"

Finn shrugged. "All I did was take some innocent pictures."

"Innocent, my ass."

"Maybe not innocent." Finn set her tea down, in case the slippery glass fell from her hand when Jack dropped another bomb. He wore an anxious look which told her he was about to do exactly that. "What did you really come over here for?"

"I kept something from you the other night at the hospital." He sat with his feet propped on one of Finn's wooden, third generation slat-backed kitchen chairs, his tumbler of tea in one hand, and the fingers of his other hand drumming a tattoo on the tabletop. The curved shade of the opaque overhead lamp cast half his face in shadows. She didn't miss the obvious look of impatience passing over his features, though. As if he wanted to be anywhere but here with her. She waited for the other shoe to drop.

Finn stared at him a moment anticipating his next words, when she glimpsed the renovated antebellum mansion next door and another problem leapt to the forefront of her beleaguered brain.

Debbie had left a note telling Finn she was going to the Arnauds'. Debbie was probably inside at this very moment trying to score with the Arnaud's teenage son, Benjy, who even in Finn's much older mind was a stone-cold hottie.

Yesterday when Debbie spotted him out the window washing his blue Corvette in the alley behind the house she texted Finn. She described him to Finn in intimate detail. Since he lived next door Finn knew good and well what he looked like, but Debbie insisted on repeating the information.

Shirtless, with his khaki shorts wet and clinging to his thighs and tiny butt, Debbie became instantly enamored. Finn read between the lines of text and diagnosed the first blush of infatuation in Debbie's desperation to tell her about her latest heartthrob.

It was the worst possible news. Considering what she knew about Debbie and her predilection for hormonally charged boys, this was definitely not a good thing. Dorie would have a heart attack if she found out.

Debbie could get into all kinds of trouble with another teenage boy. Finn narrowed her eyes at Jack's sneaker-clad feet propped on the chair and attempted to pick up the thread of their lapsed conversation with an intelligent remark. "Huh?"

"I said," Jack unnecessarily stated louder while grinning like a fool, "I forgot to tell you something the other night. Where did you wander off to?"

"Forgot to tell me or deliberately didn't?"

"Deliberately didn't." He shrugged. "You were worried about Tommy and you obviously had other things on your mind, kind of like you do right now."

She sighed. "It's Debbie. If anything happens to her while she's on my watch, Mom'll kill me. I know she's going to get into trouble with that cute Arnaud boy next door."

"Your mom won't kill you. No doubt she expects the worst."

"Probably. So why are you really here?" Jack hadn't stopped by to see her more than a few times in his adult life. Once when she had the flu he brought over soup, and once when he wanted to borrow Gert's leaf blower. Now she'd seen him two days in a row. "Why didn't you call?"

He put his glass down and dropped his feet to the cracked linoleum floor, elbows on his thighs, hands dangling between his knees. He stared at Finn. "Honestly? I didn't want you to freak out on the phone."

She snorted. "You'd rather freak me out in person? Are you kidding me? I think I can take it, whatever it is."

"Get real. You don't think anything else can freak you out?"

"Aside from seeing what I thought was a dead body? Aside from getting conked on the head? And," she continued after taking a deep breath, "aside from seeing a woman I photographed on an FBI wanted poster at the post office? Hmm, what do you think?"

"Okay, *chere*, I get your point." He chewed on his lower lip a minute, then placed his hands flat on his denim-clad thighs and sat up straight. "What I have to tell you is about you but don't forget that FBI's Most Wanted woman. If she's on their list, she's big-time serious and could well be dangerous to anyone who finds out she's here."

Worry lines fanned out from his baby blues. Now she was concerned, too. She forced a smile she wasn't feeling. "What is this thing that's about me that's going to freak me out?"

He blew out a slow breath. "When I went to investigate your crime scene I found a small voodoo doll."

"Not a full-size scarecrow?"

"No. Huh? What are you talking about?"

"Nothing."

"At the spot where your so-called body was supposed to be, I found a voodoo doll with your likeness."

She leaned forward, intrigued and more than a little creeped out. "My likeness?"

"Yup, blue jean shorts, pink tee shirt, curly red hair, even a tiny pink baseball cap imprinted with New Orleans propped on its head. It wore miniature Mardi Gras beads around the neck."

"That doesn't seem like much," Finn admitted. "Maybe I have a secret admirer. So what if it looked like me? That doesn't mean it is me."

He shook his head, his lips thinned. "Other than the fact that there was a rope tied around the neck and three pins were stuck in the chest? For some strange reason, that doesn't sound like a secret admirer to me."

"Oh."

"Yeah. A big damned oh. Don't get me wrong, I don't believe in that voodoo crap. And I don't even think for a minute that your mojo is compromised or some other bull. I do think you're on this guy's radar. It was a straight forward warning to mind your own damn business, which," he said, with a nod in her direction, "isn't a bad idea."

"Hey, I did my civic duty. I let you know," she said pointing a finger at him. *Mind her own damn business?* Yeah, like that was going to happen. It was a good thing no one saw her this afternoon stalking a scarecrow. "I'm not going to do anything else."

"I hope not. Had to let you know about the doll though."

"Did you talk to the people living there?"

"Detective that I am, I knew the body, either alive or not, fake or real had to go someplace, so I talked to the landlord. He lives on the first floor of the building. There are three apartments there on the third floor.

"He told me he'd been home all day and hadn't heard a thing. Of course, he's stone deaf and had the TV on loud enough to be heard across the river at Algiers Point."

Finn smiled.

"He told me two brothers named La Fontaine live in Apartment One. The older one works at the French Market down on Decatur and the younger one drives a horse-drawn carriage in the Quarter."

Finn nodded, urging him to continue.

"Apartment Two houses three young women. The guy gave me the universal hand gesture for a shapely woman." Jack did the same thing with both hands and Finn nodded as she fought off a grin.

"He said he didn't know where they worked and didn't care since they paid their rent on the first of the month without fail. The third place is rented to a sweet little old lady—his description—who was the first to rent an apartment when he divided up the house twenty years ago. She's quiet and seldom leaves the place. He said she even has her groceries delivered.

"'I'll probably have to call the morgue myself when she kicks the bucket'," he told me. "He said he'd hate to see her go since she's never given him a bit of trouble and always pays her rent on time.

"I asked about the brothers since they seemed the likely suspects but he didn't know if they were even home at the time."

"Now what?" Finn asked.

"I detect. I try to track down these guys and see if they know anything. Nobody was home when I knocked on their door but I'll try again tomorrow." Jack got to his feet and stuck his hands in his back pocket. "In the meantime I want you to watch yourself. I'd say it wouldn't be a bad idea to carry a gun but since you don't know diddly-squat about guns it *would* be a bad idea."

"I have Mace," she volunteered, standing up to walk him to the door.

"Guess it'll have to do." He pulled his hands from his pockets, then turned and stopped with a grip on the doorknob. He winked at her. "According to Tommy, you swing a mean backpack."

Finn cringed. "I'm afraid it's God's own truth."

Jack opened the door and stepped out onto the dark stoop. He stared at Gert's mini mansion, and shook his head.

"What?" she asked.

"Oh, it's your crazy aunt and that gigantic mausoleum she lives in."

"You should be nicer. She had exceptionally good things to say about you this morning at breakfast. Tommy, too."

"That's 'cause the woman is always on the prowl. I doubt we have anything to worry about. Neither of us has any money. Of course, we could be her pool boys. One at a time, of course."

"Very funny."

He raised one brow. "You don't think I can satisfy an older woman?"

"Let's not go there."

"Whatever you say, *chere*. So what's the game plan now? It'll be awhile before Tommy can hide in the bushes and take dirty pictures. 'Course he's always got you to do that."

"And I'm available for birthdays and bar mitzvahs." Finn laughed as she joined Jack outside the door, the sound of crickets chirping in the darkness. "Jack, I have a proposition for you if you're interested."

He turned to look at her, a twinkle in his eye. "I'm always interested in propositions."

"Of course you are," she agreed with a shake of her

head. "Part of me living here rent free is I have to do yard work for Gert and I hate yard work. If you'll come help me with it this weekend while she's out cruising, I'll cook for you. I can make—"

"Anything," he said, interrupting her. "I'll help with any yard work if I can get a home-cooked meal out of it. I eat take-out seven days a week."

"How do you know it'll be any good?"

He started down the walkway around the side of the house to the street where he'd parked his car. He stopped, turned to look at her and grinned. "I trust you. I have a feeling it'll be great. Call and give me the where and when, I'll be there." He waved. "Later, *chere*."

Finn stood staring after him. He forgot to tell her the good news.

⋙⋘

Finn settled on the couch for a little serious one-on-one time with Debbie after a dinner of her own recipe for spicy beef stew. It was damned good if she said so herself.

Debbie turned away from the flickering TV screen. Some crazy reality show where the contestants chased each other from one third world country to another. She stared at Finn with a quizzical look on her bemused face, the light of a table lamp reflecting off her youthful face. "The stew was pretty good."

"Thanks."

"In spite of the sweet potatoes."

"Thanks."

"Those were sweet potatoes, weren't they?"

Finn nodded.

"And beans?"

"Yep, black beans."

"Not bad."

This conversation couldn't get much more inane. Still she appreciated it. Finn enjoyed Debbie's company and for the first time in two days felt relaxed.

"I don't like my food mixed together. Normally," Debbie said, staring at her chipped nails. "You got remover?"

"In the bathroom medicine cabinet."

"Boys think fingernail polish is sexy." She got up to go to the bathroom. "I'm thinking about getting nipple rings. They think they're sexy, too. Do you think it will hurt?"

"Definitely." Oh, boy. She wasn't prepared for these kinds of conversations.

Debbie sauntered to the bathroom staring hard at her nails when Finn's phone chimed.

Saved by the bell.

"Hello."

"Finn, darlin' girl, how are you?"

The baritone voice on the other end of the phone belonged to Wesley. Again? What was wrong with the man? Definitely not her favorite person. Okay, he was her least favorite person. On the planet. In the entire universe. To infinity and beyond. "Yeah, what is it?"

"How's the world treating you?"

What did he want? They hadn't spoken in two years, three months and seven days, but who was counting? She had enjoyed every silent minute. And, now, twice in one day? What was up with this guy?

"The reason I'm calling is, I know how you like the Neville Brothers. They're playing at Tipitina's and I was wondering if you'd like to go."

She didn't hear any humor in his voice, or sarcasm, or nastiness. If she wasn't mistaken, he sounded sincere. Who was he kidding? She adored the Nevilles but it would be a cold day in Hell before she so much as crossed the street with him.

"You're kidding. Right?"

"Is that Weasel Wesley?" whispered Debbie, as she

entered the room holding a bottle of nail polish remover, several cotton balls and Finn's newest bottle of polish, Flame Out Red.

Finn nodded, then rolled her eyes.

Debbie held out her free hand. "I'll talk to him."

"Shh." Finn waved her away. If she couldn't handle Wes, she should throw away her mom's *I Am Woman* CD which she'd confiscated after falling in love with Helen Reddy's ode to the liberated female.

"I used to think he was all that," Deb continued, "with his Porsche, his wavy black hair, those outstanding green eyes, but, like, what a first-class jerk he turned out to be."

Finn cupped her phone. "Debbie, shush please."

"Finn, you still there?"

"I'm here. What do you want? Honestly?"

"I'm asking you out," he said.

"No, really. What do you want?"

"Seriously, I'm asking you out."

"Then no, I won't go out with you."

"Is next week good for you?"

Finn rolled her eyes. "No."

"The Nevilles will be gone after that."

"They live here, Wesley. I think they'll be playing somewhere sometime. It doesn't matter. I'm not going out with you."

"I'll check their schedule and get back to you."

"No."

"Talk soon, Finn."

Finn ended the call and stared at the phone, then at Debbie. "Do you believe him? Asking me out?"

"He always had a ginormous ego. Wasn't he, like, worried all the time about how he looked? I like the way he dressed, though, like a model or a movie star or, you know, a celebrity."

"Looked like one, too," Finn hated to admit. "He

paid more for his haircuts than I ever did. I can't believe you even noticed him. What were you? All of thirteen, fourteen?"

"Yeah." Debbie plopped down beside her, after putting her nail supplies on the end table. She moved one bare foot to the coffee table. "Like it was always all about him. No offense, Finn, but I wondered what he saw in you."

"None taken." Finn grinned. "Maybe it was my sparkling personality? My oh-so-interesting jobs? How about my falling apart Bug?"

She grinned right back. "Ha, like all of the above, I'm sure."

"It must have been my cat duty for Aunt Gert. Wes loved her cats, especially cleaning out the litter boxes."

Deb snorted. She picked up a cotton ball and the polish remover. "Like I believe that."

"All true, Debs. All true."

The phone rang again and she jumped.

"Hello?" she answered tentatively.

"Is this Finnigan?" came a familiar, older female voice Finn couldn't quite identify.

"Yes?"

"What did you do to my baby boy?"

Ah. Mrs. Boyle. Tommy and Jack's mom. She was the mama bear of all mama bears. She still lived in the same house where they grew up, a widow with nothing better to do than interfere in their lives and make sure they were being good Catholic boys. She wanted wives for them and grandchildren and soon. Since both of her boys refused to comply, she grabbed every opportunity to turn the situation around.

"Mrs. Boyle, I'm so sorry. It was an accident."

"Call me Evie, hon."

As if she could. She'd been Mrs. Boyle when Finn was a little girl and Mrs. Boyle she would forever be.

"I tried talking to Tommy when I came over to his place with my shrimp and eggplant bake but he was so drugged out on pain medication, he made absolutely no sense. He told me you pushed him down a flight of stairs. Is that the truth?"

"No. God, no. It was an accident."

"I figured as much. You Jones girls would never hurt my boys."

Finn wouldn't. She wasn't so sure about either of her sisters.

"Had to make sure. How's your folks doing down there in Florida?"

"They're good. Enjoying their retirement."

"Good for them. Give them my love the next time you talk."

"I will."

"And in the meantime, don't be pushing any of my boys down any more steps." Finn detected a slight amused tone.

"I'll try."

"You do that, *chere*. Now take care. Bye-bye."

"Mrs. Boyle. Tommy's mom," Debbie said. "Was she giving you what for?"

"I think she thought I pushed Tommy down the stairs on purpose."

"As if."

"Exactly." She went to put her phone down when it rang again. She was Miss Popularity tonight. "Hello?"

"My favorite private eye," came Tommy's familiar voice. "I'd say private dick but it is so wrong."

"Tommy, how are you?"

"Honestly? I feel like I fell down a flight of stairs."

"That's funny. You did."

"Oh, yeah. I did. That explains the cast on my leg. And the naked women dancing around my apartment."

"Naked women?"

"Not quite. They are wearing neon green g-strings."

"Tommy?" Now she was worried. As she stood up and reached for her car keys, he said, "I think it's the pain meds. And, Jonesy, I plan on being in pain a long, long time."

"Oh, thank God, Tommy, you scared me there for a minute. By the way, your mama called."

"Sorry. What did she blame you for? Her long labor with me? My lack of reproducing genes? Or was it the broken leg?"

"She said you told her I pushed you down the stairs. On purpose."

"Oh, Lordy. That woman."

"I straightened her out. I think."

"Good. You ready to go out again?"

"Oh, yeah. Can't wait. Soon I'll be tooling around in my beat-up VW taking lots of dirty pictures."

"Ain't life grand?"

"Can't complain," she said. "What happened with your hot clandestine affair?"

"Oh, man, I wish I was having a hot clandestine affair."

"You know what I mean. Is the job off now that you're incapacitated?"

"No," he said. She heard him sigh. "It's postponed until I'm back on both my feet."

"They're willing to wait for you then?"

Tommy laughed. She heard him clomping around the room, then a heartfelt sigh as he sat down. "They're willing to wait for the best damn PI in New Orleans, hell, the best damn PI in the state of Louisiana, that's f'sure."

Finn grinned. "F'sure."

They finished talking and Finn plopped down on the couch. Could she quiz Debbie about the Arnaud's teenage son and her intentions toward him without causing the girl to go ballistic? Maybe she could bribe her with food, homemade pralines or almond macaroons but if she remembered correctly, Debbie hated almonds.

"Benji Arnaud is hot," Debbie stated as she removed the chipped polish from her nails saving Finn the problem of how to broach the touchy subject.

"Oh?"

Debbie picked up the TV remote and muted the sound. She curled one bare leg beneath her, and gazed at the screen where a pair of hefty guys were traipsing through a cornfield. "Oh, yeah. Hot."

"And what are your intentions toward him?"

Debbie giggled. "Intentions? You sound like Dorie."

"Sorry, but I am responsible for you."

"I can take care of myself."

"Uh-huh, so what are you thinking about him?"

"I don't know yet."

"What about Freddy?"

Debbie rolled her eyes. "Freddy's hundreds of miles away. I still love Freddy but he's, like, not here and Benji is right next door. Isn't that great?"

"Yeah, you're right, it's wonderful." What could be wrong with agreeing with her? "He's right next door."

Her face took on a faraway look. "Finn, have you ever been in love?"

"When I was about your age, I had a majorly crush on Jack Boyle. Majorly. I thought I was in lo-ove."

"Did he know?"

"Probably."

"Wasn't Emmy dating him then?"

"Yes, but it didn't stop me from crushing on him."

"Did you tell him?"

Finn's mouth fell open. "Are you crazy? Emmy would have killed me if she thought I was trying to steal Jack away from her."

"Hmmm." Debbie's gaze wandered to the TV where a couple was now having a heated argument about whose turn it was to drive. Such serious problems. "I would have told him."

"You, Debbie, are bolder than I ever was."

She shook her head. "I, like, you know, go for what I want. I don't let anything stop me. If you really wanted Jack, you'd have done the same. It's not too late, you know."

"Who are you? Dr. Ruth?"

She turned to look at Finn with a quizzical expression on her face. "Who's Dr. Ruth?"

"The Dr. Phil of a few years ago. Go ahead and make me feel a hundred years old. How old are you anyway?" she asked rhetorically.

"Seventeen," she stated as if Finn could forget.

"I think you're a little young to be handing out unwanted advice to your older sister who, by the way, is way over her crush on Jack Boyle. And don't forget Emmy has a nasty temper. She would have had a cow if I'd made a move on Jack. She has a mean left hook."

"Oh, yeah, right. Like she'd have hit you."

Finn stared at Debbie. She forgot how much younger she was. Apparently, she didn't remember being around Emmy when she had one of her hissy fits. "If Emmy thought I was after her boyfriend, she would have slapped me silly. Then complained to Dorie how I was picking on her and being mean. I'd have ended up grounded, even though I was the one with the black eye and the swollen cheek. She knows how to manipulate things to her own advantage."

"Come on." Debbie stared at her. "Did that really happen?"

"Twice." She recalled times in her teens when she honestly hated Emmy.

"Maybe I'll have Benji run me over by the house

and, like, you know, see what's up with her." She held up her left hand in front of her face and checked to make sure the old polish was off.

"You can try but she's out of town," Finn said. "In the south of France with an up-and-coming politician. So, Debs, tell me about Benji. How old is he?"

Debbie clasped her hands to her chest. "He's seventeen just like me, has his own car, a Corvette, and he promised to show me around town."

Finn grinned. "You already know your way around town."

"He doesn't know that. Besides it's changed since Katrina."

"Unfortunately, that's true but we're getting there."

"He's so hot, I'd like to get my hands on him and—"

"Hold it!" Finn jumped to her feet. "Wait one damned minute!"

Debbie jumped to her feet and threw her arms around Finn keeping her sticky fingers away from Finn's shirt. "Gotcha."

Finn backed up so she could look into her sparkling caramel brown eyes. "What?"

"I'm kidding, Finn. Besides he said he's seeing someone else but, you know, he also said it's not serious. She's probably some Mardi Gras princess with a humungous trust fund, a tight butt and Botoxed lips."

Finn twisted around to look at Debbie's backside. "Your butt is plenty tight."

Debbie frowned. "That's not what I meant."

"I know," Finn said with a knowing grin.

"Oh."

Finn pulled her back into her arms. "Gotcha."

"I guess I deserved that," Debbie grumbled against Finn's shoulder.

"Please promise me you won't go crazy with Benji."

"Go crazy?"

"You know what I mean. No sex."

"I'll try but I can't make any promises." She rolled her eyes heavenward and then gave Finn a goofy smile. "He is so-o yummy."

God. Finn was so-o in trouble.

Jack left his third story Upper Pontalba apartment on Jackson Square with a to-go cup of coffee. He bounded onto the street to walk to work. He'd remained forever on the waiting list for the pricey apartment, but what else did he have to spend his money on? He didn't gamble, or care about clothes or cars. The car he owned, a twelve-year-old Camry, didn't often get out of the parking garage where he stored it. He had no hobbies unless he included rocking back with a cold Abita in front of ESPN. He didn't have time for anything else.

The place was ideal, close to work, restaurants and most everything else he needed. Women thought the four-story red brick building was cool because of its history and location in the heart of the French Quarter. He simply liked the convenience. Impressing women was merely a bonus.

As soon as he sat down in his chair at the precinct, Jack got a call from the coroner's office. A floater who vaguely fit the description of the body Finn had seen during her walking tour. He was identified as thirty-nine-year-old Simon La Fontaine, a part-time carriage driver with one former conviction for attempting to blackmail a tourist after eavesdropping on a conversation while driving him around the Quarter.

Jack shook his head. Why were people so stupid as to talk about anything that could be cause for blackmail while riding in a damned horse-drawn carriage?

Then he smacked his forehead, remembering where he'd heard the name before.

Simon La Fontaine, along with his brother, Peter,

lived in one of the apartments where Finn saw her so-
called dead body and where he'd found the voodoo doll.

CHAPTER SIX

Everyone who drove in the French Quarter knew parking was horribly impossible and impossibly horrible. Finn knew it and drove only when she couldn't take the streetcar. The streets were narrow, the parking limited and every driver, whether garbage hauler, taxi or delivery truck, double-parked whenever and wherever he wants.

The next morning as Finn walked along the street minding her own business, she, like everyone else, took little notice of the traffic except when stepping out into it.

So, when a dark-colored sedan with tinted windows squealed to a stop beside her, Finn barely registered it. The driver, a blonde, full-busted woman, jumped out of the car. She scampered between two parked cars and yanked Finn off her feet. Finn let out a sharp scream and shoved. Against an immoveable object.

She struggled and continued screaming but the woman hoisted Finn over her shoulder and tossed her in the back seat as if she weighed no more than a sack of flour. Finn fell against the door handle, bruising her ribs and stealing her breath. Her entire body tense, her muscles taut, Finn fought hard to calm down and think.

The woman hopped in the front seat. She hit the door locks, then, acting as if nothing unusual had happened, calmly pulled back into traffic.

"What the hell?" Finn scrambled to sit up, not easy to do with her over-loaded backpack scrunched against the seat and oxygen slowly trickling back to her lungs. She wrenched on the door handle. Of course, the woman locked all of them. Finn wasn't about to be kidnapped without an attempt to flee or, at the very least, a frantic argument. "You can't just grab someone off the street. Are you out of your mind?"

"I did, pretty easily actually. It's possible I am out of my mind, I haven't decided yet." She glanced into the rearview mirror, her brown eyes narrowed. "Nice to meet you, Finnigan Jones."

"It's Finn, and there's nothing nice about it," she answered without realizing she was speaking to the woman as she would anyone she had been introduced to. "How d'you know my name?"

"I haf my vays," she said with a terrible German accent. She turned around and grinned. "Inappropriate humor?"

"I'll say." Finn wrestled out of her backpack and set it beside her on the seat. She thought about putting her hands around the woman's neck and squeezing the life out of her but was afraid she might be armed. Or, with Finn's luck, she'd crash the car into the side of a ten-story building and kill them both. "What d'you want with me?"

"I *want* my pictures."

"What pictures?" Finn said feigning innocence. She caught the woman's scowl in the rearview mirror and gulped. Deceit probably registered on her face as though it were lit up like a B-movie marquee.

"You know what pictures."

"You mean like the one hanging on the wall of the post office?" For some reason, Finn couldn't keep from goading her. She was pissed off about being abducted but she was pretty sick of this woman as well. "Or maybe you mean the one where you and Johnny Franco, the very married Johnny Franco, are getting it on in public. Maybe I've already sent a photo that shows off your butterfly tattoo to the FBI, the one even they didn't know about."

"You're as nuts as I am. If the FBI wants me, I could be a murderer or a serial killer. Or worse."

"Or wanted for embezzling mega amounts of cash." Finn leaned forward and placed her hands on the seat in front of her so she could study the woman's sullen face in the rearview mirror. She'd be better off in the front seat so she climbed over. "Margaret Jane Barron. I know who you are, too."

She stole a sideways glance at Finn, her brow furrowed. "What's wrong with you?"

"If I keep talking and you get to know me better, maybe you won't kill me."

"I'm not going to kill you." Her eyebrows rose, nearly hitting her hairline. "You're crazier than me."

"Not by a long shot."

"Huh."

"I've been called worse than crazy," Finn admitted as her heart slowed to a more moderate rhythm. Barron might be a criminal, but maybe not a killer. Hopefully not a killer. Although anyone with enough incentive was capable of murder. "Where are you taking me?"

She turned down Canal heading toward the river. Street traffic streamed around the car. If she leaned on the horn, a dozen cars and twice as many pedestrians would notice. They wouldn't do anything, but they'd notice.

When they neared the Riverwalk and she still hadn't replied, Finn continued, "Those photos were for Johnny Franco's wife. She thought he was having an affair."

"I figured as much." She relaxed the death grip she'd

had on the steering wheel.

"How smart was it getting involved with a married guy?"

"I never said I was smart."

Finn didn't know what to say to that. Not many people would admit to their shortcomings. Still she was smart enough to embezzle thousands of dollars and get away with it. "What are you going to do with me?"

"I want those pictures. I'll do whatever it takes to get them."

"Including kidnapping," Finn prodded. "One more thing to add to your criminal resume."

"Yep. Including kidnapping."

"I don't have them on me."

"So you say. If the PI you work for has them, Johnny can't find 'em. He searched his office from top to bottom. I told Johnny he wasn't going to touch me with his hot little hands until he had those photos in those same hot little hands."

"Interesting use of words," Finn muttered. She'd seen those 'hot little hands' all over Margaret Barron's tattooed breasts.

"Oh, Johnny has talents. For a woman like myself—"

"A woman like you?" Finn said, interrupting her. "A woman who stole someone else's money, a woman fooling around with a married man or a woman on the run from the FBI?"

"Oh, please. Grow up. We're all adults here. I'm temporarily in your charming little town to say goodbye to my sister. Johnny and I hooked up, as the kids like to say. He's generous, he's horny and he's hung. He's perfect for my needs. Besides, I have to move along soon." She sighed. "I'll miss Johnny, though."

"Not if I turn you in you won't be moving along soon."

"Have you got a death wish?"

So it would seem. Finn couldn't keep her foolish mouth shut despite the desperate situation she found herself. As long as she had her criminal hands on the wheel, Finn figured Barron couldn't put them around her neck. She prayed she was right.

She pressed her mouth in a thin line. "You won't turn me in if you know what's good for you."

"You have nothing to say about it." Finn couldn't help spouting off. It was as if an alien with a desire for inflicted pain had invaded her body.

Her kidnapper smirked. "You don't have the balls to do anything about it."

It seemed they were at an impasse. True, Finn couldn't unlock the doors but she had the balls to do something about her situation. She had a cell phone. She climbed in the backseat.

"Hey, what are you doing?"

Finn pulled the phone out of her backpack and punched in 9-1-1. "I've been kidnapped. I'm in a black car with dark tinted windows near the intersection of Canal and—"

"What the hell?" Barron jerked the car to the curb. She jumped out, threw open the back door and attempted to drag Finn out of the car.

Finn latched the toes of her shoes under the seat in front of her and grabbed onto her backpack. But it was no use.

With one hard jerk, Barron managed to drag her out and toss her in the street. She tumbled against a light pole. "I'll have those pictures or you'll be sorry."

Finn struggled to her feet. "I'm already sorry."

The Barron woman hustled back to her car.

Finn edged out of the street, fighting for composure. Her heart raced and perspiration poured down her temples. She noted the make and model of the car as it pulled away. She found a scrap of paper in her pack and scribbled the license plate number and the car info in case she fell apart later. She felt damned close.

"Ma'am?" she heard from the phone still clutched in her sweating palm. "Are you still there?"

Finn dropped onto the bus bench at the curb and with shaking hands put the phone to her ear. "Sorry," she said. "Could you get NOPD Detective Jack Boyle for me?"

"Are you all right, ma'am?"

"I am now. I think."

"I'll transfer you to the detective."

"Thank you." While she waited for Jack, Finn attempted to calm down. She wasn't honestly sure what had just happened except she felt like she'd barely gotten away with her life. She took several deep breaths, wiping the sweat off her face. She was alive and all in one piece. For now.

Not for the first time she wondered if maybe the life of a PI was for her. Culinary school, even with an odious virago for an instructor, wasn't dangerous. Except to her self-esteem. Becoming a world famous chef, or even a mildly successful chef, didn't bring any death threats along with it as far as she knew.

"Boyle."

The sound of Jack's familiar masculine voice made Finn feel like crying. She choked back the lump in her throat. "Could you pick me up?"

"Right now?"

"Yes." *Please, God, right now.*

"*Ma Chere.*" She heard the note of humor in his voice. "Car trouble?"

Finn managed a wobbly laugh. "Something like that."

"Where are you?" She rattled off the location of her bus bench.

"Be there in five, if the traffic isn't a bitch. Look for a police cruiser."

"Thanks, Jack." Her voice hitched.

"You sound a little shaky."

"I've been better. I'll fill you in when you get here. I have a feeling you'll tap your FBI sources before I'm finished."

"Sit tight."

How one small woman could attract so much trouble was beyond Jack. Navigating the narrow streets of the French Quarter in a police cruiser, he arrived on Canal in no time. Seeing Finn sitting so disconsolately on the bus bench had him shaking his head.

She wore her Explore NOLA Tours pink tee, a little bit tight across her breasts and dusted with dirt and debris. Her knee had scabbed over from her ordeal with the dead body and she wore her pink cap cocked to one side with a mass of red curls escaping all around. Aside from her womanly curves and put-out expression of outrage, she looked like a cranky twelve-year-old.

Jack knew better. He'd seen the same expression on more than one woman before. She was pissed as hell about something. He was glad to know it wasn't with him. He pulled up to the curb and idly wondered why her call had been routed to him through the 9-1-1 operator.

He parked, then stepped out and walked around the front of his car. He sat down beside Finn on the bench. She took one look at him, her lower lip quivered and she burst into tears. Taking her into his arms he murmured, "It'll be all right, *chere*."

"I know," she muttered into the dampness of his shirt. "I'm mad. I'm not crying."

"Of course you're not."

"I don't." She lifted her head, tears dripping down

her cheeks. "This may look like crying to you, but it's only an emotional release."

"Yep," he agreed, "an emotional release. Not crying."

"I'm not. Get me out of here."

"Yes, ma'am," he said, gently pulling her to her feet. He grabbed her backpack, opened the passenger door and steered her inside. He walked around to his side of the cruiser and opened the door. He tossed her pack into the back seat, climbed in and put the key in the ignition. He watched as she wiped the last of her tears away with the back of both hands. "Where to?"

"I hate women who cry all the time," she said, sniffling.

"Me, too," he agreed, as he turned the air conditioning on high. "Whining, clinging, emotional wrecks. Those women are a pain in the ass."

Stricken, she stared at him with an appalled expression on her face.

He pulled into traffic. In a light voice, he said, "That's not you. I haven't seen you cry since you were five years old and Tommy chased you under the porch and kept you there by swinging a whiffle ball bat at you like you were some wild animal."

"I remember," she said with a half-hearted smile. "I hated Tommy but I hated the bugs even more."

"When you finally got out, spitting mad with tears streaming down your face and cobwebs clinging to your red head, you yelled at him every single cuss word you knew."

"Yep." Finn wiped the remaining tears away with her fingers. "Then I grabbed that plastic bat out of his hands and wailed on him."

Jack grinned in remembrance. "I thought it was great."

"I bet you did. I was sent to my room for swearing

and hitting him, and Tommy got away with nothing but a reprimand from your mom."

"Spoiled rotten, that Tommy. He always was Mom's favorite."

"That's not true."

"Is too."

She nodded her head forcing back a smile. "Okay, I see what you're doing. Trying to make me forget about crying in front of you and humiliating myself."

"What crying?" He glanced at her with a smile on his face. "Now tell me what the heck is going on. Why did I get the call about you from the 9-1-1 operator?"

"Margaret Jane Barron kidnapped me."

His mouth fell open.

Jack knew people in the New Orleans FBI office, well enough to call in a favor. The Eighth had worked with several agents on a homicide together several years back. He'd gotten to know one of the agents, Adam Deming, well. He called his number and waited for an answer.

"Special Agent Deming."

"I don't remember anything special about you back when we were working the Alton homicide together."

"Jack Boyle, as I live and breathe. How the hell are you?"

"Good. Yourself?"

"Can't complain. Good to hear from you but I'm betting this isn't a social call."

"Nope." Jack put his feet up on his desk and leaned back, relishing the idea of giving this guy important news.

"So what gives?"

"I need any information you can give me on one of your Ten Most Wanted?"

"Yeah? You're wading in deep waters here. Who you interested in?"

"Margaret Jane Barron. Wanted for major league embezzling."

"Damn. What do you know?"

"Not much but I do know she's right here in the Big Easy."

❦

All Finn had to do after her escapade with the deranged kidnapping embezzler was take a test. No cooking. No baking. No slicing, dicing or peeling. No chance of cutting off a finger or putting out an eye.

And, most importantly, no trying to please the instructor. Sit down, concentrate on the questions and handle a pen as best as she knew how. How hard could it be?

She got to class thirty minutes early. She sat in the back row enjoying the peace and quiet, her backpack stashed beneath the seat. She looked around. He stood at the front of the room. Her other nemesis. The ghost.

Dressed in a tall chef hat and white jacket, he winked at her, then folded his arms over his chest.

Finn refused to acknowledge a winking ghost and brought her gaze back to the front of the classroom where Chef Shane would hopefully appear in a few minutes.

No one came to save her. No one arrived early. She was stuck with the darned ghost. Why was he making himself known to Finn?

He sat down at the chef instructor's desk, propped his large feet on it, then placed his intertwined hands behind his head and grinned.

Really? "Why me?" Finn asked. "Is it *only* me?"

"Easy answer. You need me and, *oui*, it is you alone."

"For what? And who the hell are you anyway?"

He stuck out his chest. "I'm John Michael Winters, chef extraordinaire, ladies' man and paragon of culinary virtue. Call me John Michael."

"Why have I never heard of you?" She studied him more closely. He looked pretty good. For a ghostly manifestation. He was probably around forty with wavy chestnut hair curling around his ears, clean, manicured nails and a seamless, smiling, translucent face. And, not to forget, a see-through, though admittedly slim, body.

He snorted. "Who do you think gave Paul Prudhomme his start? Where do you think Emeril Lagasse would be without me?" He looked as disgusted as an apparition could. "They would be nothing without my advocacy, my expertise, my blessing."

"To say nothing of your modesty."

"Bah. Say what you will. I know the truth."

"Do you appear to them, too?" This was the strangest conversation Finn had ever had, or her name wasn't Finn Jones.

"Silly girl." He shook his head. "They don't need me anymore."

"And I do?"

"You bet your best sauté pan you do."

"What exactly am I supposed to do with you?"

John Michael Winters, transparent apparition and chef extraordinaire, rolled his eyes. "I'm going to mentor you."

"Really? I'm supposed to sit here and listen. Absorb your Yoda-like words of wisdom and then, someday, I, too, can become the next Martha Stewart."

He looked appalled. "I hope not. She went to prison, you know."

"Then what? I have more on my plate than class. I have two part-time jobs, a younger sex-obsessed sister I'm supposed to be keeping a close eye on, and a deranged woman wanted by the FBI chasing after me. I'm kinda busy."

He clapped his hands. "*Les applaudissements. Les*

applaudissements. Your performance is nothing if not brilliant." He shrugged his shoulders. "I simply don't care. My job is to get you through school and help you take your place as an astounding chef par excellence. With my dazzling tutelage, of course."

"Your job?" Finn stared at him. Confused much? "How did you die and get this job? You look pretty young. For a spirit."

"Thank you. I was a mere forty-two. In the prime of my life, both professionally and personally. Unfortunately before I could achieve the success I deserved I died."

"How?"

"Oysters. Very bad oysters." He pointed a finger at Finn and narrowed his eyes. "Beware of bad seafood."

Finn stifled a giggle. She thought he sounded like the portentous, fossilized old man dressed in black in every horror film she'd ever seen.

Beware of the full moon.

Walk round the moors.

Avoid the werewolf.

Finn had apparently watched too many horror movies in her life. She was paying for it now, by having a conversation with an arrogant, self-important spirit of the dead.

"And how come you don't have a male friend anyway?" he asked Finn, interrupting her movie trivia musings.

"I'm busy or didn't you catch that part?"

"You always have room for a boyfriend. Or maybe you like the girls, hmm?"

"I don't like girls." She frowned. "I mean I like girls but not in the way you mean. Not that there's anything wrong with that. You're nosy. For a ghost. And presumptuous." As if Finn knew how a ghost acted.

"I'm here to help. There's no need to insult me.

Accept the fact. A fabulously talented, experienced chef is here to give you the gift of his culinary wisdom. I'll have you know I graduated at the top of my class from Le Cordon Bleu in Paris."

"Wow," Finn said. She folded her arms on her desktop and propped her chin atop her hands as she looked up at him. "Are you going to whisper in my ear when I'm stumped on a test question?"

He nodded his head from one side to the other. "Perhaps, but you seem to be doing fine with that part." His thick brows rose. "As you well know."

"Then what? I still don't understand why me."

"Finn, Finn, Finn. Who do you think fed me those tainted oysters? A friend? Hardly. It was someone who was jealous of my talent. Someone who wanted me out of the way."

"Whoa. Anyone I'd know?"

"No, dear. It's beside the point. Water over the dam. Ancient history. The past. Over and done with. I'm dead." He waved a hand from his curly head to his wing-tipped feet. "Clearly."

"Clearly." As clearly, that is, as a ghost. One whom you could look right through and see the wall behind him. Finn's life had become as surreal as a Fellini film. Next thing she knew, she'd be having a conversation with one of Gert's cats. "Can I ask you a question?"

"Of course. Anything you like. It's what I'm here for. I think. I'm actually not clear on the details. I heard a voice."

"Like, the voice of God?"

"Do you honestly believe," he began, the haughty ghost act returning full force, "He would be interested in your career?"

"Well, to be honest, I'd like to think so."

He threw his head back in a pompous fashion. "Life mocks me even in death."

"Don't be such a drama queen. Sheesh. I think He is interested in everyone's career. But it's neither here nor there. What did the voice say to you?"

"'Help Finn.'"

"That's it?"

"*Oui*. Such is life."

"Okay, then. I'll try not to freak out when I see you. By the way, how come no one else sees you?"

"Not a clue. Maybe it's the old 'Help Finn' thing."

"I guess it makes as much sense as anything else. I wish you could show yourself to Chef Westrom."

"That witch? She deserves to be fried in her own canola oil."

Finn grinned. "Yeah. Now that's what I'm talking about. Having my very own ghost is going to be interesting."

"Don't forget what you're here for. My job may seem glamorous—"

Interrupting her insubstantial mentor, Finn said, "You think this is what passes for glamorous? I don't think so. You're dead."

He sniffed. "You don't have to be insulting. Think of me as your fairy godfather."

"Without the glass slippers, pumpkin carriage and handsome prince."

"Such a stickler are you."

"Now you really do sound like Yoda." She reached for her backpack. "I really have to go," she said lying. "Thanks for the, er, talk." She gathered her books and notes, stashed them away and stood. When she looked up, John Michael had disappeared.

Like a hallucination.

Sheesh. She sat back down. She still had a test to take.

Finn felt like Dorothy in the Wizard of Oz. Muttering beneath her breath, she said, "My, people come and go so quickly around here."

When Finn arrived home after class, all she wanted to do was down several painkillers with a shot of tequila and go to bed.

It wasn't going to happen.

"Surprise!" Debbie hollered as soon as Finn stepped out of the hot sun and into the cool AC inside her house.

Debbie looked so happy Finn didn't have the heart to tell her how awful she felt, how her head ached like hell, and her body felt like a runaway car had hit her, but she managed an upbeat, "Hi."

Debbie danced up to Finn, grabbed her backpack and tossed it aside. She took her by the hand, and pulled her into the kitchen where wonderful, spicy smells wafted out to the hall. Gert stood by the stove with a spoon in one hand and her other hand on her hip.

Debbie grinned. "Ta-da."

"You've been cooking?" Finn scanned her unusually messy kitchen with dirty bowls, pans and utensils scattered across the countertop. She dropped into a kitchen chair, propping her chin on her fist. She stared back and forth between the two smiling women. Gert wore a baby blue velour ath-leisure suit and Debbie wore a purple halter top and teeny tiny white short-shorts. Both were barefoot.

"Gert's been teaching me how to make, like, real Southern style food, crab cakes and corn maque choux. And homemade biscuits. We've fixed dinner for you 'cause of how you take such good care of Gert's cat when she's away."

"That's really nice, Debs. Of both of you."

Gert smiled. "I don't know who else I'd trust with my cats while I'm away."

Debbie fluffed her purple-tinted hair and preened like a movie starlet. Tossing her head back, she said,

"Gert did most of the work but I was, like, indispensable. She told me so."

Gert, with the careful eye of a mother hen, patted Finn on the shoulder and leaned over to stare into her face. "Bad day, hon?"

"I've had better," she admitted. Two days in a row, actually. No point worrying the two of them with her mounting problems. Like getting kidnapped by a crazy woman wanted by the FBI, seeing dead bodies and ghosts. Hell. All in all, normal days on the streets of the French Quarter.

"Hey, that's great since we cooked, Aunt Gert and me. I don't mean it's, like, a good thing you didn't have a good day but, hey, I haven't had this much fun since yesterday when Benji took me for a ride."

Finn's heart dropped and Gert's eyes locked on hers.

"Took you for a ride?" they said at the same time.

"In his totally amazing car. Like, what else?"

Gert wiped her brow with the back of her hand. "Phew, I thought it was a euphemism for, you know..." She cut her eyes to Finn. "You know."

"Yeah," Finn said, shaking her head, trying to hide a grin, "unfortunately I do know."

"What's a you-fam-ism?"

"Never mind." Finn smiled at Debbie and got to her feet. "When do we eat? I'm starved."

CHAPTER SEVEN

Jack took a long shot. He left Cordry at the precinct grumbling about paperwork. There were only a handful of voodoo shops in the Quarter. Most of them, including the one owned by Finn's uncles, sold ready-made voodoo dolls to the tourists. To get one as specific as the one of Finn he'd found at the crime scene, either the perp had to make one himself or get one of the so-called voodoo practitioners to make one for him.

He couldn't picture a man sitting down and making a doll, complete with the appropriate clothes. Between the time Finn was clobbered over the head and he arrived on the scene, no more than two hours had passed which left little time to concoct the darn thing.

He didn't know how to put one together or know how long it would take. He knew a woman who would know. She worked in her own shop and styled herself a voodoo priestess, spiritual advisor and dispensed homeopathic medicinal healing.

Jack and she had a brief affair a few years back. He ended it after several months when she got too weird for him. That, and the fact she slept with every man she met who was in possession of a functioning dick.

She called herself Marie no-last-name after the notorious New Orleans' voodoo queen of the 1800s,

Marie Laveau. The dead Marie had a tombstone in St. Louis Cemetery Number One. The tourists flocked to the site like vampires to fresh blood. They left personal items at the tomb or marked it with a big X in hopes of connecting with her, their long dead relatives or to get a wish granted. Some such lame crap. Jack didn't know or care about the details. He needed to find out if this Marie made the voodoo doll that resembled Finn.

He stepped inside and, as usual, the sheer volume of lunatic crap overwhelmed him. To say nothing of the cloying scent of incense immediately clogging his nose. The tourists may love the shop but every time Jack walked in, an overwhelming urge to shove everything off the shelves—stuffed alligators, jars of herbs, bottles of holy water, trinkets, jewelry, clothing, candles and the requisite Mardi Gras beads—played in the back of his mind. Yet, obtusely, he was deathly afraid of knocking something off accidentally and bringing a curse down on his unsuspecting head. Not that he believed in curses.

He found Marie sitting on the wood floor stacking tiny cork-stoppered vials of purple liquid on a low shelf. God only knew what they contained.

Marie used to be clean-cut, All-American, straight-A student Sally Thompson from Racine, Wisconsin. Nowadays she looked more like a circus performer. She wore her dull brown hair radically short, nearly as short as Jack's own. Piercings covered her body, in places you could see and intimate ones hidden by her clothes. She dressed in long, flowing skirts, low cut tank tops, flip-flops and multiple strands of necklaces. He couldn't count the number of holes she had in her ears, each one holding sparkly, dangly earrings.

The bell over the door had long since stopped ringing when she looked up and spotted Jack coming down the aisle, elbows tucked to his sides for safety.

"Jack Boyle," she said in a husky come-hither voice. "How *have* you been?"

"Good. How're you, Marie?" He squatted beside her and kissed her soft cheek. She smelled like freshly baked bread. He never knew if it was her perfume or her natural scent. He'd gained ten pounds while they were dating because he was always hungry when he was around her. "How's life treating you?"

"Grand. And yourself?"

He noticed she had a new, tiny fleur-de-lis piercing in her left eyebrow. The ball in her tongue peeked out as she spoke. He hated to admit it but he still found it sexy as hell. He cleared his throat. "Good enough."

"And what brings you into my little lair, as the spider said to the fly? Care to pick up where we left off?" Her lips lifted in a wicked grin. "I have a new piercing in my secret garden."

It was exactly why he'd stopped seeing her. Who talked about their hoo-ha like it was a botanical playground? Well, that and all the other men who visited her secret garden.

"Thanks for the offer, *chere*, but I'm here on police business."

"Sit yourself down here and tell me all about it, hon." She patted the floor beside her and gave him an intense smile that in the past had him returning to her time and again. Sex oozed out of her pores. She leaned across him to straighten a bottle she had placed on the shelf earlier. Her tank top dipped. She wore no bra. She wasn't overly endowed but Jack didn't care or even try to keep his eyes away from the display. She did it on purpose and they both knew it.

He ignored the offer she presented. "Did you by chance make a very specific voodoo doll two days ago?"

She frowned. "By specific, what do you mean? We

make lots of specialty items here. None of them are illegal, you know."

"Sorry. It's not you or the store I'm looking into." He'd been so distracted by Marie's charms, so to speak, he'd forgotten to tell her it wasn't the store he was investigating.

"Okay, then. I made a doll two days ago. A rush order, in fact."

"Was the doll supposed to look like a red-headed, freckled girl wearing Mardi Gras beads, a pink tee shirt and blue jean shorts?"

Her big brown eyes rounded. "How did you know? That's exactly the doll I made. The guy told me it was for his girlfriend who'd been screwing around on him. I told him sticking pins in it wasn't necessarily going to keep her from screwing around but he didn't seem to care. She didn't die, did she? Please God, say I haven't killed anyone."

"Save the prayers, *chere.* She's still alive. Did you also put a rope around the neck?"

"What for?" She shrugged. "The pins do the trick."

Of course. "What did the guy look like? Did he give you a name or credit card?"

"Ha. He said his name was Dick Smith, like that's his real name. He paid me quite nicely in cash. He was huge, like three hundred pounds, I'd guess, with a round face, thinning gray hair and a scraggly three-day-old beard. Sweating like he'd been working in the cotton fields."

Huh? The description sounded an awful lot like the floater they'd fished out of the Mississippi. Jack was more confused than ever. How could a dead man leave a voodoo doll at the site of his own death?

"He had big hands and feet. You know what they say about big hands and feet, don't you, Jack?"

He ignored the question. "How was he when he was

here?"

"What do you mean?"

"Did he seem nervous? Anxious? Was he cordial?"

"I wouldn't say cordial, but he was nervous, anxious-like, sweating like I said. Actually, he didn't seem like the kind of guy who believes in voodoo at all. But who am I to question? One customer is as good as another and he was willing to pay extra to get it done in an hour. He wasn't mad or rude to me. He was a customer. He didn't even seem interested in me, only in the doll."

"Odd behavior from a normal male, then?"

"Exactly." She smiled. "He obviously had other things on his mind."

"More important than sex."

"Hard, pardon the pun, to believe."

"If I brought in a picture do you think you could identify him?"

"Oh, sure, not a problem. I'm always happy to see you, hon, anytime you want to come by, business or pleasure."

Jack got to his feet. He shook his head. "This place is a fire hazard. What do the fire boys have to say about it?"

She looked up at him, stuck out her pierced tongue, then wiggled it back and forth. "We've worked out a compromise."

Jack shook his head again. "That's what they call it these days."

She winked. "The fire hose captain and I do."

"Marie, you are a wonder. Take care of yourself and don't do anything I wouldn't."

"I'd still do them with you, Jack," she cooed. She lifted her skirt giving him a quick, shadowed peek of her secret garden, no panties to bar the view. Winking again, she lowered the skirt and picked up another bottle to place on the shelf without glancing back at Jack.

He left the shop, the bell tinkling overhead as he stepped out on the noisy street. He released a long sigh. It had been a near miss. The woman was a magnet. He grinned as he sauntered away. The grin quickly disappeared as he thought about Finn's part in all this. What the hell did Tommy's case have to do with Finn finding a dead body? They couldn't possibly be connected. Could they?

Finn's cell chimed. She had just released her last tour group and was headed for the streetcar. She answered.

"Where are you?" Jack asked.

"I'm standing in front of the Eighth. I was on my way home."

"Stay where you are. I'll pick you up."

Before she could reply, he disconnected. Five minutes later, he pulled to the curb, reached across the seat and opened the door. "Hop in."

"Where are we going? Am I going to like it?"

"You bet." He grinned as he pulled out into the traffic. "You will have the pleasure of my company."

"The pleasure of your company, is it?"

"I won't let you forget one special minute of it. We'll both be happy and neither of us is going to have an alcoholic beverage to blame it on or children nine months from now to hang a god-awful name on."

"Where are we going?"

"We're going to go make fun of Tommy. Unless you've remembered someplace you need to be."

"Oh, joy."

Twenty minutes later, she and Jack got out of his car, and walked up the stairs to Tommy's second story apartment. Finn knocked on the door.

It swung inward with no one opening it.

Jack put his finger to his lips and drew his pistol, then motioned her away from the door.

Her heart slammed against her chest and she backed away.

Jack crouched and leveled his gun from left to right and back again, then disappeared inside.

Finn waited with perspiration dripping down her temples. She listened hard for any sign of trouble.

Silence.

Several minutes later, but what felt like a lifetime to Finn, Jack returned. He pulled her into the front room.

"What is it?" Frightened to near speechlessness she grabbed his arm. "Where's Tommy?"

"In the bathtub."

"Is he okay?" After a second thought, she continued, "he's not supposed to get his leg wet, is he? What's he doing in there?"

"He's not taking a bath. I'll show you." He holstered his gun.

"Are you sure? Is he decent?" Finn dug in her heels, unwilling to leave the front room until she was certain it was the right thing to do. She wouldn't mind seeing Tommy naked *some day* but she'd prefer he was willing and they were alone. Didn't want to embarrass the guy. Especially not with an audience. The audience being Jack.

"He's decent, as decent as Tommy ever gets," he grumbled.

"What do you mean?"

He grabbed her arm. "Come on."

They walked through the disordered front room with magazines overflowing the end table and empty cans, bottles and food containers ripening in the warm air, then through the bedroom with its unmade bed and clothes scattered all over. They stopped at the entrance to the bathroom. Finn peeked inside and gasped.

She stared at Tommy.

He lay in the bathtub with his broken leg propped on the outside edge of the tub. Someone had tied his hands in front of his stomach with what looked like black shoelaces and gray duct tape. His upper face was covered with a green, purple and gold Mardi Gras mask bedecked with sequins, flowers and ribbons. His other leg had been tied to the water spigot with a plaid belt, probably the tie to his bathrobe. He wore nothing but boxer shorts printed with pursed red lips. His mouth lay slack, and he snored, perfectly comfortable and sleeping like a baby.

Someone had written on his cast in neon pink marker. WHERE ARE MY PICTURES, SMART ASS DRUGGED OUT PI GUY?????? I NEED THEM NOW!!!!!!

"My God," Finn whispered under her breath. "Was she here?"

"Whoever she is, I'd give it a big hell yeah."

"Margaret Jane Barron. That's who. You know, the woman wanted by the FBI, the one who kidnapped me, probably tried to run me over."

"Oh, yeah, her."

She looked at his peaceful face, then up at Jack. "He doesn't even look hurt, or disturbed, or whatever, and not the least bit upset."

"You got that right." He leaned forward and shook Tommy's shoulder. "Tommy?"

Tommy's eyes blinked several times, then they opened. He looked up, his gaze puzzled. "Hi guys."

Finn squatted next to the tub. "Tommy, you in there?"

"You mean, do I know I'm tied up?"

Jack ripped the mask from Tommy's face, and tossed it to the floor. Then he worked on unknotting his leg from the spigot. "What happened?"

"That lunatic guy, Franco, who was with the woman with the big tits burst in here, two guns drawn like something out of the movies. I thought for one horrible minute he was going to shoot me but then he started screaming his head off and waving those big guns of his around. He started hollering, 'Whar's ma pitchers! Whar's ma pitchers!' I got to tell you I didn't know what the hell he was saying. He's got this weird way of talking when he's excited."

"And, you," Jack continued, "under the influence of legal drugs couldn't string a coherent sentence together to save your ass or even understand one, for that matter." He turned to Finn, struggling to untie Tommy's bathroom belt from the water faucet. "Literally."

"It's not funny, man," Tommy complained. "He could have killed me in my incapacitated condition."

"If he wanted you dead, you'd be dead." He helped Tommy out of the bathtub, held his elbow as he hobbled out of the room and set him down on the side of the unmade bed. Speechless, Finn followed.

With his hands on his hips, Jack stared at his brother. "You're supposed to be a professional, damn you. What the hell have you gotten yourself and Finn into?"

"Seriously, bro, I don't know. Other than him yelling at me, I don't remember much else about what happened until you woke me up."

Jack stood with his hands on his hips. "I tell you one thing. I'm leaving here with *all* the pain meds. From here on out, you'll have to suffer because you obviously need whatever brains you have left. Those drugs aren't doing you any favors."

"Did you know someone broke into your office?" Finn asked. She sat beside Tommy and patted his bare knee, as a mother might. Instead, she lifted her hand

and put it on his shoulder.

"Yeah, my landlord called."

"You remember the call?" Jack asked with a pained expression of his face. "Color me surprised."

"Can you cut the crap? I'm not feeling any better about this than you are. I didn't think it was a serious job or I wouldn't have handed it off to Finn. When I took it I figured it was a simple photo op, not some big FBI deal."

"Geez, Jack, cut him some slack," Finn said. "How would he know?"

"Hey, you guys are in way over your heads. I probably should know better, but I can't think how to get you out of it. And now this. What a mess."

"Why would he tie you up? I don't get it," Finn admitted.

"Because I couldn't give him the answers he wanted. I don't know where the damn digital camera got to. Seriously."

"If I didn't give it back to you I still have it in my backpack. It's in your car, Jack."

"I'll go get it but then what?" Jack said. "It's not like he left you instructions for how to get those hot shots to him, or her. Besides, the FBI wants her so except when she's harassing Finn, she's probably keeping out of sight."

Finn stared at Tommy, whose eyes still looked glazed and his expression dumbfounded. He threw up his hands. "Don't look at me like I'm the guy getting on the short bus. Those drugs seriously messed with my head. I'm lucky I can remember how to dress myself."

Both Finn and Jack gave him the once-over and grinned.

"Okay, okay, so it's not the best example but you know what I mean. For the last forty-eight hours, I've been as crazy as your average bedbug."

"Crazy or not, what's to keep those two from coming back here and really messing you up?" Jack went into the front room, gave it a hard look and then came back into the bedroom. "With the mess you've made in this place, it's hard to tell whether it's been tossed or not."

"He looked but I told him if I knew where it was I'd give it to him. I've got no reason to hang onto those pictures, especially if he was going to kill me for 'em. He looked around but I think he knew I wasn't quite right—"

Jack snorted. Finn met his expression and tried to stifle her laughter.

"I know, don't rub it in. He didn't look too hard."

Jack stared at Tommy. "You sure you're okay?"

"Yeah, I took a nice long nap in the bathtub. I'm actually feeling almost normal."

"Almost normal?" Finn said.

"Hey, you took the words right out of my mouth," Jack said, grinning.

Tommy stood up and made a shooing motion with his hands. "I've had enough of you two. It's bad enough I'm standing here in nothing but my boxers, I don't need more humiliation. He trussed me up, put the stupid Mardi Gras mask on me and I still fell asleep. I'm okay. No damage done. Nothing's missing. No new broken bones. Go home."

When neither of them moved, he said, "Please."

Finn stood up and started toward the door. "I've got things to do anyway."

"Me, too. I'm a police detective. I can detect Mardi Gras masks and drunks on Bourbon Street. I could probably solve a few murders today if I put my heart into it. I don't need to coddle my baby brother in his Valentine's boxers. Where the hell did you get those anyway?"

"None of your business." He frowned. "Have you seen my crutches?"

"Have you seen your pants?"

"Cut the crap, Jack. As soon as I get on my feet, I'm going to give you the beat-down you been asking for."

"You can try, bro. You can try."

Finn grabbed Jack's arm and dragged him to the door. "We're leaving. You two are impossible."

"We love each other," Jack said, turning his head and making sloppy kissing sounds at Tommy. "Don't we?"

"Not today," Tommy said. "Now get the hell out of here and leave me and my humiliated dignity alone."

Out on the street, Finn asked, "Is this a crime scene? Should someone be called?"

Jack looked affronted. He opened the passenger door and Finn got in. Leaning on the doorframe, he smiled at her. "Do you know what I am?"

She shrugged her shoulders.

"Thanks for the vote of confidence."

"You're welcome."

"Look, Tommy wasn't hurt, except for his pride. Nothing was taken. Nothing was even broken from what I could tell. It looks like nothing so much as a stupid prank. You and I know what it means but it's hardly a crime. Hell, he didn't even threaten him. As far as criminals go, these two are more like the Keystone Kops, fumbling around in the dark. Even the woman wanted by the FBI isn't too bright. This doesn't look like a great match of wits here."

"She is wanted for embezzling, though," Finn reminded him.

"It doesn't mean she's smart."

"She's eluded the FBI."

"So far," he conceded. "Seems to me you could have brought her in without too much trouble."

"Not hardly."

"All I'm saying is, even if we know what their crime is they don't seem like hardened criminals. Franco isn't a criminal at all, that I know of." He stood and shut her door. Walking around the front of the car, he got in the driver's seat and pulled the door shut.

"So what's the game plan?" Finn asked.

"If your befuddled brain is back, I'm taking you home."

"Geez," she said, "in all the craziness at Tommy's I completely forgot about my little lapse in the time continuum."

"Okay," Jack said sticking his key in the ignition and starting the car. He turned toward her and grinned. "All is safe in the world. No more damsels in distress. No more brothers in a drug-induced brain drain. I can go back to chasing girls and drinking like a fish."

"Sounds like a plan."

"You got it, *chere*."

After Jack brought her home, Finn rested for an hour or two before she went to school. When class dismissed, she stayed behind to study a recipe for *coq au vin* written on the whiteboard. She then copied it to her notebook. They were supposed to make it at home, then explain how it tasted and what they should have done differently.

She'd finished her scribbling when she saw a shadow pass beside her, caught for a brief moment in her peripheral vision. She stared at the corner of the room, then down the row of tables. Nothing. She was all alone with tables, ovens, mixers and a red silicone spatula left lying on the floor.

She was quite obviously losing her mind, again, or maybe freaking out after her recent escapades.

This was one too many times she'd been alone in the cooking school when she'd sensed another's presence.

She knew the security guard was still downstairs because she would have heard him on the stairs coming up.

Nonetheless, she felt...something. John Michael Winters? And she smelled something. And it wasn't the coq au vin they'd made earlier in the evening.

She stood up and turned around in a circle. She searched for the scent. It was spicy and strong, different in a way she couldn't identify.

And then she saw him again. A man. Sort of. Her own personal ghost, John Michael Winters.

"Are you for real?" she asked, belatedly realizing how rude she sounded. "Sorry, of course you are."

"*Non*," came his reply in French. He shook his not quite real head.

And the way he dressed. Yikes. This was her chef ghost again right down to his double-breasted white jacket and tall brimless toque. Finn stared, her mouth open.

He pointed at the whiteboard, drew his thumb through the line '1 cup flour', picked up the marker and wrote '¼ cup flour'. Then he disappeared like a puff of smoke, as if she'd seen nothing at all. She stared at the board. He'd picked up a marker. Who knew ghosts could do that? And he'd changed the recipe significantly. Maybe he really was here for her.

It was, without a single doubt, time to go home, get a good night's sleep and forget this day ever happened.

CHAPTER EIGHT

Jack didn't believe in coincidences. He believed in cold, hard facts. Cold, hard facts didn't lie. Cold, hard facts even a hard-ass like his partner, Cordry, couldn't dispute.

When he walked into the precinct that morning and found out about an unidentified body coming into the morgue late the night before, Jack figured it had nothing to do with him or any of his cases. He *chose* to believe it had nothing to do with him or any of his cases. Wrong again.

He stared at his computer screen. This little coincidence—actually not so little, since pushing three hundred pounds was not considered little—wouldn't disappear on its own. This was not one of Cordry's epiphanies. He was going to be righteously irritated when they had to go down to the morgue and determine the man's identity. The forensic evidence connected the dots between this corpse and Finn's disappearing body. Hell.

He rubbed his temples with the pads of his thumbs, the beginnings of a headache threatening to explode inside his head.

"Cordry."

"Huh." The man didn't bother lifting his head from the file he held in his hands. His reading glasses were low on his nose, his eyes scrunched tight as he scanned the scribbled writing.

"Have you seen this report on the dead body they pulled from the Mississippi last night?" Jack asked.

"Why would I?" he complained. "It ain't like I don't have enough dead bodies of my own to contend with."

"I guess this one's on my watch, not yours."

He lifted his shaggy head and stared over the tops of his glasses at Jack, his mouth twisted in a perturbed expression. "You got another partner I don't know about?"

Jack grinned. "Not yet."

Cordry stabbed his finger at the report in his hands. "What you pulling my crank about? Everything I know, you know, and if I can't make heads or tails out of this suck interview McCauley did, I'm laying it at your feet, *partner*."

"This isn't about the Williams case; it's about Finn Jones's missing body."

This time, Cordry grinned. "She lost her body?"

"No." Jack gave him the middle finger salute. "This is about the dead body she maintains she saw in the Quarter during her walking tour."

"Alleged dead body," Cordry prompted.

"Maybe not alleged anymore. This guy's DNA matches the blood I found at the scene."

"Hmm, don't that beat all. No coincidence then."

"Nope."

"She's not the cornflake I took her for."

"She's definitely not."

"Damn."

"You know, I've seen her sister, Emmy." As if they hadn't been discussing homicides, Cordry changed subjects without a blink. He slapped his cheek twice and whistled low. "She can play with my shield anytime."

Jack raised an eyebrow. "Good luck with that. She'd have to be pretty hard up to go for your ugly mug."

"Give me the damned case number, dickwad. I'll pull it up on my screen and see if I can solve your case for you."

"Thanks." Jack grinned. "You do realize we'll have to go down to the morgue and take a look at the guy."

"You might have to. I don't since you be the one gonna have to bring in your girlfriend for the ID."

"Thanks for the back-up."

"Anytime, partner, anytime."

"And she's not my girlfriend."

"Whatever you say, Jack-O."

"Shut-up."

Finn sliced and diced with the best of them. She could whisk, stir, whatever was called for without breaking a sweat. She loved the process and could lose herself in the work. She surprised herself when she discovered prep work calmed her, grounded her, made her forget everything else going on in her life.

On most days she didn't have a care in the world when it came to class.

On other days, it wasn't the bookwork, the cooking, or the presentations that scared her. It was the unlikely trinity of chef instructors who gave her the heebie-jeebies. They could turn a student to a dithering idiot with a frosty look or a casual put-down.

There were three, as different from each other as Larry, Moe and Curly, but not nearly as funny.

Of the two women instructors, Finn preferred the indifference of Chef Loretta Hicks over Wicked Witch Chef Westrom, who tormented her students so badly there were days when Finn doubted she was truly human. In fact, she could have sworn she'd seen slitted, silvery, snake-like eyes in her head on one occasion when class had been particularly difficult.

One of her fellow classmates fainted while another one ran from the room screaming, screeching like a bad actor in a horror movie, never to return. Finn sympathized but even if she'd wanted to follow their lead, her feet refused to leave the floor, unable to move despite the shaking of her knees.

It was her luck to have two female instructors who'd never had a good day in their lives. For kicks and giggles, they probably tortured wayward students in the basement.

Chef Loretta was plump, of average height, with the most beautiful wavy white-blonde, shoulder-length hair. Finn had only seen it on one occasion. Ordinarily she wore it tucked beneath her hat, out of sight like a nun. She had a round face, pinchable cheeks that had, no doubt, never been pinched. It was a total façade. She could trick a student with a practiced turn of phrase that left everyone in the room reeling.

Chef Westrom with her piercing black eyes often invaded Finn's sleep in nightmares. The woman looked more witch-like in Finn's dreams.

The one man, Shane O'Hurley, Chef Shane, was as jovial as Santa Claus, though he looked nothing like him. He was tall, rail thin, with thick black hair and even thicker glasses. His clear blue eyes gave him away, twinkling like the eyes of a benevolent angel. He insisted the students call him by his first name.

He'd never once barked at Finn, unlike the other two instructors. This was the problem. She was waiting for the other shoe to drop...in her clam chowder, so to speak.

These three professional chefs held her life's dream in the curve of their proverbial soup bowls. It scared the bejesus out of her. She'd rather have Chef Shane rant and rave and throw his ladle at her, than present her with his cheerful demeanor. What was wrong with the man anyway?

Today the class was taking a written test on Safety, Sanitation and Kitchen Design given by Chef—Do Not Call Me Wanda—Westrom, instead of cooking. In its way, it was relaxing. The room was quiet and peaceful, like a regular school classroom. It contained ordinary desks and a white erase board on the wall.

The sun shone through the windows like butter scorching in a hot pan. No instructor yelled or harassed or cajoled. And Finn knew the answers to the questions. Until this moment, she'd been able to concentrate and not think about her mounting problems. That was, until she saw her damnable ghost winking at her from across the room. He mouthed 'coq au vin' with raised eyebrows. She nodded and mouthed back 'thank you'. He disappeared as if satisfied with her answer.

Debbie couldn't have been more excited if she had a date with a Jonas Brother. With all the Jonas Brothers. At the same time. Oh, wait, one of them was married. Whatever. She was so-o excited.

She stood in front of the mirror admiring the violet eye shadow brushed on her lids. It matched exactly the purple color in her hair. She and Benjy were going to the zoo together, almost like a date. They had so-o much in common. They were both teenagers. They were both hormonal. They were both in love. Not in love with each other maybe, but in love with the idea of love. Or maybe in love with lust. Debbie didn't care. She was going to be with someone she liked, someone hot, someone who seemed to like her. What more could she ask for? It was a beautiful, sunny day and she was spending it with a beautiful guy. Freddy, although they texted regularly and she loved him like crazy, was far away. Benjy lived right next door. So convenient.

She checked her outfit once more before she left the house. Dressed in short jean shorts, a white camisole and a long, gray, sleeveless sweater vest which hit a scant inch below her butt, she thought she looked pretty hot. She'd painted her nails with the Purple Haze polish, the exact match for the streaks in her hair.

She grabbed her purse and slung it over her shoulder, locked the door behind her with the spare key Finn had given her and stepped out the door. When she walked up the narrow walkway beside Gert's house, she noticed the dark clouds gathering above her head. Damn. It was going to rain. Where had the sun gone? Maybe they wouldn't be going to the zoo, after all.

Debbie reached the front of Gert's house. Where were Benjy and his sexy Corvette? She didn't spot it. She did see an unfamiliar black car parked on the street right in front of Aunt Gert's house. Strange cars parked on the street all the time. This was a neighborhood the tourists liked to walk around, gawking at the mansions and taking pictures, especially of Gert's house with its many elaborate Italianate features. Or so Gert said. Whatever Italianate features were.

Debbie didn't know the first thing about architecture, Italianate or Greek Revival or Mickey Mouse but Gert loved her home and bragged on it all the time. She was tickled whenever she saw a tourist standing on the corner snapping a picture. She claimed the house was built in 1869 by a rich business guy who wanted to show off. Gert said one of the ways you could tell the house style was by the distinctive arched openings over the doors and windows. Debbie didn't know anything about that but she loved the fancy iron-lace scrollwork on the fence and around the upper gallery.

With her hands on her hips, she wondered where Benjy was. She hoped to see him step out the front door about now.

Nothing. But it was definitely getting darker. She

could smell rain in the air.

She gave him a minute and sat down on the top step of Gert's front porch, then reached inside her purse for her phone. At the same time, someone opened the door of the parked car on the street. A car door slammed and a woman Debbie didn't recognize got out. She started toward the house. She wasn't carrying a camera, a cell phone, or even a purse. Not even a smile. Something else altogether.

A gun.

An enormous, awful-looking, monstrous, blackish-colored handgun that she held outstretched in front of her.

Debbie screamed. Without thinking, she ran toward the stranger yelling as loud as she could. Shock transformed the woman's face and her mouth fell open. They slammed into each other at the curb. The other woman, her eyes round with confusion, toppled onto her butt, and hit her head on the cement. Her eyes fluttered, then rolled back in her head. The gun slithered from her hand and clattered into the street.

Shocked into silence, Debbie swiveled and ran back toward Gert's house, punching 9-1-1 into her phone.

Debbie heard Benjy's flip-flops thwack against the pavement as he strutted around the back of the Arnaud house oblivious to the drama. Debbie saw him as he came parallel to her and she screamed again. With one hand on her phone, she scrabbled in the bottom of her bag for her house key. "Benjy! That woman's got a gun!"

That woman was coming round when she spied him. Her mouth firmed into a thin white line. Shakily, she got to her feet and wobbled toward her car. She sidestepped around to the opposite side of the car, jumped in and sped away.

Benjy jerked open the gate, ran up the steps and

pulled Debbie in his arms. "Whoa," he murmured against her hair. "Who was that?"

"I don't know. Was she really, you know, going to shoot me? Like Angelina Jolie in the movies or something? I don't even know who she is. Why would she, like, even want to shoot me?"

"Maybe she was going to rob you."

"She had a gun."

They both looked to the curb as a dust cloud settled into the street where the car used to be.

The 9-1-1 operator came on and Debbie managed to give her the information she needed. She promised Debbie an officer would arrive soon.

"Look." Benjy pointed to the curb. "She doesn't have a gun anymore."

They stared at the discarded weapon as rain drops splattered around them. He picked it up. "Whoa." Turning to Debbie, he held it out to her. "It's not even real. It's plastic."

❧

Finn stood out of the rain beneath an overhang on the corner of Bourbon and Iberville munching a Lucky Dog slathered with mustard when her cell phone chimed. She juggled her hot dog in one hand and rummaged through her backpack with the other. She snagged the phone and yanked it out.

She didn't recognize the number but the area code was her mom's. Oh, no. She should at least try not to talk around the food in her mouth. She swallowed before she answered. "Uh-huh?"

"Finn! Wow! Like you wouldn't believe what happened to me."

"Try me," Finn muttered, recognizing Debbie's over-excited teenage voice. "I'm of the opinion, anything is possible at this point."

"Huh?"

Finn sighed. "Tell me what happened."

"Benjy Arnaud was going to take me to the zoo today so I was, like, hanging out in front of Gert's house waiting for him when I see this car parked out front. I didn't think much about it 'cause I know people like to walk around the neighborhood and gawk at the houses and stuff."

Finn grinned and took another bite of her dog. Those gawking people were her bread and butter. Thank God for gawkers.

"You still there?"

"Eating," she mumbled. "Go on."

"She had a gun!"

Finn coughed, then choked as a chunk of meat lodged in her throat. A passerby stopped and slapped her between the shoulder blades until she managed to swallow and began to breathe again. Finn nodded her thanks, her eyes watering. The stranger moved on without a word and disappeared into the crowd.

"Finn, did you, like, hear me? She pulled a gun on me!"

Her voice raspy, her breath ragged, Finn said, "A woman you say, did this? In broad daylight?"

"Yeah, a woman. She got out of the car nice as you please and, like, started walking toward me with this gun pointed right at my head."

Finn's heart stopped. "What, what'd she look like?"

"She was about my height, but she had big boobs and was bigger than me."

"Blonde, brown eyes?"

"She was blonde but I didn't see her eyes. Like, do you know who she is?"

"I think so. So what did you do? Run back in the house and call 9-1-1?" Finn realized she had stopped breathing again. She inhaled a hitching breath and waited for Debbie's answer with her heart in her throat.

"Not exactly." Finn heard a hesitation before Debbie

continued in an excited, high-pitched voice. "I, like, went crazy or something. I didn't even think to call the cops until after I went after her."

"You went after her?" Everything and everyone on the street looked normal through the falling rain but she felt as if her world had switched direction and was spinning out of control. What had she done? Drawing Debbie into her trouble was not what she'd intended or had any idea could even happen. But no matter what, the anger starting to build in her breast was going to be released on the devil woman. With a vengeance.

"Are you okay?"

Debbie laughed, startling Finn. "I'm awesome. I'm, like, you know, Wonder Woman."

"What did you do?" Finn looked down at the mangled hot dog and shredded bun in her hand and tossed the mess into the nearest trash container. "Don't tell me you took the gun away from her?"

"Finn, I didn't even get the chance. When she pulled the gun on me, I went into hyper-drive or something. I charged her."

"Oh, dear God."

"Yep, she made me, like, so mad I ran toward her screaming my head off. Then guess what happened?"

"I don't know, but you'd better tell me right now before I have a heart attack on Bourbon in front of all these gawking tourists."

"Gawking. Funny." Debbie laughed but didn't say anything else.

"Tell me what happened, Debs. Please."

"Nothing."

"Nothing? I doubt it. What did she do when you ran after her?"

"She must have, like, you know, panicked after I ran into her and knocked her down."

"You knocked her down?" This kept getting worse

and worse.

"Yep," Deb said with apparent self-satisfaction. "She seemed, I don't know, like dazed or something for a minute and that's when I got smart and ran back to the house."

"Thank God. Then what happened?"

"When I hit her she dropped the gun, then she got up, jumped in her car and, like, drove away without it."

Finn let out a slow breath. Leaning against the wall of the building behind her for support, she said, "She simply drove away? No one got hurt? No shots were fired?" She couldn't believe she was asking these questions as if she was a cop interrogating a witness on some overly dramatic TV show.

"No, 'cause you know what's, like, really funny?"

"Nothing. Absolutely nothing is funny about this."

"Yeah, there is. The gun wasn't even real."

"What?"

"Yeah, Benjy got there right before she drove off and he saw her, like, you know, drop the gun. He picked it up from the curb and showed it to me. It was black plastic, like a kid's toy or something. But, wow, it looked real to me."

"Did you at least call the cops then?"

"Yeah, Benjy's so smart. He even got the license plate number and the kind of car it was and everything. He's, like, a genius or something."

"Or something." Finn's mind spun with the horrible possibilities of what could have happened. What this meant. Barron knew where Finn lived. Did she know Debbie was her sister? Would she try a stunt like this again? With a real gun next time? Was it even a crime to point a child's gun at someone? She'd heard stories of people trying to rob a bank with a fake gun. From what she remembered, it didn't matter because the people thought it was real and were in fear for their lives.

Something about intent.

Finn was tempted to turn over the photos to her and forget Margaret Jane Barron ever existed. It was time for a serious talk with Tommy or Jack. Or both.

And if she ever saw that hateful woman again, she was going to go after her with something more serious than a fake plastic kid's gun. She was going to kick her butt. But not today. Today she had to catch a streetcar in a driving rain and get home to make sure Debbie was honestly okay.

❧

Finn sprinted for the streetcar, and spotted the God-awful, threatener-of-little-girls Barron woman in her car following her down the street. Finn panicked. She had to get away. With rain slashing sideways in cold drenching sheets. With lightning sparking overhead. Even with thunder booming every other minute. She had to get to Debbie.

It hadn't even been ten minutes since she'd left Bourbon, her Lucky Dog and an astonishing conversation with her baby sister.

Somehow, the woman knew Finn's tour guide schedule. How else would she have tracked her down?

The bitch was the most single-minded woman Finn ever had the misfortune to meet. Why couldn't she leave Finn alone? Leave all of them alone? Or leave town? Any normal person would simply cut their losses, head for Aruba or Switzerland or South America, and relax, for God's sake. And spend all of their embezzled money.

But, no.

Finn looked over her shoulder. Through the murk, she spotted the car getting closer but if a bolt of lightning didn't strike Finn she should get to the streetcar before M.J. Barron got to her. So much for kicking butt. Not today. Today she was too scared to think straight.

She dashed the last few feet and jumped up onto the waiting streetcar. Water dripped down her face but she managed to pull out a handful of quarters. She dropped them in the slot as the streetcar took off, and made her way down the aisle. She managed to hit every other person with her backpack and dribbled cool water in her wake.

She'd no more than sat down on the wooden bench, when charged lightning flashed and struck the top of the streetcar. The car lit up like a popping flashbulb. Electricity crackled. Thunder boomed overhead. The car shook, rumbled, grumbled and rattled, then came to a complete standstill, the smell of burnt metal hanging in the air.

Every last person aboard stared at Finn. As if this was her fault.

"What the hell?" she muttered.

"What the hell?" the car operator complained. He turned in his seat and scowled at Finn. "What did you do?"

"Get on?" she suggested as water trickled off her cap, down her clothes and puddled at her feet.

Lightning slashed overhead again, illuminating her fellow passengers' faces, scorn and disgust plainly written on each and every one.

Finn shrugged, setting off another torrent of water onto the floor. These people were the least of her problems. She stared out the window. The Barron woman was no longer following her. Apparently when Finn got on the streetcar, she gave up the chase. Temporarily. Finn released an agonizing breath. One situation averted, another staring her in the face in the form of fifteen irritated passengers.

"This wasn't my fault." She stared at the sneering faces. "I didn't do anything."

"It was running fine before you got on, missy, and

lightning don't stop the streetcar." The older woman who wore a red vinyl rain hat and slicker over her black maid's uniform spoke from the opposite bench. Finn noticed a puddle beneath the feet of her black sneakers, as well.

A young man in the seat behind Finn, a few years younger than Finn, spoke up. "Yeah, man, you brought some kind of bad mojo with you."

Finn stared. He was tall, lean and stringy, basketball player material, but still good-looking in an athletic way with big, beautiful, caramel-colored eyes and slashing black eyebrows. He wore a rain-soaked hoodie of indeterminate color pulled up over his head. She wondered what color his hair was. Under any other circumstances...oh, right, who was she kidding?

"Yeah, yeah, I got my mojo working," she sang, recalling the lyrics of an old song she'd once heard. Aggravated, she continued, "I'm a black-magic voodoo priestess who put the hex on a streetcar because I hate streetcars. Every last one of them. May they all rot in Hell." As if streetcars went to Hell. "I only got on because of you." She pointed at the young man.

"Me?" He stuck a finger at his chest.

Finn got to her feet, walked over and sat down next to him, making him scoot over toward the window to give her room. He eyed her with apprehension.

"Do I know you?" he asked, his eyes wide. Lightning struck nearby lighting up the streetcar's interior. He jumped and his eyes, if possible, widened further.

"Not yet," she said, licking the water from her lips.

He swallowed audibly, his Adam's apple bobbing.

"A woman is trying to kill me, someone put a voodoo curse on me and I found a dead body. I've been kidnapped and threatened. All in the last few days. I've had a very bad week and I could use some cheering up."

"Okay."

"You're going to cheer me up," Finn said.

"How?"

"You're going to kiss me." Why did she say this? Damned good question. She didn't have a clue about the way she was acting except it seemed like a way to diffuse the anger she felt radiating off the other passengers. Who didn't love romance? He was sexy in an uncomplicated way. And she needed cheering up in a bad way. What the hell—it was New Orleans.

She leaned in, smelling his clean, rain-washed scent. She placed her hand on his cool, stubbled cheek and waited, staring up into his avid eyes. He took the bait and kissed her. Applying a small amount of pressure, he parted her lips with his. His breath hitched, and she kissed him back. When he started to get serious with some tongue action, she pulled away.

"Can I call you?"

"Sure." She sighed. "You could but you'll fall in love with me, then break my heart when you move on to something better."

"I'm already halfway in love with you."

"Come on, you don't even know me." She frowned. "That's not love you're feeling. That's sex. What's your name anyway?"

"Jeff Smith."

"Jeff Smith. What do you know about how streetcars run?"

"Nothing." His glazed eyes, brown and wide, stared at her as if she was a super-model. He was cute and non-threatening in a good way.

She pushed back his hoodie to see his hair. Chestnut-colored and wavy, it brushed the collar of his shirt. Finn was tempted to run her fingers through it and forget about every other person on the streetcar.

"Can we cut out the crap?" The streetcar operator stood over the two of them, one hand placed on the back of their seat. "What are you two pulling here anyway? Is this some kind of terrorist act? Stopping my car?"

Stupefied, Finn stared at him. He was serious. Deadly serious. He thought they were terrorists?

Two seats back, she heard a loud female whisper. "Terrorists? Did he say terrorists? Call 9-1-1, Jeannette."

Before long every other person on the streetcar had their cell phones pulled out and were calling the cops.

Within five minutes a good half dozen police cars and, if she wasn't mistaken, the FBI and Homeland Security, surrounded the streetcar. With guns drawn, agents and officers alike approached the stranded streetcar and demanded they step out with their hands up. Every single passenger and the belligerent driver pointed out Finn and her new friend to the authorities when they hit the street.

Without a shot fired, they handcuffed Finn and her new friend, Jeff Smith, and took them into custody.

How had Finn thought her week couldn't get any worse?

Jack grabbed the phone when it rang and absent-mindedly listened because he was poring over the autopsy report on Finn's dead body. With one ear, he listened to Special Agent Adam Deming from the FBI giving him a courtesy call as a heads-up. When he heard Finn's name his mind instantly focused on what the man was saying. His mouth dropped open and perspiration beaded on his forehead. What the hell?

He'd lived in New Orleans his entire life, long enough he didn't think there was anything that could shock him anymore. He thought he'd seen and heard it all. This news shocked even him. His mind unraveled all the possible scenarios.

The FBI Terrorism Task Force had arrested Finn and some man an hour ago on terrorism charges.

No effing way!

He couldn't get up and out the door fast enough. The FBI's main office was north of Lake Pontchartrain but since it was closer, the authorities had taken the two of them to the FBI office on Poydras over in the CBD.

He arrived in the CBD after driving the cruiser like a maniac through the wet, puddled streets of the Quarter with lights flashing and siren blaring. With his blood pressure spiking, his mind racing, he was sweating like a new sailor set loose on Bourbon Street for the first time.

After he'd pulled out his cell phone and given him his time of arrival, Deming, smartly dressed in a dark suit and blue striped tie, met him in the lobby.

"Don't tell me this is serious. Please." Jack wiped the sweat from his brow then tugged on the lapels of his jacket and brushed rain drops off. "You know as well as I do Finn Jones isn't a terrorist."

A slight grin pulled at the man's mouth. "Five minutes with her convinced me. She's no more a terrorist than my Great Aunt Tilly."

He started toward the elevators, Jack following in his wake. "Then what's the problem?"

He punched the button and turned to stare at Jack, his face serious. "When she got on the streetcar it stopped dead in the street. The instant she got on. Then she met up with this smart-ass kid from Tulane and they were seen talking in whispers and kissing. Both of them carried suspicious backpacks."

Kissing? Finn? He didn't know she was seeing anyone. "Last I heard kissing in public isn't a criminal offense. And half the people in New Orleans carry a backpack. What's the big deal?"

"She had Mace in hers."

The elevator pinged and the door whooshed open. They stepped inside and it whooshed shut behind them.

"And," Jack prompted.

Deming punched the floor button and stared at Jack. "Her partner in crime was carrying a Glock in his."

"Could be legal."

When he raised his brows in question, Jack shrugged. "Well it could be. At least it wasn't a bomb. What'd Finn have to say about it?"

"She claimed she never saw the guy before today and she was rattled because some woman was trailing her as she raced to catch the streetcar. The only reason she let him kiss her, aside from the fact he was appealing, was to diffuse the situation, or so she said. Seems her fellow passengers thought she put some sort of spell on the streetcar or something. There *was* a thunderstorm with a lot of thunder and lightning at the time."

Jack shook his head. "Some woman was chasing her?"

"Yep, she said you knew who it was and I should, too. She's wanted by the FBI for embezzling."

"If it's who I think it is, she is wanted. We had this conversation. And she's been harassing Finn for a couple of days now."

The elevator pinged and stopped. Deming started walking out, then came to a complete halt, turned around to stare at Jack, his jaw slack. "Don't tell me this is the same woman you called me about?"

Jack stepped out of the elevator. "Probably."

"Let's go talk to your Miss Jones."

Finn couldn't believe they'd arrested her. Although she wasn't sure she'd actually been arrested, come to think of it. The agent who interrogated her never read her Miranda rights. He didn't handcuff her. He was adamant that she not talk to Jeff. No problem. Hard to do with the guy in an entirely different room.

Some other bozo in an ill-fitting suit stashed her in a tiny, airless office painted pea green. She suspected the door was locked and she wouldn't be able to simply walk out. He took away her backpack so she couldn't call anyone. She prayed Debbie was okay.

She knew she hadn't done anything wrong. This time. Or maybe her crazy life was catching up with her. So was exhaustion.

When Jack strolled in with the FBI agent who interviewed her, she knew things had to get better. She jumped to her feet and pulled him in for a heartfelt hug. He wrapped her in his strong, comforting arms, then looked down at her with a bemused smile. "Whoa there, Miss Jones. Isn't this a little sudden? I didn't know you had feelings for me. What'll your new boyfriend think?"

Finn stared at him, then backed out of his embrace. "You know I didn't do anything."

"I hear you murdered a streetcar while carrying a concealed weapon and will probably be charged with PDA."

Now she *was* worried. "PDA?"

"Public display of affection."

She opened her mouth to protest when he continued, "And you were associating with the criminal element. You mean to say you're not a terrorist?"

"Oh, please." She threw her arms in the air and stomped across the room. "Stop kidding around. This is serious."

"I'll say," Deming, the FBI agent, said. "Let's all take a seat and try to stay calm."

Finn obliged though she was feeling anything but

calm. She tapped her fingers on the tabletop.

The agent sat at the head of the table. Finn and Jack sat together on one side. Finn frowned at Jack, who had the audacity to wink at her.

"No one thinks you're a terrorist, Miss Jones."

"Then what am I doing here?" She looked to Jack for help. He smiled benignly. "And who is the criminal element? Jeff?"

"He was carrying a gun."

"Am I in trouble here, Jack? They haven't even read me my rights."

"This isn't a cop show, Finn. They want to talk to you, not arrest you. You don't need your rights read."

"That's true," the agent said. He tapped the tabletop with his index finger. "We realized, belatedly, after fifteen 9-1-1 calls, we might have misconstrued the situation and came in with too much force."

"You should have seen it, Jack. All these cop cars surrounded the streetcar and men in bulletproof black vests jumped out with their guns drawn. I was terrified and I wasn't the only one."

"We apologize," the agent said without a hint in his indifferent voice that he meant it. "What can you tell me about Jeffrey Smith?"

"Nothing I haven't told you already." She looked at Jack. "Honestly, I barely talked to him."

"Long enough to take advantage of him is what I hear."

"Take advantage? He kissed me after I asked him to. I didn't steal his virginity."

The agent snorted, then tried to cover it up by coughing. He looked away a moment, probably to compose himself.

"Special Agent Deming tells me he's four years younger than you are," Jack said.

"Really? Twenty-one?" At Deming's nod, she said,

"He was awfully cute. It's been awhile; I couldn't help myself."

Both Jack and the agent burst into laughter. Finn realized she wasn't in too much trouble if they could laugh about it. She released a long breath and tried to relax. Sitting alone in the FBI building with an agent and a police detective, even if she did know him, wasn't conducive to relaxation. This room looked like any old meeting room, but she suspected it was an interrogation room for hardened criminals, not harmless tour guides.

When another guy dressed in the requisite suit pushed open the door, everyone looked up. He stepped inside, then beckoned to Deming who got to his feet and walked out of the room to talk to him, shutting the door behind him.

Jack reached across the table and squeezed her hand. "Are you okay?"

"No, I'm not okay. The Barron woman was chasing after me again. After the kidnapping and all the threats, I'm not anxious to be in her company. I was doing everything I could to get away. Kissing a stranger may not be the smartest thing I ever did, but I was not myself. I don't think I've been myself for three days now and I don't much like it."

"We'll get her soon or the FBI will."

"There's more. Before this happened, I just got off the phone with Debbie and was trying to get home to her. That crazy Barron woman stopped in front of Gert's house, got out and pointed a gun at Debbie."

Jack straightened. "A gun? What happened?"

"Debbie went crazy and knocked her to the ground. Then when she came to her senses, she called the cops. By then Barron was long gone, but in her rush to get away she dropped her gun. Debbie said it was a plastic kid's gun but, damn, she scared Debbie to death. How did she know where I live? And now she's threatening

Debbie? What's up with that woman?"

"All good questions. Ones we're going to put to Deming as soon as he gets back. Meanwhile, I want to know why you were kissing a perfect stranger on the streetcar."

"I've had a bad week. Jeff smelled good, looked good and he kissed me like he meant it."

"Good for him." He lifted his hand and, none too softly, patted her cheek. "He could have been a terrorist, *chere*."

She rolled her eyes. "He also could have been the love of my life. Not that that will ever happen after getting hauled into this awful building because of me. Half of New Orleans watched and cheered as we were patted down, handcuffed and taken away. It was damned humiliating. After today he'll probably put out a restraining order on me."

"He had a Glock concealed in his backpack."

"A Glock's a gun, right?" At his nod, she continued, "Is it illegal to carry one or conceal it?"

"Not if you have a permit."

"Does he?"

"Don't know." Jack shook his head. "I'm sure they're checking."

"I kissed a perfect stranger with a gun in his backpack." Finn rubbed her temples. "I want to go home and go to bed."

"I'm sure they'll release you as soon as they ask you a million more questions."

"Wonderful."

Special Agent Deming came back inside, looked at Jack and then Finn, and then back again. "There's good news and there's bad news."

There always is, Finn thought. There always is.

CHAPTER NINE

The next morning beneath a low gray sky left over from the day before, Finn drove up St. Charles to meet Jack at the morgue. She found herself thinking about Emmy. Naturally. Nothing like dead bodies, formaldehyde and refrigerated steel vaults to remind her of her sister.

There was a good reason she was thinking about her older sister and morgues. During Emmy's senior year, her best friend, Cissy Delahunte, a Mardi Gras Carnival ball debutante, died in a car accident after the prom. Emmy had been riding in the car with her as well as their dates, one of whom, Emmy's boyfriend, had been drinking and driving. Although he walked away without a scratch, he was charged with vehicular homicide. Emmy and Cissy's date were hospitalized with broken bones and bruises, but nothing life threatening.

Emmy walked out of the hospital several days later with a broken arm, broken memories and a broken heart. She was never again the same fun-loving, joyous young woman. Finn wondered if Emmy had to identify any of the bodies. She'd never considered such a horrifying idea before but now here Finn was doing it.

"Deal with it, Finn," she muttered, reaching forward and turning up the AC a notch.

She parked on the street, marched inside and met

Jack who waited for her in the fluorescent-lit lobby. He gave her a grim nod.

As they started down the quiet hall, a sudden and unwelcome urge to giggle overwhelmed Finn. Oddly enough, it erupted when Jack took her elbow and steered her around the corner bringing them closer and closer to the morgue.

"What's the matter?"

She clapped a hand over her mouth. Tears welled in her eyes.

"Are you crying, *chere*?"

She shook her head, holding back the inappropriate laughter. What was wrong with her? A man was dead.

His steps slowed, his brow creased with worry. "It's not so bad. Honest. You won't even have to get close to him if you don't want to. The smell is hardly noticeable." He leaned in toward her and stared at her face until she looked up at him. "We can do this another time."

"No, it's not that." A giggle slipped out and she slapped her hand over her mouth again.

"You're laughing?" His mouth quirked in a quick grin, then he shook his head. "Laughing?"

"I'm sorry. I'm nervous. I've never done this before."

"It's all right. It's better than crying, but what is going on now in that messed-up brain of yours?"

"I've watched a zillion of those stupid cop shows on TV. At least once an episode the characters are standing over the autopsied body discussing something serious and earth shattering. The heart-stopping drama in their faces, really—" She threw her arms wide. "Come on, how realistic is that? It's supposed to be a real person. But this, *this*, is a real person."

"It's entertainment, I guess," he said, nodding in agreement. "But if you deal with death every day it's not entertainment."

"I know but I couldn't seem to help it. I know this is serious but I had this unbelievable urge to laugh. I was imagining those shows and me on one of them standing with my arms crossed looking at a dead body with a faux caring expression on my face. I know it's crazy and inappropriate but it hit me funny."

He shook his head, then took her arm, turned a corner and stopped in front of a metal door with nothing but a numbered plaque on the wall to indicate what was within. He tipped her chin up and stared at her face. "It's no crazier than standing beside a dead body and calling it entertainment. So buck up, *chere*, it'll only take a minute and then you can go home."

"Unless I recognize him."

"There might be more for me to do but you won't have to look at a dead body ever again."

"Unless I stumble across another one."

He reached for the door handle, his mouth twisted in a grimace. "Promise me if you see anything looking the least bit suspicious you'll turn around and run like a maniac in the opposite direction. For me, if not for yourself."

"Sounds like a plan."

"Great." He turned the handle and pushed the door open. "Let's do this."

Finn went inside and looked around. Jack crossed the room and whispered to a man seated at a cluttered desk.

The urge to giggle dried up and floated away on the disgusting fumes of formaldehyde and alcohol. And the smell of death which was probably her imagination working overtime.

Stainless steel enclosed her in every direction. After taking a quick surreptitious peek at her surroundings, she kept her gaze on Jack and refused to let it wander.

He came back to her, gently took her arm and led her away. The other man got to his feet, grabbed a handle on one of the myriad stainless steel drawers and pulled it out. Like in the movies and on TV, a body, a rather large body, lay beneath a white sheet. Finn's heart lurched.

Jack looked at her and asked in a quiet voice, "You ready?"

She nodded, slipping her hands into her jeans pockets.

He pulled back the sheet so Finn could see the closed eyes, the immobile gray slack face. It was more than enough. "It could be him but you know—" She didn't want to, but to get a closer look, Finn leaned in and stared, then backed up. "I think I know him from somewhere, but I'm not sure."

"What do you mean? From somewhere?" He ran a hand through his hair, then looked toward the ceiling.

"Do you know his name?"

He nodded. "Yes."

"So, you know who he is."

"Yes."

"Are you going to tell me?"

He pulled the sheet back over the body, and nodded to the attendant. He steered Finn out of the room and back down the hall to the front of the building. Once they were outside, she released a slow, uneven breath.

Jack turned to her. "I'm not supposed to tell you but I will anyway. His name's Simon La Fontaine. Do you recognize the name?"

"How did he die?" Finn's heartbeat slid back to normal. Emptiness hollowed out her insides. Seeing him lying dead on cold hard steel struck her how fragile life was. One day you were walking down the street minding your own business and living your life, the next day your life was over. Kaput. It seemed to Finn a person should know when he was going to die so he could prepare for it. The unfairness of it all struck her anew.

"Where'd you go?" Jack asked.

Finn shook her head, thinking hard. "I remember seeing him alive somewhere, not lying dead on a steel bed in the morgue."

Brow furrowed, he asked, "But where?"

"What can you tell me about him?"

"Dammit, Finn," he said. "I don't know where you've seen him. I know where you might have seen him but I can't put words in your mouth." He shook his head again. "Damn, damn, damn. I'd hoped you'd give me something solid I could run with."

Somehow, they'd left the building without Finn realizing when it happened. They stood on the street in the sunshine. She took in a slow, uneven breath of the thick humid air. Jack pulled the sunglasses he'd stuck on top on his head down over his eyes effectively concealing his gaze. "What?"

"You're not saying anymore, are you?" Finn asked.

"No," he said, with a quick shake of his head. "Not unless you tell me positively this is the guy you saw lying on the gallery in the Quarter."

"It kinda looks like him. It could be him, but I never said I got a good look. When I tried to, I got knocked out. Remember?"

"Don't remind me."

"So if you're not saying anything more and I'm not saying anything more, this conversation must be over."

She walked away without looking back, but she heard him mutter an obscenity beneath his breath as she reached her car.

"Damn," she said in total agreement. She wanted this whole fiasco over and done with.

Finn left Jack in front of the morgue with his mouth hanging open and obscenities falling out. She hurried on to her culinary class.

An hour and a half later, she was deep in contemplation. Giving tours, attending classes, then studying, practicing and experimenting in the kitchen, to say nothing of taking pictures for Tommy. There weren't enough hours in the day for Finn to have a normal life, or even a life of her own. A love life was out of the question. She could barely keep up with her family and friends.

After an exceptionally stressful class of slicing, dicing, julienning and jardiniering, her arm felt like it was ready to fall off at the shoulder. Her wrist and fingers ached. If this is what it took to make vegetable stock, she was thinking about becoming a *meatatarian*. She didn't know if such a word existed and what's more, she didn't care, because right now it sounded great.

She schlepped out of the classroom building wishing for a long, hot shower and a cool, soft bed. She didn't even mind she'd be alone in both of them.

The street was quiet and dark. Finn's Bug beckoned beneath the dim glow of a street lamp, the heat of the day still rising like a mirage off the street. She unlocked the door and tossed her pack in the back seat. She climbed in, pulled the door shut behind her and locked it. She closed her eyes and took a long breath, letting it out slowly. Gradually, she relaxed.

It wasn't the crazy schedule she kept or trying to keep school a secret exhausting her; it was the quite obvious fact that someone, probably Miss FBI's Most Wanted, wanted her gone. Gone. As in dead, deceased, departed and not dearly.

Finn was tired. Plain and simple.

She started her car. When it jumped to life, she

shoved it in gear and headed home.

The streets weren't busy but she was so exhausted she needed all her concentration to stay focused on her driving.

Her trip to the morgue replayed, repeatedly, in her mind. She couldn't, no matter how hard she tried, place the dead guy. She knew why. It was that odd phenomenon where if you saw someone away from his usual place you didn't recognize him. If the librarian was at the zoo, he was out of place. You knew you knew him but for the life of you, you couldn't remember where.

Of course, lying on a steel table in a morgue was out of place for anyone who'd ever crossed Finn's life.

She pulled into her parking spot behind Gert's garage, and noticed the light over the kitchen sink glowing inside her cottage. Debbie must still be up, not surprising since it wasn't quite midnight.

She fit her key in the lock and tiptoed inside so as not to wake her if she was asleep. She flipped on a table lamp inside the front room and dropped her backpack on the floor.

Simultaneous gasps sprang from the couch.

Finn was so startled she reached into her backpack for her Mace, and instead got hold of the string on a box of animal crackers first. She stopped rummaging around when she saw Debbie and the Arnaud boy hastily rearranging their clothes. Debbie wore a black sports bra and black boy leg panties; Benjy wore nothing but tented green flannel plaid Tulane boxers. He quickly turned his back to her.

"Debbie," Finn said, hanging onto her cool by a mere thread. "What the hell?"

Good God. There should be a law. She slapped her palm against her eyes and turned around.

"Finn," Debbie began, her breath coming in short

bursts, "aren't you, like, home early?"

"Like, no." She listened to the sound of rustling clothes, her eyes closed even though her back was turned.

"We were just—"

"Don't say anything. I'm not blind."

"It wasn't what it looked like," Debbie whined. "We were playing cards."

"What it looked like? Very funny." She wasn't laughing. Finn was performing deep breathing exercises to calm herself. She wasn't Debbie's mom. She wasn't Benjy's mom. But she was the adult here. And walking in on two healthy people in their underwear, yikes, well...it was her baby sister for crying out loud.

"We're dressed. You can turn around now."

She turned around. They both stood facing her—red-faced, hair mussed and clothes on but disordered.

"Are you going to tell my mom?" Benjy asked in a grudging voice. "We were just playing strip poker. Debbie was winning."

"She probably cheated," Finn muttered, then stared at the two of them. Debbie, aside from her crumpled clothes, wore a grin from ear to ear. Benjy's hair stood on end. He seemed embarrassed and uncomfortable in his inside-out tee shirt with a quite noticeable bulge in the front of his beach shorts. A deck of cards lay scattered across the coffee table. Maybe they had been playing strip poker but they'd moved on to something else before she walked in.

"Not my job," Finn said, dragging her gaze up to Benjy's crimson face. Seventeen, huh? She was twenty-five. Michael Douglas was twenty-five years *older* than Catherine Zeta Jones. Of course, Catherine wasn't an underage seventeen when they met. Besides Finn wasn't interested in teenagers and Debbie had no business doing...whatever it was she'd been doing. "I think you'd better head on home."

He ducked his head and started for the door. Before he made it, Debbie ran up to him, gave him a quick kiss and a pat on his butt. He left without another word.

"Debbie," Finn said again as she sat down. "Isn't this what got you in trouble in Florida in the first place?"

"Yeah, kinda," she said plopping down on the couch next to Finn, "but not with Benjy. Isn't he scrumptious? And we really were playing strip poker." She gestured to the pile of chips and playing cards on the coffee table. "He's really terrible."

"It doesn't matter what you started out doing." Finn brushed an errant strand of hair off her forehead. "I'm beyond tired. I'm taking a shower then falling into bed. And I'm going to forget I ever saw this. Or try to. And you're going to keep your clothes on from now on or I'm sending you home to Dan and Dorie on the next bus."

"That's it?" Debbie asked, one pierced eyebrow raised, her expression wary. "You're not going to yell or anything?"

"I'm not your Mom but I am responsible for you right now." Finn dragged herself to her feet. At the door to the hallway, she turned around and said, "Not that I think you should be having sex at all but you're at least on birth control, aren't you?"

"You asked me already and, like, *f'sure*."

Finn rolled her eyes. "*F'sure*. And using condoms?" Debbie nodded.

"Thank God. We'll talk in the morning. I am exhausted, Debs, but I do know the difference between playing cards and having sex."

"Whatever." Debbie reached for the remote. "We started out playing poker."

"Whatever." Too tired to argue or try to carry on an

intelligent conversation with a teenager, Finn left the room. Was it even possible to have an intelligent conversation with a teenager? Or was that an oxymoron?

Early the next morning Finn sat at the kitchen table eating a bowl of Cheerios. A cinnamon bagel slathered with cream cheese awaited. The sun, peeking through the yellow gingham-checked curtains, patterned bright squares across the kitchen table.

Debbie, surprisingly, was not only up, but awake and gobbling her own bowl of cereal when Finn had padded into the kitchen, barefoot and yawning. She wondered how to gracefully bring up last night's escapades. She didn't feel terribly authoritative dressed in a pink cami and dancing pink elephants pajama pants. On the other hand, Debbie wore a faded, tie-died sleep-shirt with a peace sign on the front of it.

Finn's cell phone chimed saving her. Debbie grabbed it out of Finn's backpack where it lay on the floor before Finn could even get out of her chair.

"It might be Dorie," Debbie muttered in a loud whisper. "I, need to, like, steer her clear of any mention of, you know, last night."

Finn nodded, unwilling to argue at this time of the day. She'd slept badly, tossing and turning, dreaming of morgues, dead bodies in morgues and being attacked on the street by dead bodies from morgues. Her life used to be so normal. Now it was an episode of *Bones*.

"Good morning," Debbie chirped. "This is Debbie Jones, teenage sex goddess. How may I be of service?"

Finn rolled her eyes and shoveled another spoonful of cereal in her mouth. She'd hoped to study for an exam on Computer Applications for Foodservice this morning before her first walking tour. It looked like her plan was jumping out the window along with her good intentions.

Debbie listened for thirty seconds, the expression on her cherubic face changing from humor to fascination to resignation.

"It's Tommy. He'd like to speak to you but first he told me to stop trying to, like, sell my *wares* over the phone. That I was better than that. Doesn't the guy have any sense of humor? Like, what are *wares* anyway?"

Finn held her hand out for the phone. "The man broke his leg. He broke his sense of humor at the same time. You'd be cranky, too. And, besides, he's too old for you."

Debbie plopped down at the table and took a big bite out of Finn's bagel. In a garbled voice, she said, "I think I'll stick to boys my own age. They get me."

"All too often," Finn murmured. She ate the last of her Cheerios. "Hello Tommy."

"Finn, damn, it's good to hear your voice."

"How are you?"

"I'm off the drugs. For good. Forever. And I need to get back to work. Sitting around here is driving me crazy. A man can only watch so much ESPN."

"How can I help?"

"I can't drive. Hell, I can barely fit into my car. Do you have time to drop me off at the office before you start work?"

"Can you climb the stairs?"

"I could. Slowly," he admitted. "But since the furniture store is already open, I can use their freight elevator."

"You do know I drive a Bug?"

"Damn, I wasn't thinking."

"Wait. I have an idea. I can borrow Gert's car. She won't mind. She thinks the Bug's cute. If she needs a car, she can drive mine but I think she's leaving on a cruise anyway. Her car is a boat, a Buick or something, and you should be able to stretch out in the back seat or whatever you need to do."

"Great. When can you be here?"

"How about half an hour?"

"Works for me. It will take me that long to get my pants on. You have no idea how hard it is to get dressed with a broken leg. I owe you, Jonesy."

"No, you don't. See you in thirty." Finn ended the call and placed the phone on the table. "What are your plans today?"

"Benjy is taking me to the Audubon Zoo since that kinda went by the wayside yesterday."

"Excellent." How much trouble could she get into at the zoo? "Don't forget to look for the Komodo dragon. As you would say, he's awesome."

"Okay." She leaned forward and stared at Finn.

"What?"

"When were you going to tell me about what you're doing all secret at night and in-between your walking tours?"

Finn shot to her feet. "I don't know what you're talking about. Is this your way of diverting my attention away from what you and Benji were up to last night?"

"Oh, come on, I won't tell Dorie."

"What makes you think I'm doing anything?"

"I've been here four days and, you know, you've never, like, dated much, but still you've been gone every night since I got here. I may not be smart, but, you know, I think you've been lying to me about what you're doing."

"Oh, Debbie." Finn took her into her arms and squeezed her tight. "You may be a wild child but no one ever accused you of being stupid. And since you're such a great detective, maybe you should join me and work for Tommy, too."

"Working? No thanks. I'm taking the summer off." She backed away to look Finn in the eye. "So, like, what are you doing for Tommy?"

"I want you to keep this a secret. Okay?" At her nod, she continued, "Since you're so damned smart I'll let you know. I've been going to culinary school."

"Cooking school?"

"Yep."

Debbie stuck her palm in the air. "High five!" she crowed. Finn slapped her own palm against Debbie's. "Awesome! Why do you, like, want to keep it a big secret?"

"Because no one in this family believes I'll ever be anything more than a damned tour guide. And they don't like my cooking."

"Well, you know, it has been kinda, well..."

"Bad. I know. But I like to cook and I've always wanted to be a chef and, damn-it-all-to-hell, I've gotten better."

"Hey." Debbie gave Finn a cheeky grin. "I noticed."

"Besides, I've started other things and they never went anywhere. I always got bored and dropped out so I figured it was easier to keep this quiet until I had the actual degree in my hot little hands."

"Yeah, I remember a few. Flower arranging for one," Debbie offered. "I thought I'd like messin' with flowers myself. And driving school, blech, and accounting."

"Double blech. Really hated accounting," Finn admitted. "Really, really hated it."

"And something to do with animals. What was it?"

"Animal control. Picking up strays. I couldn't do it anymore because I kept crying, especially when I knew the poor dogs would end up being put to sleep if nobody adopted them."

Debbie nodded and took another bite of Finn's bagel, which by now had, maybe, two bites left. Finn reached across the table and wiped a smudge of cream cheese from the corner of Debbie's mouth. "Thanks. I'd be bawling like a baby, too."

"We're just softies. Anyway, I like giving walking tours but it doesn't pay much and one day I'd like to say I have a career. A real career. Walking tours isn't a career."

"I still don't understand why you're keeping it all a secret." She picked up the bagel and had it halfway to her open mouth when her eyes widened. "I get it! You want to finish the school before you tell anyone so then they can't say, like, you never finish anything."

"Exactly." Finn paused. "Who says I don't finish anything?"

"Dorie. She says you're a good girl but..."

"Oh, thanks, Mom."

Debbie smirked, enjoying her moment, then finished off the bagel with one last big bite. She chewed a bit before continuing, "She says she loves you like she does all of us but she, you know, worries about you. Not as much as me, of course."

"Of course. You're on track for teenage pregnancy. Have you seen the movie *Juno*?"

"Yeah," Debbie said, grinning. "A cautionary whale."

Finn grinned right back at her. "You got it. Glad you're paying attention but try and keep your pants on, will ya?"

She shook her head. "I don't want a baby. I practice, like, you know, safe sex."

Finn put up her hand. "Good to know but I'd prefer you didn't practice sex at all. So tell me what Mom's been saying about me. This should be interesting."

"It's not, you know, like, a big deal. She says you're living here alone coasting through life like a lot of people do."

"I'm only twenty-five, for God's sake. What does

she expect me to do? Go back to college and get a PhD in Nuclear Physics?"

"I don't even know what Nuclear Physics is but I don't think it's what she means. She says she wants you to be happy."

"I am."

"And make something of yourself."

"Like Emmy?"

"I suppose so. She's popular, and she always has money. She wears Prada and has a new Coach bag, like, every year. She even drives a brand new BMW..."

"And has several boy toys paying for her extravagant lifestyle, and she lives rent-free in Mom and Dad's old house." Now she was sounding petulant and whiny. And, she had the nerve to call Debbie immature?

Debbie frowned. "You live rent-free."

"In maybe, nine-hundred square feet."

"Yeah, but, like, it's still rent-free."

"Okay, this conversation has gone on way too long and I'm not going to argue about Emmy or the house. I need to get dressed, go see Gert about swapping cars and then pick up Tommy." She took her bowl and empty plate to the sink. Debbie stood by the table with a thoughtful look on her face. "You won't tell anyone about culinary school?"

"Nope." Debbie gestured over her chest. "Cross my heart and hope to die."

"It's not worth dying over," Finn muttered. "Believe me. I want to be taken seriously for once in my life and the only way I can do it is to hand over the damned degree."

"I promise. Your secret's safe with me."

"Good. Have fun at the zoo. Wear sunscreen. Keep your clothes on."

After a quick shower, she headed out the door to see Gert about switching cars. She swapped her old, baby-sized Bug for Gert's enormous, black, brand spanking new, four-door Buick sedan, then picked up Tommy. She maneuvered him and his cast into the back seat, then drove to his office in the CBD.

She dropped him off in front of the building, found a parking spot where she managed, barely, to park Gert's boat of a car in the space. She walked Tommy through the furniture store to the freight elevator. She'd promised not to leave until he was comfortably ensconced in his office. He seemed fine, drug-free and coherent, but she could see he was in pain and somewhat awkwardly lurching around on his crutches.

As they rode up in the massive freight elevator, he said, "Thanks for all your help. You know I couldn't have done this without you."

"Tommy, you'd do the same for me. Besides, it was hysterical seeing you drugged out. And you sure looked cute in your boxers with the red kisses."

He frowned, shaking his head. "If only I could laugh with you. I don't remember much of anything. It was like being drunk for three days without the hangover. It's all pretty much a big, fat, gray fog. And I'm still covered in neon pink marker."

When the elevator opened, they stepped out and headed down the hall toward Tommy's office. He opened the unlocked door and with a look of pure disgust on his face, took in the disaster of papers tossed all over the carpeted floor, files scattered and drawers pulled out of the desk. It would take him all day to put things right.

"Franco."

"Yep, or his girlfriend," Finn agreed. "They really want those pictures."

"And you've still got them, don't you?"

"Yes, I do." She handed the camera over. "I'm damned glad to get rid of it."

"Just a sec." He hobbled over to the wall where his PI certificate hung and pushed it aside. Finn was astounded to see a wall safe hidden behind it. He twisted the dial a few times, unlocked the combination and pulled the door open. "Give it to me."

Finn heaved a big sigh. He took one look at the camera, shook his head, then set it inside and shut the door with a resounding thud. He gave the lock a spin and swung the framed diploma back in place so nothing looked any different.

"Wow," Finn muttered. "That thing has been nothing but a pain in the ass."

"And the leg." Tommy limped to the desk and gingerly settled himself in his chair. "What I want to know is who wants it more, Franco or his lady friend, the FBI's Most Wanted?"

"Good question." She set her backpack on the floor, and sat down across from Tommy. "Here's a couple more thoughts for you to ponder. Franco attacked you here, then came to your apartment to harass you. Since you were incoherent, he couldn't get the answers he wanted so he trussed you up like a Thanksgiving turkey. Gotta ask why?"

"Out of spite, maybe."

"Maybe. Then the Barron woman kidnapped me, did I tell you about that?"

"What? No way!"

Finn proceeded to relate the story of her kidnapping and abrupt dumping on Canal Street.

"You weren't hurt?"

She shook her head. "Only my pride."

"Wow, this keeps getting weirder and weirder." He frowned. "I'm worried about you. I don't want you involved in something like this."

"Much too late, boys and girls."

Finn turned at the sound of the deep voice.

Johnny Franco, tall, lean and menacing, stood in the doorway, brandishing a weapon. Not, Finn noticed, the same weapon he'd been "holding" in the photos she'd taken of him and his lover. No, this time, he held a gun. What looked like the biggest handgun Finn had ever seen. Behind her, she heard Tommy mutter an obscenity under his breath, his fingers tapping the tabletop.

Finn's heart fluttered. She felt exactly the same way.

"This has gone on long enough," Franco said. "You two should know I'm serious. I want them pictures and I want them now. If you don't hand 'em over, I'll shoot ya, both of ya."

Tommy got to his feet and shuffled around the edge of the desk.

"You best not be reaching for no gun," Franco warned, his beady eyes never leaving Tommy, the barrel wavering between him and Finn.

"Don't be an ass, Franco. I can hardly stand up, much less pull a gun on you."

"Yeah, heard dat one before."

Tommy moved to stand in front of Finn who couldn't have gotten out of her chair if her life depended on it. She swallowed the lump in her throat, her brain frantically scrambling for something to do to defend herself.

"Franco, you don't want to do this. Getting involved with a felon is one thing, but murder is a death sentence. Don't even go there."

"Margaret is mine and I protect what's mine. If she don't want those pictures circulating, then neither do I. I love her."

"And she's leaving you as soon as she says good-bye to her sister," Finn muttered. "You're nothing to her but a good time, a quick roller coaster ride."

"Shut up, Finn," Tommy whispered.

"What do you know about it?" Franco asked. "Like she been talkin' to you."

"Yes, she has. She gave me all the gruesome details. You're nothing to her—"

"Finn!" Tommy said, grabbing her shoulder in a tight squeeze. "Shut the hell up."

The elevator doors down the hall opened with a chime. Franco, standing in the doorjamb, turned to look. What he saw apparently shocked him because he took one last hateful glare at Finn and Tommy, then bolted away.

Without warning, two uniformed cops burst through the door. Finn bounded to her feet ready to defend herself. When she saw who it was, she sat back down, arms tucked to her sides.

Tommy explained the situation in a matter of seconds. The police left in as big a rush as when they arrived.

"How did they know?" Finn asked, waiting for her heart to return to a normal rhythm.

"My cell phone was on my desk, right at my elbow. When I spotted Franco, I simply texted the address to 9-1-1."

"No way. I didn't even notice."

"Neither did Franco, thank God. Otherwise we might both be dead." He tapped his desktop with one finger. "This is something more than protecting his lady friend. No one can be that desperate to get back a few lousy photos. He's as crazy as any murderer."

"You think Franco's a murderer?"

"I don't know. He's more than an exposed lover, though. Did you see the look in his eye? Stone cold. Something strange is going on here. Did she really talk to you?"

"A little bit." Finn let out a long, slow breath and got to her feet. "I've got to get to my walking tour. I'm going to be late."

Tommy took hold of her arm. "Please be careful."

"I will. I have Mace in my backpack."

"Use it if you have to. Ask questions later. Franco is one dangerous dude. I don't know what he'll try next. I don't even want to think about it."

"I don't either."

"He's probably running from the cops now so you should be safe for a few hours. At least long enough to get your tour in."

Finn hugged Tommy. "Thanks."

"No, thank you," he said hugging her back. "I'm as sorry as can be for getting you involved in this. I feel like a total jerk."

"Who knew? It looked like every other job I've done. Simple and uncomplicated. Snap a few pictures and be done with it. You collect your money and I go on to the next job with a little extra cash in my pocket."

"It sure looked like it, didn't it? The cops have to grab that dude before he kills someone. If he hasn't already."

Finn couldn't even comprehend such a thing.

"All I know for sure is he's dangerous and out of control."

Finn left Tommy with a look of anger on his normally placid face. She had a walking tour, people waiting for her. She hoped she got through it with all her parts intact.

CHAPTER TEN

Jack knew the corpse wasn't going anywhere this time. Dead bodies didn't move of their own volition. He sure as hell, though, wanted to talk to Simon La Fontaine's brother, Peter. First off, the man needed to know his brother was dead. Jack had a few other questions he wanted answered.

He stared unseeing at the words on the flickering computer screen in front of him. Why was he having problems locating this guy? He wasn't at home. He wasn't at his job in the French Market and he hadn't called in. He wasn't answering his cell phone. No one knew where he was.

When no one knew where you were, it meant one of two things. Either you didn't want to be found or you were dead. Which also meant if this guy was alive, he probably knew something about his brother's death and that was why he couldn't be found.

Jack tried to put the facts together. Finn saw a dead body. The body disappeared. The guy Finn looked at in the morgue, Simon La Fontaine, was probably shot elsewhere and dumped in the Mississippi. Two men, other than the super, lived in the same building where Finn was knocked out. One was dead. One was missing. Were both of them dead?

Jack rubbed his aching head. Last night out on the

town, drinking and chasing girls had seemed like a great idea. At the time. Now he wondered why. Sadly, he'd gone home alone, not quite drunk, not quite sober and not quite sure why he continued to punish his aging body.

Cordry said he was looking for something. Yeah, he was looking for something. He was looking to have a good time, then get laid. Not necessarily in that order.

It was past time he stopped acting like a horny teenager. The mornings came too early and the headaches lasted too long. Soon he'd have a beer belly and he'd be spending every night sitting in his recliner in front of the TV watching the golf channel. Alone.

The hell with it.

One problem at a time. If he could find Peter La Fontaine he'd be a happy man. He stood up and stretched his arms over his head. He couldn't sit in this stuffy, airless office one minute longer. Grabbing Cordry by the arm, he said, "We're outta here."

Cordry got slowly to his feet. "What's the plan?"

"We're gonna find the other La Fontaine brother one way or the other."

"Where we lookin' first?"

Jack pulled his car keys out of his pants pocket. "We're going to his place of business, a little fruit and vegetable stand down on Decatur in the French Market. Someone he works with has to know where he is."

"Maybe he's at one of the funeral homes planning his brother's burial."

"Possible, but if that's the case why didn't he tell someone at work?" Jack pushed through the doors and took a deep breath. He winced at the blinding sunshine, then put on his shades. "My head hurts like a bitch."

"I suppose that means you're not taking any crap from me today."

"Got that right." He started down the banquette.

"And I'm going to find La Fontaine if it's the last thing I do. He knows something about his brother's death or my name's not Jack Boyle."

"My hero," Cordry cooed.

"In your dreams."

The noon sun shone brightly through the floor to ceiling windows reflecting off the stainless steel tables, the stainless steel kitchen equipment, even the stainless steel bowls. Finn turned away from the glare as she watched one of her fellow schoolmates bend over the table as he painstakingly slowly diced onions into tiny blocks the size of the tip of his pinky finger.

Finn had finished her fine dice of perfectly formed carrots and they lay in neat little squares in a bowl in front of her. She'd practiced on so many at home her skin had turned the same red as her hair.

Cynthia, a young woman who grew up in a backwater bayou and was a good seven years younger than Finn stood across the table. She frowned as she finished slicing and dicing her own green peppers.

The young man, Eli Southern, caught her staring. "What?"

"Nothing," Cynthia drawled, trying, not terribly hard, to hide an obvious smirk.

Eli, a twenty-year-old with a baby face still blooming with acne, didn't have a clue. About anything. Finn figured he'd been told his entire childhood how wonderful he was, how he could do no wrong. Now he believed it. He was, without question, the slowest guy in the class. It didn't matter what they were doing. He was slow.

"Am I doing something wrong?" he asked, anger simmering below the surface of his blushing face.

"Not exactly wrong." Finn eyed the angle of his chef hat, which was listing toward his left eye. She wasn't about to stick her nose in this business. She appreciated where it was on her face too much, and wanted it to stay there with no change in its shape. Eli looked as if he could rearrange it without a thought.

"Excuse me?" He put his oh-so-sharp knife carefully on the table and stared daggers at her.

Oh, boy. She waited as Eli's egotistic, self-important personality reared its ugly culinary head. When would Finn learn to keep her mouth shut?

"You slow," offered Cynthia with a grin from the other side of the table. "An *onyon* shouldn't take no ten minutes to slice up."

"Yeah? You're the expert now?" He glared at pint-sized Cynthia who, with her winsome brunette good looks and sparkling brown eyes reveled in her mile-long Cajun drawl. She looked and acted no older than Debbie but had twice the attitude. If such a thing was possible.

Finn felt about as old as Gert caught between the two of them and their ratcheting bickering. She hoped one of the instructors would walk in soon and straighten out this fiasco. Or, at least separate the combatants.

The other students had stopped what they were doing. They watched the drama unfold.

"It just so happens I'm taking my time to get it right." Eli flung his thin shoulders back and looked down his pampered nose at Cynthia. "Something you would know nothing about, little girl."

"Mo-ron," she barked, sneering at him. Several more heads lifted and turned their way. "Admit it, junior. You is slow."

Finn wisely clamped her mouth shut and kept both eyes on the various long-handled, sharp-bladed knives strewn about the table.

"What would you know?" Eli asked, his voice rising, his eyes slanted in anger. "You're not even passing this class. Even Finn is better than you are."

"Thanks," Finn murmured.

Cynthia calmly lay down her knife and walked across the room to where both the red fire alarm lever and the fire- suppression system lever attached to the wall. One you pulled in case of an everyday fire and one you pulled in case of a grease fire. One would sprinkle water from the ceiling, the other a foam substance that worked to put out a grease fire. Finn swallowed hard, looking in all directions for help.

At the beginning of the term, one of the first classroom lessons had been to study the difference between the two fire suppression systems and when you needed to use one over the other. It was not an easy lesson, nor one easily forgotten. To pull either were serious matters in a culinary classroom and Cynthia, bent on mayhem, seemed on the verge of pulling either. Or both.

Finn heard several gasps as Cynthia raised her hand to within inches of the wall. Instead of touching either one, she turned off the lights casting the room in gray shadows.

"What're you doing?" Eli asked, his face ashen, looking to Finn for help. He didn't seem quite as confident as he had mere minutes ago.

"I expect you not to disrespect me. I's not gonna sit back and let you go on like I's some kind of *cooyon.*"

"Oh, hell," Eli murmured, casting a fearful expression at Finn.

"Oh, hell," Finn reiterated between clenched teeth. She edged across the room toward Cynthia with not a single clue about what she was going to do to prevent a disaster.

Thank God, a smiling Chef Shane chose that moment to walk into the classroom. He took a glimpse around the darkened room, sized up the volatile situation and his smile vanished. He flipped on the lights and then looked at Cynthia, hand raised, fingers outstretched. He calmly walked to her side, clasped his hand around her wrist and lowered her arm. She glared at him. Without a change in his expression, he asked, "What's going on here, Miss Cynthia?"

Eli, of course, couldn't keep his mouth shut. "She insulted me."

"Oh, my," Chef Shane said, placing his free hand over his heart. "Did she hurt your poor wittle feelings?"

Eli's face reddened further.

"Back to work, class," Chef Shane said as he maneuvered Cynthia back to her table. "The drama is over. Now let me see those sweet veggies you all have been attacking."

Finn heaved a sigh of relief. Another disaster averted. If only her life were this simple.

After her early morning class, Finn headed for the Quarter and her first tour of the day. Although sunny and humid, Finn thought it would be a wonderful day to walk the streets of her beloved city since the temperature hadn't reached eighty yet.

She'd woken this morning feeling wonderful and more relaxed than she had in a week. Why? She'd seen and done it all. After the little fiasco in class this morning, what was left? All the craziness was finished. Over and done with. Nothing could possibly happen today which could shock her, scare her or send her screaming into the bayou.

Debbie and her new boyfriend were going to the zoo where the most intrepid teenager would be hard pressed to find any more trouble than a melting ice cream cone.

The Barron woman was still out there but Jack promised Finn the FBI was on the case. Anyway, Finn would be surrounded by tourists and French Quarter residents alike. People she loved. Safety in numbers.

According to a phone text earlier, this morning's tour group consisted of ten people. Finn had been pleasantly surprised. Groups of more than six had been few and far between since Katrina devastated the city.

After changing, she left the house with a smile on her face dressed in her tour uniform of pink cap and pink tee, khaki cargo shorts and packed-to-the-max backpack. Finn found herself grinning as she came around the fence in front of the police headquarters. Eight smiling, expectant faces stood waiting for her in front of the praline shop next door.

She hoisted her backpack in place and greeted everyone with a hello. She handed out strings of cheap gold, green and purple Mardi Gras beads. They draped them around their necks, the men somewhat reluctantly. After a bit, everyone loosened up.

Finn made small talk by asking them where they were from. She told a few jokes while they waited for the last two to show.

An older, overweight, bald gentleman dressed in a Hawaiian shirt and baggy black pants came waddling toward the group, followed by a medium-tall woman wearing dark glasses and an oversized straw sun hat which completely covered her hair and most of her face. A white tee stretched tight across her breasts. She sported black spandex biker shorts, and looked ready for the *Tour de France*. Interesting choices. Even for New Orleans.

"Is this the walking tour?" the gentleman asked.

She assured him it was, then handed him a string of beads, then one to his quiet companion who stood nearly hidden behind him.

Finn explained how long it would take for the tour, how to stay together, what she would be talking about and then began walking backward down the street, her face to her group. The woman with the hat stuck close.

She'd given this tour hundreds of times so she didn't need to think about what she said or where they headed. She merely needed to watch where she was going, and avoid gawking tourists and crazy bicyclists. As she described the first brick building, she stopped and began her spiel. She couldn't help noticing the last woman who'd joined the group. Instead of putting the beads around her neck, she seemed to be moving them in her hand like rosary beads. Finn couldn't see much of her face beneath the wide brim of her hat and the black lenses of her sunglasses but something about her disturbed Finn. Her easy feelings of earlier in the day evaporated.

"Any questions?" Finn asked before she started along to the next stop.

"Yes," the sun-hatted woman said. "How long have you been doing this?"

"Giving walking tours?" Finn asked. At her nod she said, "Five years."

"And how many more years do you think you can do it without something happening to you?"

Okay, as questions went it was an odd one but Finn had heard worse. She was once asked how much she weighed by a boy of ten who actually had the temerity to pat her on the butt. Another time, someone asked why the city smelled bad. The topper was when a twenty-something girl asked when the Mardi Gras parade began. Since it had been July, Finn hated to inform her there was more than one parade—in March—and she'd missed all of them by approximately four months. The devastated girl actually broke down and cried.

"I'm going to school right now," Finn said by way of explanation. "I expect if I ever graduate, I'll get another job in the career field I'm studying. Right now I like doing the tours so you don't have to worry I won't be here the next time you're in New Orleans."

The last sentence produced a few smiles and easy laughter. The woman frowned. "We'll see about that."

Again, a peculiar thing to say but Finn didn't let it keep her from smiling and continuing on down the block, talking and walking backward. It was then when she recognized her. Finn cleared her throat, not knowing where to look.

She stopped the group in front of the St. Louis Cathedral beside the iron fence surrounding Jackson Square. By rote but in a wavering voice, Finn explained about the history of the building, the oldest active cathedral in the United States, and the two buildings on either side of it, the *Cabildo* and the *Presbytere*. She kept one eye on her late arrival, who seemed to be doing the same to Finn. While she'd had men scrutinize her, she'd never had a woman do it. It was a bit unnerving since she was unsure what the Barron woman would do next.

Finn tried, without much luck, to concentrate on the job at hand. When they moved up Pirate's Alley, Margaret caught up to Finn and walked along beside her.

"You don't recognize me, do you?"

"Yes." Finn hoped someone from her group would eavesdrop. "Where did you say you were from?"

"Tacoma, Washington."

"Nice city?"

"You've never been there?"

"No," Finn admitted, shaking her head. "Between school and work I don't get the chance to go anywhere except run away from deranged kidnappers."

She snorted. "It's a good place to be from but I don't ever plan to go back."

"Going to stay here then and get arrested? Lots of people come to New Orleans and never go home. It's a great city to live in. We have great weather and the best people and I could collect that nice reward money."

"Not likely, sister. Way too hot."

Finn's heart skipped a beat. She stared, slowing her pace. "You really are crazy if you're still here when you know they're after you."

She had the audacity to smirk. She lifted her glasses to her forehead so Finn could look into her avaricious eyes. She leaned in close and whispered, "And yet here I am."

Finn checked on her tourists. They were enjoying a juggling street entertainer and weren't even looking her way, except to amble along behind.

"Haven't you done enough?" Finn asked.

"I still don't have my pictures and I don't want you selling them to the highest bidder."

"What? Like the FBI? I hate to tell you but they already have one shot, a pretty good likeness, too. Or haven't you seen it on the post office wall? I guess the few I took don't compare to the thousands already up.

"Besides," Finn continued, "what are you going to do in front of all these people? You don't have a car so you can't kidnap me. I wonder if they've added that to your long list of crimes? In fact, without a car, what can you do? You can't even harass an innocent teenage girl."

"I could shoot you."

"With your toy gun? But it wouldn't get you your pictures, now, would it?"

"You sound pretty cocky."

"After the few days you've given me, I figure I'm pretty safe surrounded by hundreds of tourists."

Barron sighed. "I want the pictures. I'm not a bad person. I've never hurt anyone in my life. You've driven me to act this way."

"Driven you to act crazy? Why don't you leave?

Forget the pictures. Forget New Orleans. Find a sunny beach on an island in the Caribbean somewhere and spend all your ill-gotten money."

"You're so righteous. You don't even know me."

"I know you embezzled someone else's money. I know you scared Debbie and tried to kill me when I—"

"I never tried to kill you. Ever." She stood with her legs spread wide, daring Finn to argue.

"Really? Call me doubtful. No matter what you've done to me, I'll never forgive you for scaring my little sister."

"Your little sister is perfectly capable of taking care of herself. I have the bruises to prove it."

"Where are we headed next?" one of Finn's tourists asked with a tap on her shoulder.

Finn had nearly forgotten about the rest of the tour group. "Our next stop is one of the most haunted buildings in the city with a spooky history I think you'll like."

"Cool," came the reply.

"Cool," mimicked the Barron woman.

Finn refused to acknowledge her. She had been a thorn in her backside long enough. She wished she could pull out her cell phone without her seeing. She'd have the FBI here in mere seconds and they would be all over her butt. It was a lovely thought and kept Finn on track with her tour.

After describing the horrors that took place in the haunted building, they had to walk another two blocks to get to Finn's next stop.

Of course, then the wanted woman wanted to talk. Again.

"I understand your reluctance to hand over the pictures. I do. I'm a wanted fugitive. I'm forever in your rearview mirror."

"Why do you keep coming after me? I'm a minion. I

take pictures. I'm nothing. Just go away." Finn swiped sweat from her forehead. She eyed the nearby streets, hoping to spot a cop. Of course, there wasn't one anywhere around. Her tourists looked happy, taking in the sights, not the least suspicious of their conversation or the fact that a woman on the FBI's Top Ten Most Wanted was in their midst.

"Don't even think about it. I can read your mind, you know," Barron warned. "I've got a gun in my pocket."

She wore a sleeveless filmy white tank that concealed nothing. The tip of an iridescent blue, tattooed butterfly wing peeked above the ruffled edge. She also wore those awful tight spandex running shorts. If she had a gun on her, it was inside a body cavity. There was no gun. She was harmless. At the moment.

To get rid of her, Finn lied. "I think Tommy gave the camera to the FBI since they seem rather interested in you. If I were in your shoes, I'd forget about the pictures and leave town."

"You don't understand. I can't leave without them."

"Why not?"

"Are we almost to the next building?" asked one of Finn's tourists, interrupting their conversation.

"I'm sorry. This woman was asking me some questions about the history of New Orleans. We should have been sharing with the group. It's in the next block. See the yellow awning up ahead? That's where we'll stop. In the shade."

"Thanks."

Barron grabbed Finn's arm. Her eyes were frantic. "It's Johnny. He has a terrible temper. He says he'll kill someone if we don't get the pictures."

"Why? His wife already suspects he's fooling around on him. What difference does it make? You're the one in trouble."

"He told me," she said, lowering her voice so only Finn could hear, "he's already killed someone over this."

Finn snorted. "He's bluffing. Why would he kill anyone? It doesn't make sense." She shook her head as she crossed the street checking behind her to make sure her group was still following. "Doesn't make any more sense than the fact I'm having a conversation with a wanted woman who's been trying to kill me."

"Come on," Barron whined. "I haven't been trying to kill you. You should be more afraid of Johnny than me. He's a dangerous man."

"You pointed a gun at Debbie."

"It wasn't even real."

"Which is beside the point. It scared her to death and probably added another line to your FBI poster."

"Give them to me. Please."

"I don't have 'em."

"I believe him when he said he had to kill someone over this affair."

"All the more reason to go, leave New Orleans," Finn said, "leave Franco and never look back."

They'd come to Finn's next building and her tourists were looking at her expectantly. She turned to them with a bright smile and spoke from memory. When she finished and turned to talk to Barron again, the woman was halfway down the block, the sway of her biker short-encased rear end disappearing around the corner. Finn should tell Jack about this conversation but she could already hear him.

Did Johnny Franco actually kill someone? Was it an idle threat? If he did, where's the body? Where's the evidence? And where is Barron now? What do you want me to do about it?

Jack was such a stickler for the facts. Along with Margaret Jane Barron, Finn put all thoughts of murder and mayhem away and concentrated on her paying customers. Except for Debbie and getting through school, they were more important than anything or anyone else right now.

When Finn tossed her backpack into the rear seat of her car to go home her cell phone chimed. She plucked it out as she climbed into the hot car.

"How's it going with Debbie?"

A phone call from Dorie couldn't have come at a more opportune time. Finn really needed to talk to an adult and her mom would do fine. Jack was good up to a point. As was Tommy. Both were men, however. Testosterone-infused men in their prime. Not what a stressed-out, PMSing woman like Finn needed right now. What she needed was a best friend. Gert usually filled the role but she'd left the day before on one of her man-hunting cruises. Finn never talked to Emmy about girl things or—God forbid—feelings. She was as bad as men when it came to discussing emotions.

"Mom, good to hear from you. I've had a helluva week."

"Debbie?" she asked. "It's Debbie, isn't it? I'm sorry she's such a handful. A boy. Is it a boy? Sex with a boy?"

"No, it's not Debbie or a boy." She tried without success to get the image of Benjy's teen-aged, decidedly under-aged, body out of her head. Debbie had explained about the strip poker and Finn believed her. Sort of. It would have led to sex and Debbie wasn't afraid to admit it but fortunately, for everyone involved, Finn had walked in before anything happened. "It's not Debbie. Much. She's been fun to have around."

"Honestly? I'm not sure I believe you."

Finn adjusted the rearview mirror and looked at the lopsided hat on her head. She tossed it in the rear, then frowned at the way her curly hair looked now, crushed on one side and sticking out on the other. She ran her hand through the strands trying to make it presentable. "It's true. She's made friends with Benjy Arnaud from next door. He seems like a nice boy and they're the same age."

"A nice boy? They're all nice. There's the problem. They don't know how to say no to Debbie. She's quite persuasive."

"I wouldn't think she'd need much persuasion to convince a teenage boy to have sex with her."

"That's certainly true. I think she could talk a boy who has signed one of those purity contracts—"

"Purity contracts?" Finn had no clue what Dorie was talking about.

"You know. The kids sign a contract to wait until marriage to have sex. I think it's through their church or something."

"Seriously?"

"As a heart attack."

"Wow." She couldn't even imagine how it would work.

"So, if it's not Debbie who's giving you fits, who is?"

"It's a long and convoluted story you probably won't even believe."

"Try me."

Finn took a deep breath and settled into her car wishing she had a glass of iced tea at hand. By the time she'd told Dorie about the dead body, how she got a lump on her head, the FBI's Most Wanted woman chasing her all over town, Tommy's broken leg, and how she got arrested for terrorizing a streetcar, the ice would have melted and the tea would have been the color of the underside of a dead mouse.

Silence met her on the other end of the phone.

"Mom? Dorie? You still there?" She hadn't even

told her about the ghost. Or Debbie's own adventure with the Barron woman on Gert's front lawn.

"Mom?"

"Finn, honey, maybe you'd better put Debbie on a bus and send her on home."

"She's fine."

She waited through another silent pause while her Mom digested what Finn had told her. Maybe it was too much information long distance. Maybe she should have told her about the mundane. What mundane? She'd had the wildest week of her life barring the week Wesley stood her up at the altar. Maybe she should have waited for Gert to get back from her cruise and have her tell Dorie. Gert took everything in stride. Dorie tended to get a bit more excited.

"Are you telling me everything?"

"No, but I don't think Debbie is in any real danger or I would send her home."

"Any real danger?" she repeated, her voice rising again. "What do you mean? Like there's such a thing as un-real danger."

"I'm sorry if you think I've put Debbie in a position to get hurt. I don't think I have. Debbie is a much more savvy girl than you probably think. She can handle herself."

"Oh, she's savvy, but not in a good way. She knows how to manipulate boys, your dad and me, too. I'm concerned about both of you. It sounds as if you have a criminal after you. How do you know she's not dangerous?"

"I don't. It's a feeling I have about her. True, she's embezzled money but I don't think she's capable of real harm. I wouldn't want to go out and have a Hurricane with her, but I don't think she'd shoot me or anything."

"How comforting. So then why is she still chasing you?"

"Honestly? I don't know. She says she only wants the photos but why does she want them? If she'd leave the country, it wouldn't matter if every single person in the French Quarter had her picture and was handing it out on the corner with a free Lucky Dog. After all, it's on the wall at the post office. It's not like she isn't already known."

Dorie sighed. Finn heard her moving around. Maybe getting comfortable if such a thing was even possible with this convoluted conversation. "She may not seem like a dangerous person, Finn, but she's a felon, she's wanted by the FBI and she's chasing you. Obviously, her situation is dicey. She's not playing with all her marbles. She could do anything."

"I've thought of that. I have. Jack has talked to the FBI so they know she's here in New Orleans. They have a description of the car she's been driving. It's only a matter of time before they catch her. I'll be careful in the meantime. Don't you worry about Debbie. She's good and she's been fun to have around."

"Fun?" Dorie snorted as if she didn't believe her. "If you think she's fun you can keep her until the first day of school but I don't want to hear one more word about you confronting that awful thief."

"I promise I will stay as far away from her as I can." It was an easy promise to make since she'd left her not fifteen minutes ago on Royal Street. She had no more desire to be in her esteemed presence than she did to walk naked around Jackson Square.

"You take good care of yourself, Finn. Have you talked to Emmy since Debbie's been there?"

"No."

"Have they talked?"

"Not that I know of."

"I'm going to give that girl a piece of my mind. There's no way she can be so busy she can't take time to talk to Debbie. Even if she is on vacation in the south of France with a race car driver."

Ever the voice of reason—Not—and she had no idea why she was defending Emmy, Finn asked, "Does Emmy even know she's here? Maybe she didn't get the message."

"She got the message. And, she's going to get another one from her mother before this day is out. Maybe I'll post a nasty comment about her on my Facebook page. Or unfriend her."

"*You* have a Facebook page?" Her mother? Dorie? The queen of the cell phone but allergic to the Internet.

"All the people in our little senior community down here have them. It's how we stay in touch. Need to with all the classes, lunches, golf dates, all the important stuff."

"Really."

"Swear to you, it's God's own truth."

"Wow." Finn was flabbergasted. She didn't even have a Facebook page but she'd watched Debbie when she was on the computer for hours on end. Finn failed to see the humanity-robbing appeal of Facebook. She hardly had the time anyway. Wow. Her mother.

"Gotta go, Finn, and update my Facebook page. You take care and take good care of my baby. I'll send more money. She can eat you out of house and home."

"Not necessary. Debbie will be fine. I promise."

She prayed it was a promise she could keep. As things stood right now, she wasn't sure she could even keep herself safe.

CHAPTER ELEVEN

Ordinarily the one person Finn could count on was Tommy. He never changed. He was happy-go-lucky, confident, and secure in his masculinity. He never questioned her choice of clothes, friends or jobs. He knew about her attending culinary class and had nothing but good things to say about it.

Of course, now he was cranky about the broken leg and somewhat drugged, not out of his mind anymore but not himself. Still a good friend deserved all the help she could muster.

She wanted to make sure Tommy was better before she went to her next class. She also needed to know if he'd learned anything more about Margaret Jane Barron's business. Miraculously Finn found a couple of free hours in the middle of her day and set to work cooking.

Several hours later, with all this in mind, dressed in clean jeans and a purple tank top, she hopped into her car and turned the key. Nothing. She tried several more times thinking the battery must be dead. Gert's monster cruiser needed gas and, of course, Finn had no money.

She toted several bags down the street to catch the St. Charles Avenue streetcar cursing cars and life in general. Loaded down with plastic containers of home-cooked food, the enticing fragrance drew friendly looks all around her once she got aboard.

Not that she should feel guilty about Tommy's broken leg. She did, couldn't help it. If Franco hadn't shown up, it wouldn't have happened but since he did and she was trying to fend him off she felt as if it was her fault. Partially. And she had taken the incriminating photos.

Thus, the food offerings.

She got off the streetcar a block from his building, shuffled down the street, then up a flight of stairs to his door, the heavy plastic bags full of food nearly dragging on the ground.

She stopped a moment to catch her breath, then knocked and called out his name.

He opened the door for her with a huge grin. He wore a yellow Sponge Bob t-shirt and plaid, flannel pajama pants with one leg sliced open to accommodate his cast. "My favorite culinary student bearing gifts." He sniffed, then rolled his eyes. "And if I'm not mistaken, gifts of homemade food. I love ya, sweetheart."

"Back at ya. Can I come in or do you want to eat it out here on the gallery?"

"Sorry." Holding one crutch, he hobbled aside to let her in. "Lost myself in the sweet aroma. Smells like gumbo. Yes?"

"Yes. Shrimp gumbo with fresh-baked brioche. I pulled the bread pudding out of the oven not thirty minutes ago."

He shut the door behind her. "Did I say I love you? If I didn't it bears repeating."

"You did. Sit yourself down on the couch and I'll dish it up. What would you like to drink?" She opened up cupboards in his galley kitchen searching for bowls and plates.

"Bring me an Abita. I think I can handle a beer. I'm

feeling like a new man already." He rubbed his stomach.

"Have you eaten at all today?"

"Oh, sure. I had a bowl of Wheaties for breakfast and a bag of potato chips for lunch."

"The breakfast *and* lunch of champions."

"You got it."

She found utensils in a drawer and before long, the two of them were eating gumbo and mopping up the leftover juices with hunks of the brioche. The look of ecstasy on his face surprised her. She imagined it was how he looked in the midst of hot, mindless sex. It was arousing in the extreme and a bonus side effect she'd never imagined. This cooking thing might work out better for her than even she'd originally thought.

"Have you saved room for dessert?" she asked.

"Do alligators eat Cajuns in the bayou?"

She grinned.

"Bring it on."

Finn stood up and took the empty bowl from his hands. As she backed away, she stepped on his crutch causing it to snap back, smack into the right side of Tommy's head.

"Yeow!" He hollered, his hands flying up to cover his face. "Damn it all to hell."

"Oh, my God. Tommy? Are you okay? Can you see?" She dropped the dishes on the coffee table. She pried his hands away from his face, kneeling beside him on the couch. Gently she examined his right eye.

He winced as she touched his face, one eye squinting, the other half closed. His right cheek and right eye were already turning red and beginning to swell. Finn sat back on her heels.

"Is it still there?" Tommy asked, his voice tight.

"Your eye?" At his nod she continued, "Yeah, God, I'm so sorry, I think I've given you a shiner."

"Ha, there's another story for ya." He leaned back against the couch, cupping his forehead, rubbing his brow. "You can tell people I tried to take advantage of you and you clobbered me with my own damned crutch. It'll make for a more interesting story than you stepped on it and it miraculously found its way to my eye."

Confused, she asked, "Why would I lie?"

"Because otherwise you'll look clumsy. This way it makes me look like a rascal, a ladies' man. I'm the love-struck moron who couldn't help making a pass at you."

"No, you'll be the big fat jerk with a black eye and a hard-on."

He laughed. "Your great cooking might give me one anyway."

"Seriously, are you okay?"

"I will be as soon as you bring me a dish of that bread pudding. With bourbon sauce?"

She got to her feet. "Absolutely. It'll take me a minute to put it together, but yeah, bread pudding with bourbon sauce coming up. You sure you're okay?"

"Bring ice, too. For my face."

"Good idea."

"Then I have a tale to tell you."

"About what?"

"Just you wait." He tried to wink and ended up wincing.

Ten minutes later, she finished whisking the sauce on the stove and then mounded two bowls with warm pudding. She poured hot bourbon sauce over both and stuck two spoons in the bowls. She returned with her hands full of dessert when a knock came at the door. She handed Tommy his as he hollered, "It's open."

"Is it smart to say that?" Finn whispered sitting down next to him.

With his free hand, Tommy reached beneath the couch cushion and pulled out a large, lethal-looking gun. He pointed it at the door.

"Wow." Finn edged a few inches away never taking her gaze off the weapon.

"No one is going to catch me unprepared again even if I'm laid up with a damned broken leg." He squinted down the barrel.

"Shooting isn't necessary," drawled a familiar voice. "If you want me to go, I'll go right back out the door without a word."

They both looked up to see Jack staring at them with his hands on his hips, a slight frown turning down the corners of his mouth. He wore a lightweight jacket over a black tee and faded blue jeans. The coat didn't do anything to disguise the bulge of his shoulder-holstered gun. Apparently, he came as prepared as Tommy.

"Jack, big bro, good to see ya," Tommy said as he stashed his gun beneath him. "You can never be too careful these days."

"Try locking your door." Jack turned toward Finn. "Terrorized any streetcars lately?"

She pursed her lips. "Maybe. Maybe not."

He snorted. "Anyway, I'm glad you're here. Wanted to talk to both of you. Kill two birds with one stone." He turned toward Tommy, studying his face. "What's wrong with your eye?"

Tommy grinned, took a bite of bread pudding, savored it, taking his time before he answered. "Finn here clobbered me with my crutch as I was trying to cop a feel."

"No kidding." Jack smiled and raised his palm to her. She gave him a high five and tried not to grin. "Good job. He's going to have a beautiful black eye."

Finn rolled her eyes. "It was an accident."

"So you say," Tommy mumbled between bites.

Jack leaned in close, studying the contents of their bowls. "I thought I smelled something mouth-watering when I walked in. Bread pudding? Bourbon sauce?"

At Finn's nod, he asked, "Any left?" He wandered into the kitchen and helped himself. "Who made it?"

Finn shook her head, touching her finger to her lips. He shrugged his shoulders but kept on eating. "I picked food up for Tommy at the deli near home."

"Good idea. Poor baby brother doesn't need to break any other body parts fooling around in the kitchen. Besides he can't cook worth a lick."

Jack settled into the chair opposite the coffee table with a huge bowl of dessert. After one bite, he said, "This is great. Still warm, pudding-like, not so hard you have to cut it with a knife. Just the way I like it."

"Just the way it's supposed to be." Tommy put his bowl on the coffee table, holding onto the spoon as he licked off the last of the sauce. "So, what did you want to talk about?" He dropped the clean spoon into the bowl. Smacking his lips, Tommy settled back against the couch, turned to Finn and winked. His swollen eye barely blinked.

Jack didn't notice, intent on eating. "Wow. Is this the best bread pudding or what? I didn't think anyone could beat The Gumbo Shop's."

"Thank you," Finn answered without thinking. She grimaced but Jack was too busy eating to notice. Tommy patted her knee and mouthed, "good job", then gestured with his fingers a key twisted to his lips, then tossed away.

Jack witnessed the last motion but, oddly enough, didn't say anything about it. "I've got news but it'll wait. I'm not letting go of this bowl until every last bite is gone."

Finn got up to go to the kitchen to hide her astonishment. She put the leftover gumbo in the refrigerator and cleaned up while Jack finished. She left the pan of bread pudding and the bowl of bourbon sauce out in case anyone wanted seconds.

"Okay, I'm ready." Jack set his bowl on the coffee table.

Finn returned and took her place beside Tommy, tucking her legs beneath her.

"Here's the latest. The FBI is not only looking for Barron, they want to talk to Johnny Franco."

"How come?" Tommy asked. "Because he's an asshat?"

"Not only. Seems lover-boy has a record. He's not supposed to associate with suspected criminals. I think Finn's lady friend qualifies."

"A record for what?" Finn leaned forward, giving Jack her undivided attention.

"Assault with a deadly weapon on a U.S. marshal, no less. Served two, on a two to five, at Angola."

"No kidding," Tommy said. "Doesn't surprise me."

"No kidding." Jack scowled back and forth between Tommy and Finn. "You kids sure know how to pick 'em."

"We didn't, bro," Tommy explained, then with a grin, continued, "Mrs. Franco picked me because I'm the best PI in the city."

"What else?" Finn could tell by the look on Jack's face there was more.

"The story is he nearly killed two guys in a bar fight. A witness said one of the men asked Franco something rude like, 'Who'd your mama screw to give you that ugly mug' or something equally stupid and Franco went crazy on him, first bashing a beer bottle over his head. When the guy's pal, the marshal, tried to intervene, he attacked him too but this time hitting him with his gun. Several witnesses said they'd never seen anything like it. He was a madman, pistol-whipping the poor sap. The marshal was in the hospital for three months, the other guy a month. Ordinarily a couple guys in a bar fight, you get probation but since Franco used deadly force and nearly killed these two, one of them the afore-mentioned marshal, the judge threw the book at him."

"Whoa." Tommy shook his head. "A real sweetheart."

"Yeah, there's even more. When he got out, not a month later, one of these guys, not the marshal, the other guy, shows up dead in an alley in Algiers. The murder is still unsolved."

"They think Franco did it?" Tommy asked.

"No way to know for sure but I wouldn't put it past him. I'd say, all in all, you two are lucky he hasn't gone berserker on your sorry butts."

"Over a couple of pictures? Overkill much." Tommy struggled to his feet. "Excuse me. Nature calls." He winked at Finn as he started from the room. "And, no thanks, I can handle this myself. It's amazing what getting off those pain meds can do. I can take a piss all by myself."

"We're so proud," Jack muttered.

"Screw you." The sound of Tommy's voice vanished behind the closing of the bathroom door.

"What happens now?" Finn asked.

"There's a warrant out for his arrest."

"Good. I think. And in the meantime?"

"Keep your eyes open and your Mace handy."

"That's it?"

Jack studied her as he chewed his lower lip. "I'm sorry. We can send extra patrol cars to cruise past your house but until something happens, our hands are tied. We're looking for him but it's a big city and he's one man. The FBI is looking for Miss Embezzlement, too. Maybe they'll get lucky and find them together."

"Like I did. Accidentally."

"Like you did, on purpose."

"Did you hear what she did to Debbie?"

"Yup. I'm sure it was scary for Debbie but it makes it even clearer since she used a toy gun, Barron's not the dangerous one. It's Franco you got to watch out for."

"What's Franco?" Tommy asked as he hobbled back into the room and took his seat on the couch.

"The more dangerous of the two."

"I agree." Tommy nodded as he reached for his forgotten beer. "She stole the money and has been threatening you, Finn, but that's all, threatening. Franco's the one who pulled the gun on us. He's out of control for whatever reason and from what you've told us, Jack, he's volatile."

"Volatile is the word," Jack agreed.

"You two aren't making me feel any better." Finn regarded one brother, then the other. "I think I should hide under my bed until you arrest him."

"I'd feel better if you did," Jack said in all seriousness. He nodded to Tommy's beer. "Got any more of those?"

"Help yourself."

"Finn?" he asked as he shoved to his feet.

"No thanks. I should get going. I put the gumbo in the fridge, but I left out the pudding in case you want more. I'll grab my stuff later." She got up, kissed Tommy on the cheek and waved good-bye to Jack. "See you Saturday, Jack, for the weeding?"

"Wouldn't miss it."

When the door closed behind Finn, Tommy and Jack stared at each other a long moment.

"She made the food, didn't she?"

Tommy nodded. "You knew?"

"That she's in cooking school?" When Tommy

nodded again, he said, "Yup."

"You gonna say anything?"

"Nope."

"Good."

"Hate to say it, but I've got more bad news," Jack said, stretching his legs out full length in front of him and folding his arms over his chest.

"Lay it on me. I thought I could tell something was up by the sick look on your face."

Jack took a breath and let it out slowly. "We retrieved a body out of the river. His name is Simon La Fontaine. He works as a carriage driver in the Quarter and he's one of two brothers who live in the building where Finn saw her body. Looks like he was beaten to death, but after being in the river awhile...well, let's say, it's hard to say positively."

"Yeah? Is it Finn's body?"

"Don't know. Possibly. Took her to the morgue but she couldn't identify him."

"What does the brother have to say?"

"He's missing. Tell you the truth. I'm worried. Both of those clowns, Franco and his girlfriend, have been sniffing around Finn and you way too much. You, I'm not so worried about, you can take care of yourself. Even with a broken leg."

"Thanks for the vote of confidence, bro."

"But I'm worried about Finn."

"Yeah, me, too."

"What are we going to do about her?"

After leaving Tommy's place Finn stood alone in the neutral zone waiting for the streetcar. She squinted her eyes against the setting sun, a yellow sphere teetering on the horizon. A woman across the street corralled three little girls and a baby in a stroller. Finn wondered what it would be like having four kids. She cringed. She didn't think of herself as the motherly type. Even the thought of one child, to say nothing of four, gave her a feeling of pure, unadulterated terror.

Maybe, sometime in the future—the far, far distant future—she might find the idea of motherhood appealing. For now baby-sitting Debbie was proving to be difficult enough. Of course, a baby didn't talk back, pierce her tiny belly button or get it on with every available boy. Then again, Debbie had been a sweet-natured silent baby once upon a time, too.

The streetcar arrived with a clang and a rumble, startling her out of her reverie. Finn climbed aboard, paid her fare and found an empty bench. The car overflowed with smiling, purple and red clad, Red Hat ladies. Purple blouses and red pants, purple pants and red blouses, and every combination of red and purple on their clothes. Finn didn't realize you could even buy shoes and hats in some of those shades.

The women were certainly happy, until Finn sat down and the streetcar failed to move. Died. Dead in the water, or at least in the middle of the street.

Oh, no.

Not again.

"What'd you do?" one of the Red Hatters asked, a quizzical expression creasing her face, the crimson feathers on her hat bobbing like a yo-yo.

"Me?" Finn pointed at herself. "Are you talking to me?"

At her insistent nod, Finn continued, "I got on the streetcar?"

"And it stopped," the stranger complained.

"It stopped to pick me up," Finn groused. She saw the driver, who had left his seat and was even now coming down the aisle, scowl at Finn. Along with everyone else on board. *Oh, good.* At least it wasn't the same driver who thought she was a terrorist.

"What you do?" he asked, stopping next to her, his

hands on his non-existent hips. "You killed dis car."

"I didn't do anything," she said, feeling her cheeks heat with embarrassment. Everyone stared at her with apparent anger on their once smiling faces.

"You brought dis bad gris-gris with you, den, din't you?" he insisted.

"No, no. It wasn't me. I didn't do anything."

"How come we're not moving?" someone hollered from the back.

"Dis gal, she put de hoodoo on dis streetcar," one of the Red Hatters said.

"I didn't," Finn said. "Honest."

The woman in the seat behind her wearing a red straw boater leaned forward and whispered, "You best leave, gal, before the natives get restless."

"Seems like they already are," Finn whispered back. "I killed a streetcar once this week and Homeland Security wasn't happy."

"What?" The woman frowned, her thin lips narrowing. "Go on now, honey. I have a gun in my pocketbook and a cell phone. I can call Homeland Security as well as the next person."

At this point Finn had to wonder which was worse. Staying or leaving. While the natives argued about the best way to string Finn up without getting arrested, she slipped out the side door.

When she hit the opposite side of the street she sprinted away, took a sharp right and disappeared among the crowds.

Twenty minutes later, she found a park bench outside Jackson Square. Her head throbbed and her throat hurt. She placed her backpack beside her and slumped against the seat.

She was beginning to think whoever put the voodoo doll Jack found at the scene of the disappearing body had truly put a spell on her. Since then everything in her life had spiraled out of control. It was past time for her to take back her life. She hated to spend the money, but when she felt like she could walk without falling over, she traipsed down to Decatur and caught a taxi to take her home. No more streetcars for now. If ever.

"I really like Benjy," Debbie informed Finn over dinner that evening. She grinned. Wearing Finn's old Pedro for President t-shirt and black leggings, her multi-colored hair tousled, her eye-shadow neon green, she looked as young and fresh as the teenager she was.

Despite feeling as if she'd missed a beat or eight in the awkward two-step of her life, Finn had managed to throw together a simple baked potato soup and garlic toast for the two of them to eat after her silent, thank-you-God, peaceful cab ride home.

"That's wonderful, Debs," Finn said, after swallowing the spoonful of hot soup she'd put in her mouth. "Please don't get too attached. You're going home in a few weeks. You wouldn't want to break his poor fragile heart."

It was hard to say with a straight face. She doubted teenage boys had hearts, fragile or otherwise.

Debbie snickered. "I, like, doubt that's gonna happen."

Finn enjoyed Debbie's company, finding it oddly tranquil. The normalcy of simply sitting down and eating reminded her of their childhood with three talkative girls vying for attention around the dinner table.

Debbie broke off a piece of bread, tossed it in her mouth and thoughtfully munched. "I guess I have to go home and start school pretty soon."

"I suppose so. Freddy awaits."

"Freddy." Debbie got a faraway look in her caramel-colored eyes and broke off another piece of bread. Holding it in her hand before she popped it in her mouth, she gave Finn a sly grin. "How could I forget about Freddy?"

"How *is* the relevant question. Benjy perhaps?"

She nodded in agreement. "Benjy is, like, hot and all, but Freddy, he's, you know..."

"The yin to your yang? The Abbott to your Costello? The peanut butter to your jelly?"

"Huh?"

Finn shook her head. "The love of your short life."

Debbie grinned back. "That's it, *f'sure*. He rocks my world."

"So says Dorie."

Debbie pursed her mouth, holding back an incorrigible grin. She waggled her eyebrows up and down.

"She has seen him in all his glory, hasn't she?" Finn returned the grin.

"'Fraid so."

"Let's not go there. I heard more than enough when I talked to Dorie the other day. You've been giving her fits." Finn stood up to clear the table.

Debbie slowed in the act of reaching for her glass of milk. "I don't know what you mean."

"Doesn't matter. I know you'll be good from now on out."

"Why not? I've been good while I've been here, haven't I?"

Finn playfully smacked her shoulder as she turned for the sink. "You mean except for playing strip poker with Benjy and attacking a woman when she pointed a gun at you. Why, you've had a regular day at the beach."

"I didn't know you had a beach here." When she saw Finn's smirk, she stopped speaking. "I'm kidding. I, like, knew that. I lived here before we moved to Florida, you know."

"You were, what, ten?, when you moved away. Maybe you didn't remember New Orleans isn't exactly a thriving beach community."

"Very funny." Before she handed Finn her glass, she tipped it up and swallowed the last of her milk. "Who was that woman anyway? She looked really mad."

"It's a long story."

"I've got time."

"Yeah, but I don't know if I have the stomach for it right now. Maybe later. You should know what to do if she comes back again, though."

Her eyes widened. "Will she?"

"I hope like hell not. Let's watch some TV, let me relax a bit, then I'll give you the scoop. Is *Dancing With the Stars* on tonight?"

The doorbell buzzed. Debbie looked at Finn and Finn looked at Debbie, her brows raised. "Expecting anybody?"

"Nope." Debbie moved toward the front door. "Maybe it's Benjy and, like, you know, he's come over to beg me to stay here forever and ever."

"Very funny." Finn grabbed a dishtowel and dried her hands. She followed Debbie into the front room, and said a silent prayer that Barron hadn't decided to make a house call.

When Debbie reached to open the door, Finn nudged her aside and snuck a peek through the security-eye in the door. She shook her head and stepped aside, letting Debbie open the door.

It wasn't the Barron woman standing on the other side of the door. It wasn't Tommy on crutches or Jack borrowing trouble. It wasn't even a neighbor come to borrow a cup of sugar.

Debbie stared.

Finn stared.

Wesley Ellis St. Clare III stood outside the door and

grinned, his teeth sparkling fresh-from-the-dentist white, his eyes twinkling, his wavy professionally scissor-trimmed hair perfect. Wearing a pink oxford cloth shirt and knife-pleat khakis with boat shoes and no socks, and oddly enough in the heat of a sweltering Louisiana summer, a lavender sweater tied around his shoulders, he held up a pair of tickets. "I've come to take you out."

Debbie snorted. Turning toward Finn, she said in a stage whisper, "Wow. Slow learner much."

"Wes, what are you doing here?"

"We're going to see the Nevilles."

"No, we're not."

He waved the tickets in his hand. "Sure we are, got 'em right here."

"No. We're not."

"I'll go with you," Debbie chimed in.

"Shut up," Finn said without any heat behind her words. "Don't you have something to do, someplace to go, some guy to seduce?"

"Nope. I'm, like, gonna stay for the fireworks."

"There won't be any. Wes is leaving. Isn't he, Wes?"

Oddly enough, his shoulders drooped. His smile withered, his trouser creases wilted, even his sweater looked less lavender. He placed his free hand on his hip. "You're still angry, aren't you? Why don't you invite me in and we can discuss this like adults."

"Wes, don't you get it? We don't have anything to discuss. We're done. Finished. Over and out. Read the credits at the end of this horror movie."

Debbie giggled. "Even I get it."

"Okay. This time, I'll back off," Wes said, turning to go. "You must be PMSing or something. Otherwise—"

"Otherwise I'd have my purse in my hand so fast your head would spin. Otherwise I'd be out the door before you had a chance to turn around. Are you crazy?

"I am not PMSing. I simply don't want to go out with you. Try and get this through your thick skull. No way. No how. Not ever."

"No," Debbie said. "Is the word in your vocabulary, Weasel Wesley?"

He stared at Debbie, his mouth dropping open, then he turned back to Finn. His cheeks bloomed with blotchy color. "I didn't know you felt this way about me, Debbie. I thought we were best buds."

"I was thirteen the last time we saw each other, Weasel. You broke my sister's heart. Like, how could we ever be best buds? Are you, like, for real?"

Finn took Debbie in her arms and hugged her. "You're the best sister ever."

Thankfully, Wes left. He turned halfway down the walkway. Over his shoulder, he caught Finn's stare and winked. The man was unbelievable, irrationally confident. Was it possible he still didn't get it?

Absolutely possible. Probable, in fact.

Finn shut the door, taking Debbie by the shoulder and steering her toward the couch. "I love you. Chocolate?"

"I love you back. And, hell yeah, to the chocolate. Now before we turn on the TV, tell me what's with the woman with the fake gun?"

"You really want to know?"

"I'll say. Like, why would anyone pull a gun on sweet little ol' me? I don't even know her. I'm innocent."

"Innocent? Now that's a stretch." Finn went into the kitchen and grabbed the emergency bag of peanut M&Ms out of the pantry. Debbie lay sprawled in the corner of the couch, her eyes bright and inquisitive, a slight smile curving her lips.

She handed the bag to Debbie. She ripped open the package and tossed a few into her mouth.

"Sit tight, Debs. Have I got a story for you."

CHAPTER TWELVE

The name of the class was Boring Things You Need to Accomplish to Graduate This Damnable Culinary Program. Okay, not really. It was Purchasing and Storeroom Procedures, which amounted to the same thing. Finn hated it. It was uninteresting, unexciting and downright awful. She particularly hated it today when her mind was on other things, things like people who wanted her dead. She reminded herself that someday this would all be over. No running from one tour to the next, from one class to another, taking sordid pictures for Tommy with little time to eat, sleep or have a life. One day she would be a professional- –a chef with her own kitchen. No Johnny Franco or FBI's Most Wanted woman chasing after her.

Today she'd take notes, learn, explore and try not to fall asleep or think up ways to get the chef instructor, Wanda Westrom, fired. The woman herself paced in front of the class, a bead of sweat tracking down her forehead. No cooking—oh, no, not today—they were in a classroom and the instructor seemed to think they were all idiots.

She was intent on humiliating someone.

She was intent on clearing the room of someone. Or several someones.

She was intent on making someone cry.

In other words, she was being herself.

"So, Eli," she asked, an evil twinkle in her eye, "what do you think of the concept?"

Since Finn had been woolgathering, she had no idea what concept Chef referred to and was overjoyed the woman hadn't called on her. She cringed when she spotted Eli, one of the twelve other students in this class. From the panicked look on Eli's face, he had no idea either. His face reddened. If possible, he was sweating even more than the Wicked Witch. His mouth opened and closed several times as he gasped for air, or the answer.

"I don't know," he managed.

"Do you plan on passing this class, young man?" Chef Westrom's strident voice penetrated every nerve ending in Finn's body.

Eli visibly shook as he answered in a quivery voice, "I hope so."

"So do I," she said, "but I don't see it happening."

"You don't?" he replied, his tone indicating his belief that such a thing was at least possible.

"Never mind." She scanned the other expectant, terrified faces. She extracted a sheaf of papers from a manila folder. A groan emanated from behind Finn. "Right you are, boys and girls."

With a smirk on her face, Cynthia of the bad disposition, chimed in, "Pop quiz, hotshot."

Chef Instructor Westrom might have smiled. It was hard to say for sure. Her lips twitched. "That's correct, Cynthia. Pop quiz. Twelve delightful questions for twelve delightful students. You should know the answers. Otherwise, you might as well go watch movies with Cynthia to hone your movie references because you'll never graduate or go on to become average chefs."

One of the younger girls in the front row raised her

hand. If Finn had been closer to her, she would have yanked it down. No good ever came from raising a hand and asking a stupid question. Not when the woman was in one of her evil moods. And Finn knew, without a single doubt, the question was going to be moronic.

"What's on your mind, Elspeth?"

Elspeth? What kind of idiot parents named their child Elspeth? What an unfortunate name. Almost as bad as Finnigan.

"What movie are you talking about, Chef Westrom?"

The instructor's face reddened, her eyes widened and the sweat trickling down her forehead dripped onto the floor. Oh, boy. Here it comes.

The evil witch was about to cast a spell on poor Elspeth. Finn imagined her turning the poor girl into a toad. Or maybe in this case, a tureen of turtle soup.

From the corner of her eye, Finn saw her ghostly chef friend standing beside Chef Westrom and gesturing with his hands like he was trying to choke her.

Finn hid a grin behind a hand. He winked at Finn as the instructor began to cough. Her face, already red, turned a deeper magenta color. She reached for her water bottle, took a long drink. A puzzled expression crossed her face.

When her breathing returned to normal, she handed out the test papers without replying to Elspeth's ridiculous question. Finn's ghost threw up his hands. He scowled, then stalked up the aisle and stopped beside Finn's chair. She looked but, of course, no one saw him but her. The whole idea she could see a ghost still blew her mind.

"She's ten times worse," he drawled, "than the worst chef I've seen in all the years of classes at this school. I know you can't reply without looking like a lunatic or drawing the wrath of the foolish woman. I merely wanted you to know I feel your pain."

Finn took the sheet of paper the student in front of her passed back but her eyes never left Chef John Michael.

"You'll do fine. As they say, this, too, shall pass. Whoever they are. Watch out for question number four. It's a bit tricky. Remember proper storing temps. Until next time." He disappeared.

Finn swallowed hard and looked around. No one watched her. Most of them had pulled out a pen and were starting the test. She caught the instructor staring at her. "Ten minutes, Miss Jones. Time's a wasting."

Finn got the hint, took a pen from her backpack and began. Was everyone else's life as complicated? Given her week, she'd bet a year's tuition no one's life was more screwed up than her own.

The test covered the things they'd been studying in this class. She knew the answer to the first question and the rest fell in line as easily. With special attention on question four, it came to her right away. If only her life could be so simple.

As Finn stepped out the door after school, her cell phone buzzed. She looked at the number and didn't recognize it. She stopped walking, stepped back against the building into the shade and flipped it open. "Hello?"

"Finnigan Jones?"

"Yes?"

"This is Margaret Barron."

Finn's heart skipped a beat. "No way. How did you get this number?"

"I haf my ways. I believe I've said this before."

"What do you want? Do you know there's a warrant out for Johnny Franco's arrest?" Finn paused to take a needed breath. "It's only a matter of time before the FBI finds you. And him. You should leave New Orleans. The whole country, for that matter."

"It's why I called. I'm tired of running. I'm tired of putting up with Johnny. Even great sex isn't worth putting up with his bull. I'm outta here. I said good-bye to my sis. I'm headed to an island with boat drinks, sandy beaches and plenty of sunshine. I want to see buff young men in nothing but surfer shorts every single day for the rest of my natural life."

"Some country with no extradition policy with the United States."

"Exactly."

"Why are you telling me this?" Finn asked. If this wasn't one of the craziest conversations of her life, she was a future Miss America.

"I'm trying to say I'm sorry. Honestly. I never meant to scare you or your sister. I'm not like this. I don't even kill bugs. Johnny kept at me to get those pictures but I don't care anymore. I simply want to go away."

"What about the money? Doesn't Franco want a piece of it?" Finn couldn't believe she was having this conversation. They were actually talking like two normal people.

Barron chuckled. "Oh, he wants it all right but it's safely stashed away where he can never get at it. He seems to think I want to set up housekeeping here in New Orleans with him. Like I'd actually do it. I can't stay here. Eventually the FBI will find me and then where would I be?"

"So, you're calling me because...?"

"To say I'm sorry. To say I'm leaving. To say be careful of Johnny. I know he has a terrible temper, but I don't know what he's capable of."

"You think after you're gone, he's gonna keep after us for those pictures?"

"Exactly what I think. It doesn't matter to me. I'm disappearing. Margaret Jane Barron will be no longer. New name. New face. New body. Watch out, Jennifer Aniston."

Finn shook her head. The woman might find a great plastic surgeon who could work wonders, the best in the entire world, but she would look no more like Jennifer Aniston afterward than Finn herself. "Good luck with that."

"Thanks, dear, it's been real."

Not real. It had been a nightmare. With Franco still in the picture, she doubted it was over yet. When she realized she had the phone to her ear and was listening to nothing but dead air, she called Jack with the news. Thank God, one of her nemeses was leaving town. One down, one to go.

Since Gert left on cruise patrol Finn was officially on cat duty. After her afternoon class, she went home and grabbed a bite to eat with Debbie. She felt a little guilty for having left her alone so much of the time she'd been visiting.

It was nearing twilight when she let herself into Gert's back door. She opened the gate and walked past several antique lawn ornaments and a contemporary lap pool to get to the back door.

Gert had a great sense of style yet the yard desperately needed a little TLC, a lot of TLC actually, weeds sprouting everywhere, overgrown bushes in need of trimming, branches and twigs littering the brick walkways and grassy areas. Soon she and Jack would be tackling it all.

She passed a hundred-year-old magnolia tree and smiled at the eccentric garden gnomes and elves scattered about the base of the trunk. She half expected them to come to life, jump up and start jabbering at her. Or worse.

The kittens, Maggie and Jake, met her at the kitchen door, mewing, winding around her legs and begging for attention. She flipped on the overhead light, picked them up and cuddled their warm bodies.

She stood in the massive kitchen with its black and white tiled floors, black granite countertops and ten-foot high ceilings. She wondered for the hundredth time how Gert kept from going crazy in the huge mansion all by herself.

It had at least thirteen rooms, marble fireplaces and antique carpets in nearly every one. Each magnificent room had been decorated with Louis XVI furniture, extensive draperies and overpriced paintings. Whenever Finn stepped inside she tiptoed around terrified she was going to break something. Gert merely laughed at her.

She went into the laundry room to feed and water the entire crew. When she opened the bag of cat food, the crackle brought forth Angelina. Her elegant black tail swished back and forth. Scarlett wandered in looking sleek and regal, her fluffy white coat gleaming and lustrous.

Finn filled six food bowls, set them in a line in front of the dryer, then from the oversized laundry sink emptied and re-filled the water dispenser. She placed it on the floor.

She leaned against the washing machine, watched the cats eat and relished the peace and quiet. The only sound that of the air conditioning quietly turning on and off and the mantle clock ticking distantly from the dining room.

When Archie, an orange tabby, tiptoed in, he stared at Finn a moment, then lined up with the other four and began to eat.

She proceeded to clean out the litter boxes beside the dryer. After washing her hands, she studied the cats as they delicately ate their way through the food then licked their whiskers and paws. Such single-minded dedication to eating and grooming. Such simple lives. If only.

Drew still hadn't shown up. Sure, he was a cat and had his own agenda. And true, he was only one of six in Gert's menagerie but he was the one she'd saved from the clutches of death. Or whatever it was they did to cats people no longer wanted. Finn called his name. Again.

She took the cat-sitting job seriously and wanted each cat accounted for before she left.

If she didn't find him soon and get him fed, Finn was going to be late for her pathetically voyeuristic job of photo taking. Where could the darn cat be anyway?

"Drew, honey? Here, kitty, kitty." She wandered from one room to the next looking under beds, behind furniture, around the bend. "Kitty, kitty."

Archie followed in her wake, meowing pitifully.

Drew was named after the Saints' quarterback and he was Gert's favorite. Finn had to find him and make sure he was okay.

Where was he? Like the real-life New Orleans Saint he was named after, Drew Brees, this Drew could normally be counted on for top shelf behavior. Not so much when he was a kitten, however. Once, thankfully not on Finn's watch, he pulled a bedspread off a bed by pulling on a single thread and then shredding the thing until there was nothing left but square- inch quilting-sized pieces. Another time he managed to get the bag of cat food off the counter and made his way through half of it before falling down sick, his belly bloated like a balloon, and scaring Gert half to death.

Finn knew he hadn't devoured another week's worth of cat food this time since none was missing. She didn't mind the cat-sitting, even cleaning up the poop, but she didn't want to make any vet visits. She'd done it once before and it was no picnic. It had been Scarlett several months back and thankfully, it was nothing but an eye infection.

She came back to the laundry room. No Drew. She went through the kitchen one more time calling his name. She toured through the dining room and the den, slowly this time, turning on the lights as she went, checking beneath chairs, behind furniture and drapes, calling out his name and feeling downright foolish. When he wanted to eat, he'd appear. You could lead a horse to water but...blah, blah, blah.

Still she'd feel better if she knew he was okay. She wasn't going to leave until she at least saw him.

She climbed the stairs and checked the hallway, the guest rooms, the bathrooms, even opened the door of the linen closet and peeked inside.

When she entered the lovely master bedroom, Gert's room, she was captivated as always. Bathed in the warm late afternoon light coming through the bank of west windows, the comfy-looking bed would have enticed Goldilocks.

An unmoving orange-striped tail stuck out beneath the edge of the front window's drapes and lay on the carpeted floor like an s-shaped banana.

"Oh, no." Finn's heart jittered in her chest as she rushed across the room.

She shoved the drapes aside, knelt on the floor and gently touched the body. Thank God he was still warm and alive, though his breathing hitched in and out. She was no doctor, wasn't certain how much longer he would last or if this was even serious. She did know she was making a trip to the vet again.

Finn held him against her chest and rushed downstairs.

"Later, cats," she hollered as she snagged her keys off the counter passing through the kitchen at a run. Her

mind spun through all the options. She was done with
tours and culinary classes for the day but she was
supposed to be on booty patrol for Tommy later on. It
was still two hours away so she should be fine. If Drew
was fine.

She jump in her car and arrived at Gert's vet's office
in ten minutes, after having run two red lights and
avoiding killing an avid bicyclist intent on riding in the
middle of the street.

She dashed into the single story building holding the
still breathing Drew who, as far as Finn could tell,
needed to be on life support.

No other four-legged patients waited. The thin,
young, blonde receptionist, dressed in a blue smock
with kittens bouncing all over it, looked up expectantly,
her big brown eyes wide, her mouth a round "oh" of
surprise.

"I'm cat sitting for my aunt, Gert Charboneau," Finn
explained gasping hard after her mad dash from the car.
"This one, his name is Drew, he's sick. He's not
breathing right."

"You're lucky you got here when you did. I was
getting ready to close." She peered at the cat in Finn's
arms. "Is this the cat who ate the bedspread?" She got
to her feet and came around the partition, which
separated her desk from the waiting area.

"The one and only. He was fine yesterday. I don't
know what's wrong."

She tucked her finger beneath the cat's chin, studied
his half-staff eyelids and the tongue lolling out his
mouth. "Did he eat something he shouldn't have?"

"I looked but I didn't see anything."

"Has he been outside?"

"Only in the fenced yard. Gert doesn't let them
wander the neighborhood or anything."

"Doc Mac isn't with anyone right now so we can

take him right in. Follow me."

Finn held Drew tight in her arms and followed the young woman down a short hallway to an examination room.

"I'm sorry I didn't catch your name," said the receptionist, aka the vet assistant, as it turned out when she pulled strange utensils from a drawer and lay them out on a counter.

"Finn Jones. I'm cat-sitting for my Aunt Gert."

"Cruising, is she?"

Was there nothing Gert didn't discuss with virtual strangers? "So to speak. And you are?"

"Karen Manning."

At Finn's look of surprise she shook her head and smiled. "No relation to the football Mannings. Unfortunately. I'd sure like some tickets." She took Drew from Finn, then stuck a thermometer in Drew, not in the mouth, and Finn turned away. She wasn't squeamish, well, maybe a little, but she figured Drew would appreciate the privacy.

The door opened and Doc Mac entered the room. He was a handsome man of about sixty. He had a full head of thick salt and pepper hair cut short, deep-set dark chocolate eyes and a mouth bracketed by fine lines, indicating a man who smiled often. Finn knew because Gert often spoke of him as an, unfortunately, happily married man with a passel of children and grandchildren. Unlike the awful smock Karen wore, he was dressed in faded, worn blue jeans and a dark red chambray shirt.

Introductions were made, symptoms discussed and a thorough exam ensued. Finn sat in a plastic chair worrying and observing from a safe distance and discreetly checking her watch for the time.

According to Tommy, the subject of the current investigation and his paramour had reservations at

Brennan's for eight. Tommy gave Finn a description of him and the car he'd be driving. She planned on parking outside the restaurant, waiting for them to leave, and then following. Somewhere along the way, snapping a few incriminating photos.

She figured they couldn't eat and be back on the street in less than ninety minutes so Finn had plenty of time.

"I'd like to keep Drew overnight for observation," Doc Mac said in his relaxed, deep drawl. "I don't like his labored breathing. We've drawn blood and we'll take x-rays but it will be a while to get back all the results. I think I know what the problem is, but until I know for sure I can't get him on the right medication or procedure."

"What do you think it is?" Finn asked.

"At first guess? Pneumonia."

"Cats get pneumonia?"

"Sure, they can get almost anything people get." He turned to go. "Have Karen get your cell phone number and I'll call you as soon as I know anything."

"Thanks, Doc Mac. I appreciate you seeing me so late and without an appointment."

"It's what we're here for." He grinned, his hands still stroking Drew's tabby fur. "Gert is a favorite of ours."

"And a good customer," Karen added.

He chuckled. "Of course. That, too. We love Gert. She has such an infectious energy and vitality. If I weren't already in love with my Grace, I'd be pounding down her door. She's quite a woman."

"She is," Finn agreed. "You'd have to stand in line though."

He laughed.

Karen picked up Drew, then patted Finn's arm. "Don't you worry."

Doc Mac escorted Finn to the door. "We can't have

our Super Bowl MVP's namesake down for the count at the start of the season."

"Thanks, both of you. I'll be waiting to hear from you then."

Finn left the clinic still worried about Drew but confident he was in the best hands possible. She prayed she wouldn't have to give Gert any bad news on her return.

In the dank darkness on the bank of the Mississippi, Finn couldn't make out the couple parked in the car. She'd followed them from Brennan's where they'd probably paid a fortune for their meal. Brennan's was one of the *chi-chi* places to eat in New Orleans. Their reputation was well deserved, but Finn could name a half dozen other restaurants where the food was as good at a fraction of the price. If you gave up service and ambience, which was not necessarily a given, you more than made up for it in your wallet.

Finn's own restaurant would never be Brennan's, but it would be fine all the same with the best shrimp and andouille jambalaya in the Quarter, if not the entire city.

She sighed. It cost her nothing to dream, although as she peered into the inky black of the night, the cloud-covered half- moon gave off precious little light. She considered the smelly riverbank might not be the best place to daydream...in the nighttime.

She tiptoed closer, gauging each careful step, edging around weeds and who knew what else, breathing through her mouth to avoid the strange smelly mixture of wet dog and decomposition. She gave a little prayer there weren't any snakes or other creepy crawlies hiding in the grass.

The couple she was supposed to photograph had chosen a spot to park beneath the wide, overhanging branches of a cottonwood tree, upriver, far from the

Riverwalk, the nosy tourists and good lighting. It was proving nearly impossible to get close to the pair without giving herself away.

Damn them. She needed this money shot and unless they got out of the car, she wasn't going to get it this far from the city's lights. Flash for the camera was probably out of the question.

Finn slapped at an insect munching on her neck. If she didn't move out of these thick weeds soon, a voracious mosquito herd was going to reduce her to nothing but one giant, itching red welt.

In a painful crouch, she slipped through the dense undergrowth and came to within ten feet of the car. Any closer and she'd be seen. The soft muddy ground at her feet squelched beneath her sandals. Cold mud oozed up between her toes. She groaned. A tugboat blasted several short whistles in the near distance as it pushed a barge against the strong river current. Rustling in the weeds at her feet made her want to run for her life.

Another mosquito buzzed at her ear and she waved it away. She was ready to leave when the driver's side door opened, the interior light came on and out stepped the wandering middle-aged husband, tall, lean and sporting a grizzled, graying, week-old beard. Finn sighed in disgust as she snapped her pictures when she saw the heavy chains around his neck, the open-necked white sports shirt displaying a hairy chest and the diamond-studded pinkie ring. He was a walking cliché. She stared with her digital camera squeezed close to her eye when the passenger door opened.

She pressed the button and got several shots of a somewhat chubby, extremely young—*okay, be honest, Finn*—jailbait-young, girl stepped out. She left her door open washing the near area in the thin light. It illuminated her unlined face.

If she was sixteen, and Finn guessed she was closer

to thirteen, for God's sake, Finn would gracefully admit her mistake, stand on a bench in Jackson Square, naked, and sing the Star Spangled Banner. God. How bad was this?

Should she call Tommy?

Should she call the cops?

Should she start screaming bloody murder?

Or should she grab the girl and hightail it back to her own car parked far away?

She stared, her heart in her throat, as the pervert walked around his sedan. His teenage paramour met him halfway. He leaned her over the back of the car and kissed her bare shoulder.

Finn half expected the jerk to tilt her head, bare his exposed canines and bite her on the fragile column of her neck.

"I vant to bite you on the neck," he whispered, laughing. Pushing aside her long dark hair, he bit her.

Oh. Dear. God.

The teenager groaned in apparent ecstasy, her hands on the car trunk. His hands roamed over her firm backside as he nibbled her neck. Finn clicked away, ecstatic herself to be getting the shots she wanted, yet disgusted she had to watch this display of male stupidity and possible criminal activity.

"Honeybun?" cooed the young girl.

"Yeah, what is it?" He chewed on her neck much the same way the mosquitoes were chewing on Finn's. She smacked at another one where it buzzed in her ear, loud as a 747.

"Are we gonna do it right here? Standing up like a couple of cows?"

"I thought you liked it this way, baby."

"You like it like that, Delbert. I don't."

Baby. How accurate. Cradle robbing was more like it. Finn's mind whirred. Should she leave? She had her pictures. She could exit the scene without a sound, but the idea of this pervert getting away with sex with an underage girl rankled.

She made up her mind. Stowing the camera in her pocket, she stiffened her spine. Stomping forward, she yelled, "Hey! Delbert?"

His head lifted. His hand came out from under the girl's shirt where he'd been fondling her pert young breasts. "What the hell?"

"Is that the cops?" she asked in a thin voice.

"Young lady, how old are you?"

"Fourteen."

She knew it. "What's your name?"

Finn stepped into the light from the car. Up close, the perv wasn't as old as he looked from a distance. Still too old to be with a teenager but the beard was apparently prematurely gray.

"You don't have to answer her, Bonnie."

"Yes, you do, Bonnie. Bonnie what?"

"Bonnie Blue Beaufort." She stood at the back of the car, unmoving, her mouth wide, her eyes wider, her hands clenching and unclenching at her sides.

Delbert stalked around the car and back to the driver's door. He reached inside, turned the key and started the car. "We're outta here."

Finn ignored him. "Whoa, interesting name. Parents fans of *Gone With The Wind*?"

Delbert watched Finn while gesturing for the teenager to get in the car.

"I guess."

"Get in the car, baby. She's not showing us any ID so she's not a cop. You don't have to say anything to her. Let's go."

The truth hit Finn like a Saints nose tackle. "You knew all along she was fourteen, didn't you, you jackass pervert."

"No," he lied. "She told me she was eighteen."

"I never did," Bonnie complained. "You knew exactly how old I was. He promised to buy me a new I-Pod if I'd have sex with him."

"No way," Finn said, her pulse pounding in defense of wayward, teenage girls who cut this close a line to prostitution. This could have been Debbie. Finn reacted without thinking about the consequences. She reached the open driver's side door and held onto it as she leaned into the car to turn it off. Delbert tried to wrestle her hand away while attempting to get in the car himself.

"Get in the car," he bellowed. Bonnie turned toward her door. As she came parallel to the passenger side, Finn reached across Delbert and shoved the gearshift between the seats into first. The car drifted forward and edged closer to the dark riverbank.

Bonnie backed away, and stood watching. Her mouth hung open gaping like a landed trout.

Delbert screeched like a crow, then scrambled to stop the car. His hand fumbled on the gearshift while trying to push Finn out of the way. The car rolled forward. Finn toppled over and landed on her backside in the mud with a cringe-inducing squelch.

She stared, appalled, as the car picked up speed and lurched toward the river. She scrambled to her feet.

Delbert, realizing he couldn't stop the car either, jumped, free falling over Finn in the process.

The car, rolling in slow motion, picked up speed like a sprinter at the tape. It tipped hood first, slipping into the river with a quiet splash. Within minutes, it disappeared into the darkness of the water.

The three of them stood at the bank, mouths open, trying to see past the darkness.

Uh-oh.

Finn may have saved a young girl from a pervert but

she was in a world of hurt now. She'd drowned an innocent car.

"Wow," Bonnie murmured, staring at Finn. "You drowned Delbert's car."

He stood staring over the water, his hand over his mouth. He removed it to speak. "Not any car either. That was my old man's brand new Buick. He picked it up from the dealership two weeks ago. I promised to take good care of it."

"You don't have a car?" Finn asked.

"Yes. No. Not at the moment."

"How old are you?"

"Not that it's any of your damned business but I'm thirty-one."

"Going on eleven? How do you afford dinner at Brennan's?"

"You were following us?"

"Yes," Finn admitted. At this point what did she have to lose?

"Who are you?"

"I'm doing my job."

"For who?"

"Do you have a wife?"

"Yeah."

"You do?" Bonnie looked crushed.

"What is wrong with you?" Finn couldn't contain her outrage. "You borrow your dad's car so you can impress underage girls and have sex with them, *and* you have a wife? You're a degenerate."

"What do *you* know? I have a job. I have a car. It's in the shop. You're the one going to jail for stalking us," Delbert threatened.

"I doubt it. If anything, you are. You tried to have sex with this girl. She's fourteen, for God's sake." Finn pulled out her cell phone and called 9-1-1.

Five minutes later and well into a heated argument

with Delbert, the cops arrived. After a ton of accusations, finger pointing and general mayhem, they let everyone go. They arrested no one since no crime had been committed. No sex occurred since Finn intervened. No one deliberately pushed the car into the river even though Delbert insisted Finn had done just that. When she explained her side of the story, that she was trying to save Bonnie from the clutches of an evil, perverted older man, Delbert received a tongue lashing about carousing with teenage girls. The cops didn't ask nor did they seem to care what Finn was doing there in spite of Delbert's feeble explanations.

He and Bonnie wandered away, probably to get away from Finn. They waited without a word to each other for the tow truck to arrive to pull the car from the river. It hadn't completely drowned. The right side of the rear bumper rose out of the water, the moon glistening off the chrome, like the last hours of the Titanic.

Finn made a feeble attempt to wipe the mud off her backside then she grabbed her backpack and headed for her car. She looked up when Jack arrived and groaned.

"What? Again with the cops? This is becoming a regular occurrence with you." He wrapped his arm around her shoulder and grinned. "At least this time you didn't get hauled off to jail."

He walked her to her car, brushed a kiss across her cheek and watched as she drove away. She was so tired she didn't even want to think what he meant by that tender show of affection.

CHAPTER THIRTEEN

Her misadventures on the river wrapped up, Finn drove home as carefully as a drunk, avoiding any possibility of further disaster. Something repulsively smelly clung to the seat of her pants with its last dying gasp. She held her breath.

She pulled into the narrow, shadowed spot beside her tiny house, then went inside and dropped her stuff inside the back door. She called out a hello to Debbie to say where she was headed, and walked over to Gert's house.

Loud meowing drifted to her before she even got the key in the lock. She was late for their usual feeding time. Since cats were self-reliant and adaptable, and this bunch had plenty of playmates, Finn didn't feel guilty about leaving them alone for long periods. Like all day. She did feel a twinge of guilt about serving dinner late.

Finn sidestepped several felines who wound their tails around her ankles when she stepped inside. She slipped off her shoes and bent down to pick up Scarlett to snuggle her warmth against her neck.

"Scarlett, you are a beauty," she stated staring at her little round face and emerald green eyes.

Jake rubbed up against her leg purring. She patted him on the head and put Scarlett back on the floor.

"Okay, Drew's still at the vet, who's missing?" she

counted heads as she headed toward the laundry room. With the upside-down watering devices empty, Finn knew it needed refilling as well as the cat food dishes.

Four cats followed her. She flipped on the light, reached into the pantry for the bag of food, still searching for the missing cat. Generally when she came over to feed them morning or night, they followed her around like baby ducklings.

As they ate, Finn studied them to see who was missing. After some deliberation, she saw it was Archie who was not quarterbacking his housemates.

She left to go find him. It felt like déjà vu all over again.

"Here, kitty, kitty," she called feeling a little foolish but since no one but the other cats could hear her she kept on. She turned on lights as she wandered through the dining room with its cypress wood floor, Queen Anne table and Chippendale chairs, then into the cheery parlor checking on and beneath the Victorian sofa and behind the piano. She lifted the drapes and kept calling, "Kitty, kitty, time for dinner, Archie honey. Come and get it."

She wandered into the entrance hall with its gorgeous leaded-glass double doors. Streetlight poured through pooling on the floor and reflecting off the dual mirrors on either side. She startled herself with how bad she looked. Her hair fell in a disarray of tangled curls around her head. A streak of dirt dusted one cheekbone and her face was as pale as her new boyfriend, the chef ghost. She didn't need to check her backside. She could feel the dampness through the denim and smell...something awful.

She shook her head. No wonder Archie was a no-show. With her homeless street-person look, she'd probably scared him off. She trudged up the cypress stairs, past the stained-glass windows and stopped in the hall. Which direction? With six bedrooms, it could take her all night to check. She decided to go with the most logical and look in Gert's first.

It was the prettiest room in the house. The walls were painted the faintest shade of turquoise, which in the light of day made the room look like the Caribbean. Underneath the three bay windows stood a charming brass and iron bed with a pure white chenille bedspread. Curled up on one of the pillows at the head of the bed lay Archie, sound asleep and purring with a deep resonance that Finn found surprising.

Finn walked past the fireplace and the loveseat and looked down at the sleeping cat.

When she reached out to pet him, his eyes flew open and he hissed at her, the fur along his back rising in a deeply defined ridge.

"Hey, now, Quarterback, is that any way to treat me? Haven't you heard about not biting the hand that feeds you?" Archie stretched, got to his feet and hissed again. Finn backed away. "Okay, mister, you know where the kibble is."

He jumped off the bed and strode out of the room, his tail twitching, his head high.

Finn shook her head and laughed. "I have such a way with the men."

She went downstairs to clean out the litter boxes.

With that disgusting chore out of the way, she checked once more on the multitudes. Maggie and Jake were still eating, but the rest of the crew had left the laundry room. She went back through to the kitchen and found Archie laying on his side in front of the back door, not moving, no tail twitching, his breathing labored, his sides heaving. He didn't even hiss when she bent down to take a closer look. He barely moved when she picked him up.

Deja vu all over again? She grabbed her car keys and

made the mad dash to the vet's office. Fifteen minutes later, she rushed inside and found the same woman, Karen Manning, at the front desk.

She smiled. "Drew is ready to be picked up. I didn't even have to call you. Luckily this is our night to stay open late." When she saw the cat cradled in Finn's arms she jumped to her feet.

"Oh, boy. You're having a time of it, aren't you?"

Finn handed the cat over. "You could say that."

Again, she followed the woman down the hallway and into the examination room. Doc Mac stood at the sink washing his hands. He turned at their entrance, his smile turning to a frown as he saw the cat in Karen's hands.

"Gert is going to wonder about leaving her cats in my care next time." Finn sat down in the same plastic chair as she had before.

"Oh, I doubt it. When she sees the cats fully recuperated she'll thank you for taking such good care of them." Karen handed Archie into Doc Mac's hands. The cat gave a half-hearted hiss, his sides heaving and his eyes wide.

After an examination that Finn thought seemed much too short, he turned to Finn with a grin.

"What is it?" Finn whispered.

"Archie is going to be a mommy."

Finn jumped to her feet. "No way. I thought Archie was a male."

"Archie is and always has been a female. Gert's little joke, I guess, naming her Archie. In a few hours, she is going to have a brood of kittens to mother."

"Wow." Finn didn't know if she was more relieved or more flabbergasted. She idly wondered who had fathered them.

"So I should take him home?" She was no midwife.

Doc Mac smiled, then patted her shoulder. "You can

take *her* home and she will manage fine on her own. Drew's ready to go home as well."

"What about Archie? What do I need to do?"

"Don't you worry, hon," Karen said. "Archie doesn't need you at all. Find a nice dark, quiet spot and put down plenty of towels. She'll do all the rest."

"You're going to be an aunt," Doc Mac stated as he handed Archie to her. Karen got Drew and handed him to her.

With her hands full of cats, Finn said, "Wow. What am I going to say to Gert?"

"*Mazel tov*?" Karen suggested with a wry grin.

Later the next day Gert, tanned and rested, got back from her cruise. She stuck her blonde head in at Finn's back door, minutes past the dinner hour, finding Finn and Debbie hard at work over a game of Scrabble at the kitchen table.

"You'll never guess what happened while I was away," Gert said, hands on hips. "Or maybe you already know."

Debbie tilted her head. "What? Like did you get engaged or something?"

"No, silly. My Archie had five little kittens."

"Archie?" Debbie questioned. "Isn't that, like, a guy's name?"

"Like, yeah, Gert," Finn mimicked. "Like Archie Manning, quarterback extraordinaire? Did you know *he* was a *she*?"

"I've always known Archie was a female. I liked the name and I'm a Saints fan so I named her after one of their more famous players."

"And they're doing okay? The kittens? I mean, she was acting a little grumpy when I fed them last night but I figured he, she, was being a cat."

"Oh, she's fine. Doing the motherly thing."

Finn took the moment to explain about Drew's

illness but Gert took it all in stride. With six cats, Finn guessed she spent a lot of time at the vet's office. After all, they knew Gert by name.

Finn remembered what Gert said the last time she'd returned from her cruise. "When are you going on your date with your taxi driver?"

Gert gasped holding a hand to her red sequin-covered chest. "For a moment I flashed on Danny DeVito in the TV show *Taxi*. Yeesh. I'm not that bad off, am I?"

"I've seen that show!" Debbie's face transformed from Scrabble concentration to joyful recollection. "That's so funny, Aunt Gert. He's, like, the meanest boss ever."

"And short," Gert added, then demonstrated by putting her hand shoulder high. She rolled her eyes sending Debbie into a fit of giggles.

"And bald," Finn added, grinning.

"And grumpy," Debbie managed between giggles.

"None of which describes *my* taxi driver," Gert said, pulling up a chair and checking out the game board. "He's tall dark, and handsome. I'm supposed to call him this week about our date. So who's winning?"

"Finn," Debbie groused. "She knows all these cool cooking words, like none I ever heard of."

Debbie missed Finn's shake of the head, her futile attempt to keep the secret of culinary school to herself.

"Like braise?" Apparently, Gert didn't pick up on the acknowledgement as she stared at the board. She smiled at Finn as she studied it with no other apparent reason than to see what words they'd played. "And bake? That's a big one."

"No, bake was mine," Debbie bragged.

Finn caught Gert up on the latest gossip she'd missed while she was away. All the adventures Finn and Debbie had survived. Even Gert was surprised.

Thank God, Chef Shane was teaching today because Cynthia was on the warpath.

It was bad enough Finn arrived late to class. When she entered the room and tiptoed in past him, he merely nodded. She heard the last phrase angrily tossed by Cynthia toward Eli as she stepped up to their workstation. "Try not to be stupid today."

Lovely. The girl was relentless, humorless and downright irritating. That was on a good day.

"What are we doing today?" Finn asked, donning her chef jacket.

Both Cynthia and Eli's heads swiveled in Finn's direction. They stared at her as if she were an alien with two heads. Cynthia sneered, baring small kibble-sized teeth.

Finn sneered right back. "Could you at least try to get along?"

"Why?"

"Don't even bother, Finn," Eli said, his voice resigned. "She's gonna do what she's gonna do. You can't change a tiger's stripes."

"As if I'd want to change." Cynthia cocked her head and looked off in the opposite direction.

Finn felt like the non-descript referee for the WWE. She reached beneath the worktable and pulled out a large stainless steel mixing bowl. "Let's do the work and try not to talk."

"Fine by me," Eli said.

"Whatever," Cynthia muttered.

They were supposed to make beignets from scratch, and then using three different cooking oils compare the differences. They combined yeast with warm water and measured out the sugar into a work bowl. Finn kept one eye on Cynthia as she mixed her ingredients. Stirring with her own wooden spoon, she followed Eli's steady work and Cynthia's frenetic movements. Finn couldn't help noticing her eyes dilating with each ingredient she added to her bowl.

They measured and mixed in relative quiet, handing each other the next required ingredients—salt, egg and evaporated milk and actually working well together for a change albeit with Cynthia's raised brows and haughty demeanor.

They added flour and shortening. Finn began to think everything might work out today when the kneading began. Both Cynthia and Eli concentrated on the simple enjoyable movement. If nothing else, it allowed Cynthia to work out her aggression.

After placing the ball in an oiled bowl to let rise and double in size, they moved to the classroom for a primer on the joys of *Written Expression*. Finn never imagined she'd have to learn grammatical structure when she signed up for culinary arts.

Later, they returned to the kitchen, rolled out the dough, cut it into diamond shapes and placed them on a baking sheet to rise again. They adjourned to the classroom one last time for a class on Public Speaking. Neither this class nor the last one thrilled Finn, but at least it was quiet. No students fell asleep because they were frothing with anticipation for the thrill of frying delightfully tasty doughnuts.

Everything was going along smoothly with Eli heating up canola oil, Cynthia cottonseed oil and Finn vegetable oil until Eli took a misstep. As he stood in front of the hot stove getting ready to place the dough into his pan of sizzling oil, Cynthia purposely elbowed him. The dough plopped on the floor with a nasty squishing sound.

He spun around, eyes flashing, anger apparent in his stiff posture. "What the hell did ya do that for?"

Cynthia grabbed the baking sheet out of his hands and set it aside.

Finn watched horrified, her own baking sheet in one hand and a towel in the other.

Cynthia dropped her first beignet into the oil from a height of several inches and chortled as it fell. Thick, roiling oil splashed onto the stove, the floor and the nearby countertop. The second one she dropped from a height of a foot. This time the oil splashed on her as well. Finn flinched and backed away. That had to hurt like hell. Cynthia didn't so much as blink, her facial expression vacant, eyes a blank stare.

The oil splattered onto the adjacent burner where Finn had removed her own pan of sizzling oil in hopes of avoiding more destruction. Then it did what hot oil does when it strikes a hot surface. It burst into flames. Within minutes, a scorching conflagration rose up the metal vent and then poured out the edges.

Cynthia ignored the searing heat and devastation of the developing fire, and dropped her third beignet into the bubbling oil from a height of several feet.

Finn came to her senses and jerked the bowl out of Cynthia's hands, then roughly pushed her away. Cynthia fell back against the workstation behind her. With wide eyes, she stared as the fire spread from the stove to the adjacent counter, heat and oily flames spewing upward, engulfing everything in its path.

Waving a small kitchen towel, Eli attempted to put out the advancing fire. Fanning the flames was more like it.

Then every boring safety class he'd ever sat through deserted his slow-moving brain. He picked up a pitcher of water and tossed it on the fire. Flames flashed and spread around them as if he'd doused them with gasoline. The blaze shot to the ceiling.

Finn rushed across the room and pulled the fire suppression handle. A blaring alarm sounded at the same time as cool chemical-smelling foam rained down on their heads.

Chef Shane hollered for everyone to get out. They couldn't leave fast enough, scrambling over each other to pile through the door. Eli trailed the last of them.

Cynthia stood before the stove as if in a hypnotic trance, admiring her work. Finn dragged her toward the door. She seemed to realize what she'd done and ran screaming from the room.

Finn shivered, soaked and desperate not to inhale the toxic fumes. She took a last look around the smoke-filled room. She didn't want to leave until she was certain everyone was out.

Chef Shane took her arm and escorted her from the room, out into the hall, and down the stairs. They passed several firemen, bulky in their fire gear and hauling hoses, coming up.

"Oil fire," Chef Shane yelled as they passed.

The class, as well as Chef Shane and Finn, dashed through the front door and out the building. Finn leaned against it and took several deep, clear, oxygen-filled breaths, ignoring her wet clothes and the smell of chemicals clinging to her every pore.

Chef Shane stood beside her, bent over, hands on knees pulling in deep draughts of fresh air himself.

Finn asked. "Are you okay?"

He straightened, his face pale. "I should be asking the same thing of you. You might not know it but you saved lives today by pulling that fire alarm."

"I was way late in stopping Cynthia. She seemed hell-bent on burning down the place."

He shrugged. "Unfortunately, I didn't see her. You were the one I saw in front of the building fire. So did another student, Jim Harwell. He told me you started the fire."

At her astonished look, he nodded.

"You pulled the fire alarm. And you were the one

standing in front of the fire before that."

Finn goggled at him. "Trying to put it out. Eli saw it."

"Perhaps you were only trying to help, but we have rules. Rather strict rules. Not burning down the school is at the top of the list."

"But I didn't." She rubbed the back of her neck.

"There will be a hearing later on that you'll be required to attend where you can defend your actions."

"A tribunal of all the chef instructors?" Finn asked, already knowing she had one black checkmark against her with Chef Westrom.

"Yes, and the Director of Education." He patted the soaked shoulder of her chef coat, then winced and wiped the flat of his hand against his thigh. "Even with a good word from me and Eli's testimony, I think you'll be reprimanded."

"I was afraid of that." She dropped her head and closed her eyes.

"I'll do my best to make you the victim here, even the hero, but you'll probably be suspended regardless. You can always re-apply next semester. If it's any consolation, Cynthia and Eli will be suspended as well."

Little consolation for doing the right thing and ending up with nothing. She felt her dreams going up in smoke right along with the building. "Thank you."

"You've been an outstanding student, Finn. Someday you'll look back on this day and laugh."

At her doubtful expression, he smiled. "You will. And some day after that you'll be a chef, a wonderfully brilliant chef."

"Thank you." This time she meant it but it seemed a long way off.

Finn talked to the school administrators, the fire

marshal, the police, the EMTs and every other possible person who had an interest. After all that, there was only one place left to go.

The place where every red-blooded woman went when she needed a lift. No, not the mall. That was for teenagers. No, not a bar, although a stiff drink didn't sound half-bad. No, she went to her hairdresser. M.F.'s Hair to Dye For.

Gert was the one who had put Finn onto Mary Frances O'Shea. Since then, they'd been great friends. M.F. was the only person able to tame Finn's flyaway red curls. She also knew all the gossip and dirt on everybody in town. She knew what the local radio personalities and journalists were up to, as well as the mayor, the governor and both senators.

You could count on M.F. to keep on talking and not ask any questions. Finn often wondered how she coaxed information out of everyone but she managed. The whole of New Orleans loved her for it.

Finn had no idea how old the woman was. She and Gert shared plastic surgeons. She always looked great. No wrinkles, no sagging chin-line, obviously no gray hair among the black. She wore the latest styles, even if they were a little young for her, and she never commented on Finn's less than sartorial attire.

Although she'd scuttled the white jacket and hat after her fire fiasco, underneath she still wore her pink tour tee and denim shorts. They looked lovely with her chef clogs, which she'd forgotten to change out of. Oh, well. She still needed a haircut and, more importantly, a shampoo.

She parked in the lot behind the shop located on Decatur between a Chinese restaurant and a head shop.

M.F. took one look at Finn when she walked in the door and gasped, her scissor-holding hand stalled in mid-air. "What the holy hell happened to you?"

"I helped start a fire, and then put it out. Long story."

"My Lord above. You smell like...what do you smell like? Are you okay?"

"I will be once I get this hair washed."

A lady sitting in a chair by the window reading a magazine took one appalled look at Finn. "I'm next, hon, but you need M.F.'s tender loving care more than I do. I'll peruse the latest *People*. And see what Brad and Angelina are up to."

"Thank you," Finn said, taking the spot next to her. When she saw her wrinkle her nose she moved to the far end seat.

"I'm almost finished here, Finn."

Finn leaned back and closed her eyes. The next thing she knew M.F. sat beside her shaking her shoulder. Finn opened her eyes. M.F. stared at her with compassion in her sparkling hazel eyes. "I'm ready for you now."

Finn blinked the sleep from her eyes. The woman who offered her spot to Finn was looking at her over the edge of the magazine and quite obviously not reading. Otherwise, they were alone.

Finn got to her feet and followed M.F. to the back of the room where a row of sinks lined the salmon-colored wall. "How long was I out?"

"Only about twenty minutes." She pushed Finn into a chair and turned on the water. "You looked exhausted."

Finn leaned her head back. "It has been one hell of a few days."

"Are you in trouble?"

"Probably."

"With the law?"

"I don't know. Maybe. I expect you'll see it on the news."

"Oh, hon, you close your eyes, lay your head back and I'll get this awful guck out of your hair. Then we'll see if we can tame those beautiful strawberry locks of yours while you tell me everything."

"Concentrate on the guck, M.F. The curls are hopeless."

"Not in my hands, they're not. I'm the best. I work miracles every day."

"You can try."

Finn left an hour later looking better, certainly smelling better, but not feeling much better.

As she sat in M.F.'s chair, the dreadful truth set in. She was a twenty-five-year-old woman with a dead-end job, a half-dead car and a dead ghost for a friend. Of course, all ghosts were dead. She had no boyfriend and no prospects on the horizon. Furthermore, if she couldn't get back to school for six months her dreams lay shattered and broken at her feet. She'd have to move to Mississippi or Alabama to find a school to take her if this one didn't accept her back.

Jack was nothing if not persistent. He was going to find Simon La Fontaine's brother, Peter, if it killed him. The man had been at work at his job at the French Market selling fruits and veggies on the day before his brother died and at the time, he seemed fine to his fellow employees. His boss said he was reliable, likeable, if a bit odd and superstitious. He never missed a day of work.

He hadn't shown up at the market the next day nor had he called on the day his brother disappeared. Nor any day since.

He interviewed all the employees, then Jack widened his search to the cheap motels in the Faubourg-Marigny neighborhood, in particular the Bywater section, a stone's throw down river from the French Quarter and his workplace. The area was a haven to musicians and artists and a place where a person could easily disappear.

Armed with his badge and a photograph of Peter La Fontaine, it took Jack only four stops at four motels to locate him.

The motel was a grungy two-story nineteenth century brick building with what looked like castle turrets on the roof. Long gone was any semblance of ambience. He suspected it now rented on an hourly basis if one so chose. La Fontaine was in a back room on the second story. The room looked out over a dark alley and was plenty private.

Jack chatted up the young, red-faced, stammering boy-manager, and learned La Fontaine only left his room to pick up fast food. He refused to let anyone in to clean up. He had allowed another woman in, who in the boy's own words, "dressed like a maid but was no way scrubbing out the toilet or changing the sheets".

Jack agreed. A "maid" who knocked on his door was more likely a stupid euphemism for a local prostitute. Jack didn't care one way or the other, as long as he could talk to the man. The manager went on to tell him he figured Peter was a fugitive from the law. He wasn't surprised when Jack showed up. When Jack asked him why he hadn't called earlier, he merely shrugged.

Jack crossed the threadbare carpet in the dingy, moldy-smelling lobby and took the steps two at a time to the second story. He strode down the musty, dark hall and before knocking on the chipped, vermilion-painted door to Number Eleven, he unsnapped his shoulder holster and palmed his weapon. He pulled back his jacket to leave his right arm free. He knocked and stepped aside. "Peter La Fontaine? NOPD. I'd like to talk to you."

From inside the room came the muffled reply, "I ain't done nothin'."

"You're not in trouble, sir. I'd like a word."

"Got nothin' to say."

"Wouldn't you like to take care of your brother's remains? I know you know he's dead."

"Cursed, he was."

Huh? Jack scratched his head. "Open up, Pete. Let's talk."

"It's Peter."

"Peter, then. I'd like a word."

Surprisingly, the door opened. Jack shifted back another step to study the man. He held up his hands to show Jack he was unarmed. He looked terrible—bleak sunken eyes, unshaven, faded green t-shirt stained with food, gray sweat pants torn and droopy.

"I loved him, my brother," he muttered, choking back tears. "He deserved better than some crazy woman cursing him like dat."

"You're right. Can I come in?"

He gestured for Jack to enter and stepped aside. The thin brown drapes were drawn. The room was as dark as the inside of a cave and as cool. The temperature couldn't have been much above fifty-five. Why so cold? He should have brought Cordry along. He knew how to deal with crazy.

"Peter. Can I call you Peter?"

The man shuffled back inside, pulling the door shut and locking them both inside.

Jack jerked the drapes open, exposing the dusty, shabby room to the bright light of day.

"Hey, whatcha doin'? I like de dark."

And *de cold*, Jack thought about adding but refrained from doing so. "The dark makes me nervous. You understand how it is."

"Yeah, but she could see me, dat devil woman."

"What woman would that be?" Jack pulled out a chair from the perfunctory desk piled high with fast food wrappers and soda containers, the straws jutting out the tops like a line of toy soldiers, and sat down.

Peter rested on the side of the bed, his large hands dangling between his knees, his head bowed. Dressed as he was, he looked more like a deranged homeless person than a conscientious employee and loving brother. Jack had checked out the apartment they shared. The brothers lived a Spartan existence but the place was neat and clean. The forty-two inch television and comfortable couch spoke of people who spent a lot of time there.

"Dat woman," he said, his chin trembling. "Dat woman what kilt Simon."

"I'm sorry for your loss, Peter, but he wasn't killed by any woman."

He lifted his head. "What you say?"

"I'm saying a strong man probably killed Simon. One who could lift him. Do you know if Simon was trying his blackmail schemes again?"

He rolled his head back and forth on his neck, then closed his eyes. When he opened them, he stared at Jack with an aggrieved expression. "Damn him. Ah tole him when he gets back from Angola, 'You stay on de straight and narrow. Don't you be blackmailing no body.' Hear me?"

"And did he?"

He shook his head in an exaggerated manner. He leaned forward, his elbows on his knees. "I don't know. I s'pose not. What 'bout dat voodoo women den?"

Jack shrugged his shoulders. "I don't know who you're talking about."

"You know." He stood up and paced a few feet away, then gave Jack the once-over. "Dat redhead woman, the voodoo priestess." He made the sign of the cross and paced back to sit on the rumpled bed again.

Finn? Did he think Finn was a voodoo priestess? It

was laughable. Finn looked like the girl next door. Finn *was* the girl next door.

"She put de bad juju on Simon. I saw her with mine own eyes."

"Was she conscious at the time?" Jack was doing everything in his control not to laugh in the man's face.

"She was in some kind of spell. Her dominant hand was pointed right at Simon like de conjurer she be." He demonstrated by pointing his index finger at Jack. "I tell you, she was fixing de tricks on him."

Jack swallowed his laughter. When he interviewed him, Peter's boss told him the man was superstitious. Jack figured he avoided black cats and kept a rabbit's foot in his pocket. He hadn't counted on this full-on Hoodoo stuff.

Peter stared a moment at Jack, then squinted at him. "You in it, too?"

"No. No. I avoid those people." Except the few times he'd been with Marie. She hadn't put a spell on him unless he counted the times she kept him in bed long after he should have been gone.

"She not only kilt Simon, she put de hex on me."

"How's that?" Jack waited expectantly, hating to hear the ridiculous answer.

"I gone de im-po-tent."

"Huh? Important?"

"I can't get it up no mo'."

Jack choked. "That is a problem."

"You know dey put de saltpeter in decoctions."

"I hate to burst your bubble but if you can't get it up it's your own problem. The redhead is a tour guide in the Quarter. She's harmless."

Peter shook his head. "But in her satchel, I saw. She carries de bag of tricks."

"She carries a backpack full of a lot of nutty things, but a voodoo priestess she's not." At his look of full-on horror, Jack continued, "I promise you. We think we know who killed your brother. No magic involved. It was a twenty-two to the back of the head that did him in."

He still looked doubtful. He sat on the edge of the bed, and stared at Jack. "No question?"

"None, whatsoever. As to your other little problem, I'd say that's probably stress induced. Now what can you tell me about your brother on the day he died?"

The poor man calmed down long enough to relay everything he knew, which wasn't much. When they finished, he asked, "Can I go home now. Go back to work?"

"We don't have anyone in custody yet but it's only a matter of time. You're safe."

The man gave him a heartfelt hug. It took everything he had not to pull away.

CHAPTER FOURTEEN

"Is it true voodoo is still practiced in New Orleans?"

Finn smiled at the eager young man asking the question. In spite of feeling as low as possible after getting suspended from school, here, at least, was someone who could make her smile. Maybe life wasn't awful.

She wrapped up her afternoon walking tour. She was on her way to her uncles' voodoo shop before letting the tourists go their separate ways. They'd been walking along the street admiring the building beside them when this guy advanced on Finn with a decidedly playful gleam in his eye.

Voodoo? It was hardly an original question. She'd heard it too many times to count. Her own inner devil, though, prompted her to give a different answer each time.

She leaned in as if giving him, and only him, an intimate reply. "We-ell, I don't practice it myself but—"

"You know people who do?" he finished for her. He seemed a bit older than the usual pimply teenager or annoying young adult who usually asked this type of question. And, for some reason, it was generally a girl.

"My two uncles own a voodoo shop," Finn said. "That's where we're headed now. You'll have to ask

them. I'm sure they have lots of colorful stories." She
had one of her own but so far she hadn't seen any effect
from her personal voodoo doll—no unexplained pains
anywhere on her body, no sore throat caused by a rope
around the neck. If he'd asked, she would have said she
didn't believe in such things, but the folklore was good
fodder for the tourists. Believe it or don't; to each his
own.

She herded the small group of six around the corner.
They stopped beneath an overhang long enough to
listen to a solo saxophonist playing for a few tourists.
Since Finn had extra time, she listened with one ear as
well, the upbeat music escalating with the increased
crowd noise. It was a typical day, warm, sultry, the
earthy scent of the river wafting into the Quarter.

When a mule-drawn carriage stopped to wait for a
car to pass and caught her attention, she studied the
driver. A dim memory floated to the front of her
mind—Finn taking pictures with her digital camera of a
couple kissing while sitting in just such a carriage.
Franco and Barron. The beginning of her many
problems.

As she watched, her mind drifting, the driver turned
around to say something to the couple. He gestured to
the restaurant to their right. Finn couldn't hear what he
was saying but knew that his chatter wasn't much
different from her own. A thought nagged at her,
something about the driver. The way he moved or sat,
something she couldn't put her finger on.

When he turned around to drive on, a snippet of the
couple's conversation penetrated the noise around her.

"We need to find an ATM," the male passenger said.
"I'm about out of cash."

Finn saw the woman's lips move but the sharp clip-
clop of the horse's hooves and the pedestrian and street
noise drowned her out.

"Oh. My. God." Pieces of the past week fell into place like the tumblers in a combination lock. Finn clutched her chest.

She hadn't realized she'd spoken aloud until several of her tourists turned to look at her with a question in their eyes.

Finn paused to take a breath and collect herself. In a slow, measured voice, she said, "It's time to move on, folks."

This was it! This was the recollection that had nagged at her. Why she'd thought she'd seen the man at the morgue before but couldn't place him. She *had* seen him before. He was the carriage driver in the pictures she'd taken of Franco and his ladylove.

He hadn't been the focus of the photos so his face had quickly deserted her brain but she knew that he was in a few of those shots. All she'd been concerned with at the time had been capturing the images of Franco and his girlfriend for the paying customer, Clarissa Franco.

How had the driver ended up dead? Why? She couldn't put all the pieces together. Her mind whirled with myriad possibilities.

Jack would know.

They arrived at her uncles' shop with Finn clueless how they got there. Attempting to compose herself as her group crowded inside, she stopped to greet her uncles with hugs and kisses, something she did twice a day. They always acted like they hadn't seen her in months. The act tickled her because they loved it as much as she did. For the benefit of the tourists, Finis asked after the family when they both were perfectly aware of everything going on with Dorie and Dan, and, of course, Debbie. It was all Finn could do to keep from rolling her eyes.

Finn knew, as they spoke together, Debbie was even now in the backroom of their store learning how to string beads for a bracelet or how to put a curse on someone or some other crazy thing they'd concocted for her. God only knew. Finn didn't want to know.

She shifted from one foot to the other impatiently waiting for her tourists to buy their key chains, shot glasses and Mardi Gras beads so she could talk to Jack.

When they met together outside the shop several minutes later, she hurriedly herded them along to their original meeting place. She accepted their thanks and their tips and wished them well, all the while her brain whirled with questions.

Even though she stood next to the police precinct, she called Jack rather than go inside to see him and put up with that particular indignity again.

"Jack?" she said after tapping in his cell phone number.

"Finn?"

"The one and only. Have I got news for you."

"Oh, yeah? Me, too."

"You first," Finn suggested.

"I know where your voodoo doll came from and the guy who had it made seems pretty harmless. Nutty as a fruitcake but harmless."

"Was it your old girlfriend, Marie, who made the doll?"

"Yep. She was pretty helpful."

Finn knew Marie. In fact, most everyone who spent any time in the Quarter knew Marie. She was the kind of woman, who, if a man and a woman walked into her store, the woman became invisible and the man became the undivided focus of her salacious attention. "I'm sure she was *very* helpful, but why did he do it?"

Jack laughed. He knew how Finn felt about Marie. He knew how all women felt about Marie.

"First things first. What d'you know?"

"I remembered where I saw that guy in the morgue

before."

"So you know his name?"

"I don't, but I know he was a carriage driver."

"How does he connect to Franco?"

"You know how Franco wants those pictures so bad, the ones I took of him and the Barron woman?"

"Uh-huh."

"I thought he was worried about her pictures being circulated to the cops or feds or whoever, but there's someone else in those shots."

He snorted. "You got pictures of a threesome or something? I need to get Tommy to show me those pictures."

"Will you get your head out of your pants? There's no threesome. Before they found that quiet spot to make out, they took a carriage ride and I took photos of that, too."

"You mean to tell me," Jack said, the tone of his voice indicating a trace of humor, "that you can put the carriage driver and Franco together?"

"Not only is that what I'm saying but Tommy has the pictures to prove it."

"This keeps getting better and better."

"Only you would think that. A man is dead here."

"I know, but look at it this way. The guy had one conviction already for attempted blackmail and now, not only was he seen with a woman with a boatload of embezzled cash who's wanted by the FBI, but with a former felon known for his wicked bad temper."

"The plot thickens."

"Yes indeed."

The gears clicked in Finn's brain. "So it's not much of a stretch to put him, your guy, whatever his name is, eavesdropping on Franco and Barron while they're obliviously discussing her millions and trying to cash in on it, forgive my pun. Maybe said driver tries to extort money from Franco or his girlfriend, and then Franco objects to paying him anything and he kills the man. Seeing as how he's known for his temper. I could totally see that happening."

"I'll make a detective out of you yet, Nancy Drew."

"Thanks."

"Now all we need is proof."

"The pictures aren't enough?"

"That only proves they were together. The forensics guys are doing their thing. We have to hope that Franco left his DNA somewhere on the body. It's been in the river and isn't in the best condition. Maybe on his clothes."

Disappointed, Finn asked, "There's nothing else you can do?"

"Oh no, *chere*. The greatest detective in New Orleans is on the case. I've got other irons in the fire."

"So what do I do in the meantime?"

"Stay safe. This is big. I mean it. I'll get those pictures from Tommy. They might shed some light on the case. No pun intended. We know Franco's dangerous. With the photos, I might be able to get a warrant for his arrest for murder and not just for associating with the Barron woman. It's thin but I happen to know a judge."

"Knowing is everything in this city. Is she gorgeous?" Finn read the Times Picayune every morning over her bowl of Cheerios. She knew how these things worked.

"You got that right, Miss Jones. Knowing is everything. And she does happen to be gorgeous. This helps. It's like a jigsaw puzzle and what you've told me puts a few more pieces in place."

"Glad I could help. Glad I remembered."

"Keep your head down. This will all be over soon. Take good care and I'll talk to you as soon as I know something. I'll see you at Gert's tomorrow."

"Bye, Jack."

"Bye, *chere*."

Wow. For a few hours she'd managed to forget how lousy she felt about the culinary school "incident" and the sidetracking of her career. Amazing how a little distance and someone else's problems put her own in perspective. She was alive, single and healthy. Life could be a whole lot worse.

The next afternoon, Finn stood still long enough to admire Gert's garden. It was beyond beautiful. Magnificent described it, with lush jungle-like vegetation and an all-encompassing quiet found only in the Garden District. Giant banana trees and elephant ear plants vied for attention with spiky dracaena and spider plants in potted terracotta containers. Colorful flowers abounded galore. The glorious magnolia tree shaded a three-tiered gurgling fountain. Gert added a contemporary lap pool along the high-backed brick border wall when she married health-conscious husband number three.

A seasoned brick walkway wound through the yard, front to back and side to side, but even it looked a bit bedraggled, overgrown and weed-strewn. However, the scene improved once Jack walked through the gate and graced it with his confident, masculine presence.

He came prepared to work wearing khaki utility shorts, work boots and a short-sleeved white t-shirt, which showed off his lean, muscled arms and broad chest. Finn couldn't quite take her eyes off those damnable boots. She'd once seen a picture in a *Playgirl* magazine of a guy dressed in work boots...nothing but work boots, a hardhat and an impressive erection. Oooh. Boy. Finn dragged her thoughts away. She had a real live man in front of her. No need for erotic images. Of course, this one was fully dressed.

Jack brought his own pair of gardening gloves and wore his ever-present sunglasses. Bent over, staring at something in the fountain, was perhaps his best side, but certainly not his worst, and it took Finn's mind off naked men in nothing but work boots.

Finn stared. She really, really hated to leave him alone with the weeds but if she was going to prepare a dinner of biscuits, her own version of *cochon de lait*— the essential Louisiana-style pulled pork, and her homemade barbecue sauce made with peppers, cane syrup, vinegar and her newly discovered secret spice ingredient, crushed tamarind, she had to hop to it. She already had the pork in the oven where it had been simmering for hours. It smelled like heaven on a platter, the scent drifting in the air.

He turned, caught her staring and grinned. "Smells great."

"Thanks. I could help," she offered, gesturing to the yard.

"Nah. Get inside and put your apron on." He swatted her backside with the gloves. "I think I know the difference between a weed and a plant."

She hoped so.

Thirty minutes later Jack came in the house, sweaty, dirty and grinning. He marched to the sink, turned on the cold-water tap and stuck his head beneath. Finn idly wondered what had happened to the gardening gloves. When he came up sputtering and swiping water from his face, he said, "Nothing like manual labor to make you appreciate your day job."

She handed him a dishtowel. He wiped off his face and started for the door, dropping it on the counter. "Had to take a break and tell you my stomach's rumbling from the terrific smells coming from in here. Almost done. See you in a few."

One hour later, Finn stepped outside. She shaded her

eyes with one hand as she took in the yard. "Wow. It looks great."

Jack wiped his brow with the back of his hand, then pointed out the places he'd worked. As he moved around the yard, he said, "I couldn't wear those damned gloves. They made my hands sweat."

"Some weeds can make your hands itch," she warned. "You can even get a rash or blisters."

"Is that the voice of experience?"

Finn nodded.

"I'll be okay. I've never had any problems before."

Famous last words. Within thirty minutes, she looked out the window and he was scratching his face and arms. Surreptitiously he scratched an even more personal area. Finn tried not to stare as she remembered he'd come in and used the bathroom. She fought a grin. She located an antihistamine and the calamine lotion in the bathroom medicine cabinet.

She gave the sauce one last stir, humming a song to herself, before she rescued Jack. When she heard an odd scraping noise and voices coming from the yard, she peeked out the window over the kitchen sink. She gasped.

Jack stood with his back to her, a rake raised threateningly in his hands, wildly gesturing and yelling obscenities loud enough to be heard on the street out front.

She couldn't see who he was yelling at but the angry tone didn't sound like Jack. She couldn't ever recall hearing him raise his voice. Easy-going Jack seldom got mad. Except with Tommy. And her. This Jack, however, was extremely, crazily, mad-scientist psycho.

Finn forgot all about the itch medicine and rushed out the kitchen door into the yard still holding the spoon she'd been using. The sun blinded her. She shielded her eyes and stepped from the sun into the shade of a tree.

Again, she heard Jack swear loudly.

"Jack?"

He swiveled, brandishing the rake like the deadly weapon he'd made it, his eyes wild, his face stark with an emotion Finn couldn't quite read. "Go inside, Finn, lock the door and call 9-1-1."

She couldn't move. Johnny Franco held a gun on Jack. A huge, black gun that looked big enough to blow both of them to Kingdom Come.

He pointed it at her, a sneer on his smug face. "No, stay, sweet-cheeks, and watch me shoot your boyfriend."

"He's not my boyfriend." Okay, that was a stupid thing to say. It was the first thing that came to her rattled mind, but stupid all the same. Common sense returned when she opened her mouth to speak. Okay, not common sense. Common sense dictated that she turn her butt around and go back in the house. But she couldn't abandon Jack. "Why shoot him? He hasn't done anything to you."

Franco glared at Finn, his piercing eyes dark as Hell on a moonless night. "He's keeping me from you. And it's you I want to shoot, bitch." He swiveled the gun toward her. Finn stood rooted in place, incapable of movement, unable to look anywhere else. "I killed one man because of you. I can do it again. I ain't afraid to shoot no woman."

Franco focused on her, his furious, black eyes narrowed, his jaw tense. Jack shifted a fraction to his left. He positioned the rake on his shoulder, and swung it like a baseball bat. It crashed against Franco's gun hand. Franco howled like an alley cat and dropped the weapon.

Jack kicked it beneath a flowering basket of impatiens. It disappeared from view. He raised the rake to hit Franco again but Franco grabbed the handle with his uninjured hand. They wrestled over control, trampling the newly de-weeded flowerbeds.

They tripped over each other's feet and fell into a patch of weeds. Neither man held the rake. Finn rushed forward and grabbed it. She followed the men at a safe distance searching for her chance to do something, anything to help, as they wrangled in the dirt like a couple of pissed-off kids, cussing, fists flying, kicking, scratching, anything to maim each other.

Finn edged closer to Franco and Jack. She zigged and zagged. They zigged and zagged. She avoided flying fists and spinning legs and got behind Franco.

When they moved to within inches of the lap pool, Finn held her breath. Franco took a step back, and Jack took a step back, then dropped his head and bulled forward, his arms outstretched, hollering at Finn to get out of the way. The two men fell into the pool with a loud splash, kicking up twin fountains of cold water. Both men sank to the bottom.

Franco hit the bottom first, then bounced up through the water. When he attempted to climb out, Finn seized the opportunity. She didn't hesitate. She took the flat end of the rake and hit him as hard as she could over the head. He fell back into the pool as if in slow motion, drifting toward the bottom again. She winced when she saw Jack. He surfaced, sputtering and spewing water, bedraggled and irritated. He gave Franco a disgusted look, then swam down to retrieve the unconscious man.

When he got him to the surface, she helped haul the deadweight from the water. They left him on the deck, alive and breathing.

Jack climbed out and lay on his back wheezing, his sunglasses missing, his clothing soaked and clinging to his body, his hair dark with dripping water. His no-longer-white shirt had one shoulder ripped off and the scrap of fabric clung to his wrist. He gave Finn a slight grin. "Nice job, *chere*, 'though I really would've liked to take my new boots off before I went for a swim."

"I'll try to warn you the next time."

He shook his head. "See if you can get my cell out of my pocket and call the cops. If it still works. I don't think I can move. That jackass weighs a ton and hits like Evander Holyfield."

"Your phone won't work now. You just want me to put my hand in your pocket."

"True on the second count, but I have a waterproof cover. Should be fine."

She kneeled beside him and pointed. "This pocket?"

When he nodded, she yanked the phone from his tight, wet pants and ignored his grin. "Are you okay?"

"No." He rolled to his side, then when Finn handed him the phone he slowly sat up and gave the 9-1-1 operator the pertinent information, then disconnected. "I hoped you killed the son-of-a-bitch. He fights mean."

Finn looked at the inert, waterlogged man. Blood dribbled from the back of his head. "Would I be in trouble if I killed him?"

"Not as far as I'm concerned."

"What should we do with him?"

Jack glared at Franco's prone body. "As long as he stays put, we're fine. You were impressive, *chere*. You could give any action star a run for his money. Watch out, Jason Statham."

"Or Bruce Willis. Or Arnold Schwarzenegger. Or Steven Sagal. I don't know Jason Statham. Is he famous?"

He laughed out loud. "Don't get to the movies much, do ya?"

"Who's got the time?" she complained as she worriedly contemplated Franco. "I can't believe we're having this conversation with him right there, out cold. He tried to kill you."

"And you."

"What's wrong with him anyway? He said he killed someone else. Who? And, geez, it's a bunch of photos. What difference does it make to him whether I see them or the whole damned world does?"

"He's a psycho."

"Is that the technical police term?" She couldn't believe any of this. It was like an episode of *CSI*. She couldn't help returning his infectious grin.

"Yep. Did you see where that gun got to?"

Finn walked over to the potted red impatiens she saw it slide beneath earlier. When she spotted the dark metal of the gun's grip peeking out from an over-hanging bloom, she pointed. "There. It's right there."

Jack struggled to his feet, limped over to where she stood, his boots squishing, water droplets following him like a trail of breadcrumbs. He reached into his back pocket for the gardening gloves he'd stuck there earlier and picked up the gun with one of them. "Some days I hate these guys."

"What guys?"

"The bad guys."

Sirens wailed in the distance. Finn gave Jack a grim smile. "The cavalry is arriving."

"About time." He absent-mindedly scratched at his forearm.

"Do we need an ambulance for Franco?"

"Not that I care, but I'll let the EMTs make that call."

"You're a cop," she reminded him.

"Not today. Today I'm a gardener." He took in the trampled yard and scratched his arm again. "And not a very good one."

Finn eyed the damage. "The flowers'll bounce back. You didn't break too many stems. Without all the weeds, it still looks better than it did." He'd stacked a pile of pulled weeds in one corner of the yard. "Of course now I'll have to call the pool guy. There seems to be an awful lot of dirt in it."

"Very funny. Be careful or I'll sic the cops on you, too." He swung his gaze around as several police pushed open the garden gate and stepped into the yard, guns drawn, gazes wary. Jack pulled his badge from his shorts pocket and held it high. "At ease, boys. I'm on your side. The jerk is out cold thanks to Finn here, my fearless savior."

As they gave their statements to the police officer, the other one cuffed Franco moments after he came to. He growled at the officer and glared at Finn. "It ain't over, bitch."

"Shut up." Jack gestured with one hand in a shooing fashion. "Get that ass out of here."

"What now?" Finn asked.

The cops were gone.

Franco was gone.

Jack sat down at an outdoor table and removed his wet socks, boots and ripped tee. Maybe it was the adrenaline but he looked even more delicious than usual with his broad bronzed shoulders and washboard abs.

He leaned back and closed his eyes, allowing himself to relax and dry out in the sun. He opened one eye and looked up at Finn. "Let's eat. Gert got any beer in there?"

"I'm sure she does."

"You want me to come inside and drip all over or should I stay out here?"

"Stay. I'll serve. You deserve a little pampering."

"Got that right." He leaned back, stretched out his legs and crossed his ankles in front of him. "Detective Boyle saves the day again."

Finn brought the food out on a large tray. They ate together, laughing over Franco's antics even knowing they could've been killed. The dunk into the water must have cooled off Jack's itching because Finn forgot all about the anti-itch medicines she had been going to give him.

He regaled her with the story of Peter La Fontaine and how he thought she'd put a spell on him that cost him his ability to get it up. He thought it was hilarious. She refused to take the blame for scaring the poor man into erectile dysfunction.

She sent Jack off an hour later with leftovers then cleaned up. She hadn't told him about being suspended from school even though it weighed heavily on her mind. He didn't know she'd even been in school so what was the point? Still, she didn't want to lie to Jack even by omission. What did that mean about their strange relationship?

CHAPTER FIFTEEN

Somehow, the school's administrative offices weren't damaged in the fire. The rooms on several floors smelled of smoke but the insurance company's ionizer equipment was working overtime to clear the air. The kitchen classroom where the fire occurred was the only room with major damage. Several other rooms had water damage. Finn and her two cohorts had effectively put school on hold for everyone.

She sat in the reception area cooling her heels, waiting to have her feet, so to speak, held to the fire. Called on the carpet. Berated. Admonished. Rebuked. Or all of the above. Whatever happened there would be no kissing and making up.

From her intense study of the intricate blue and gray woven carpet at her feet, she saw a shadow pass in front of her. Chef John Michael sat down next to her wearing his usual white double-breasted chef coat and white toque. Finn straightened and leaned away as she stared through him at the wall at their backs.

"You set my home on fire."

Finn cleared her throat. Thank God, they were alone. She was in enough trouble without being seen talking to herself. "It was an accident."

"This never happened on my watch before."

"Of course not," Finn snapped. "Mister Perfect here

who trained Emeril to be the millionaire he is today. You think teaching cooking to the masses on TV is *my* idea of a chef?"

She startled him into a brief chuckle. "I didn't perceive it. *Non.* You think there is something wrong with TV?"

"Have you ever actually watched him in action?"

"Non."

"Then save your advice. I just meant I want to cook in a real restaurant, one meal at a time."

"I was merely going to say that you've mucked up any chance you have of becoming a TV chef or anything else for that matter. You're going to be suspended, even if it wasn't strictly your fault."

"I'll be back."

"Of course you will, Arnold." He rolled his eyes, then folded his arms across his chest looking decidedly haughty. "In the meantime I have to put up with the stench of this place. *L'horreur.* I could have been hurt, you know."

"You're dead."

"You're an expert?"

Finn studied his arrogant face. He seemed more irascible than usual. Maybe it was the fire. "What's wrong? Really."

"Nothing." He sighed, staring heavenward.

"You're not French at all, are you? It's all a front."

"Of course I am," he replied, the snotty factor in place.

"It doesn't matter to me. You're a ghost. Who cares if you're English, French or an Indian maharishi?"

"I care. I'm a Cordon Bleu-trained chef who—"

"Is dead."

"—who had the most excellent training ever. What does it matter if I'm actually French or not?"

"Exactly. It doesn't matter to me at all," Finn said.

"And you can stop putting on airs. I'm less than impressed." She actually was impressed that he'd attended the Cordon Bleu School but she wasn't about to tell him so.

"This from the young lady who set her own school on fire."

"It was an accident," Finn reiterated, sick to death of the entire conversation. "Do you think we could put this love fest on hold for a few days? I'm sorry it happened. Let's leave it at that."

"Fine," he said.

"Fine," she said.

They sat in mutual silence a few minutes. Finn watched the dust motes in the air. When she turned to look at him or rather through him, she caught him smiling. "What now?"

"I am not happy. Okay, not really, but you wrecked my home."

She raised her brows.

"Such as it is. Still it's my home, cooking school or not. It's mine and has been for years."

"And now it's waterlogged, smells like a bar after hours and is a little charred around the edges."

"Exactly."

"Get over it, Chef Boy-Ar-Dee."

"Oh." He grabbed his chest. "*L'insulte*. I'm devastated."

"I don't remember you having a sense of humor."

"That was before I saw you in action in the classroom with the incomparable Miss Cynthia." He threw his arms wide and sang out, "Mental."

"Got that right. I can't believe no one else caught on to her act before now."

"It takes a village."

She rolled her eyes. "Oh, shut up. It takes a witch doctor."

"I hear footsteps. The instructors are coming to take a bite out of your posterior. Take care not to burn any other buildings down while you're away."

"Does that mean you think I'll be back?" she whispered.

"Of course. It's your destination."

"Wow," Finn said to herself. Her chef ghost disappeared. Chef Shane stood in his place dressed in his whites.

"Wow?" he questioned.

"Nothing," Finn said as her cheeks heated. "I was thinking aloud."

"Okay, then, we're ready to see you. Are you ready to see us?"

"As ready as I will ever be."

"Good luck."

"Thanks."

Beneath the pale yellow halogen light from the pole overhead Finn sat in her car in the hospital parking lot after her visit with Jack. She groaned aloud. She beat her head against the wheel once. Then twice for good measure. It didn't make her feel any better but what the hell. It didn't make her feel any worse either.

If this hadn't been the week from hell, she didn't know what was.

She couldn't believe she'd incapacitated Tommy. Twice. And now, Jack. She'd managed to put two grown men out of commission without even trying. Tommy could at least move but Jack looked worse and felt worse if his loud complaining meant anything. Who knew he'd be allergic to poison ivy and her special bbq sauce ingredient, tamarind? He was itching and vomiting equally.

If one didn't know better one might think she was out to get the Boyle brothers. Nothing could be further from the truth. She liked them. This is what she did to her friends--broke their legs, gave them black eyes, gave them food poisoning and allowed them to cover nearly every square inch of their skin with poison ivy. And these were the people she liked. Why couldn't she be this effective against the bad guys?

Furthermore, she'd put two streetcars out of commission and burned down a perfectly good building. Accidentally.

She had to face it. That voodoo doll must have cast a spell on her. She was bad luck. Next thing you knew, she'd get arrested for scaring little kids. Or sideswiping the mayor's limousine. Or setting back civilization by several hundred years. With the Boyle brothers out of commission, she was on her own. Well, the FBI might help if she called them. Then again, they might not. They might be afraid of her. Thank goodness all the crazies chasing her were either in custody or out of the country sunbathing on a Caribbean island.

She stiffened her spine, dug out her car keys and started the Bug.

To hell with Johnny Franco, Margaret Jane Barron and both La Fontaine brothers, one alive and impotent, and one dead. She could take care of her own damn self. She was going home to fix herself something fattening to eat before heading to bed and sleeping for a solid eight.

∞

"Margaritas?" Tommy stared into Finn's grocery bags as she stood at his door shortly before eight the next night.

Finn lifted her heavily laden grocery sack. "I didn't know what you had so I bought everything we'd need, including the gonzo extra-large bottle of tequila."

"Hot damn." He shuffled to the side to let Finn in. His crutches, she noted, were propped in the corner beginning to collect dust.

"The kitchen is all yours. I'd help but I'd get in the

way."

"Sit," Finn ordered, waving him to the couch. "If I can't handle a batch of Margaritas, I might as well throw away my apron. Oh, yeah, I already have."

"You said something on the phone about getting kicked out of school? What'd you do? Get caught in the storage room checking out the head chef's sausage?"

"Not exactly." She choked back tears. "I'm out, though. As soon as I've numbed myself, I'll tell you all the gruesome details."

"Gruesome, huh. You must be feeling awful if you can joke about it."

"It's either that or cry. I feel terrible. I've already cried a million tears and I still get all weepy whenever I think about it."

"Stop already," Tommy ordered. "I can't handle it. Get those Margaritas in the blender. I've got chips and salsa. We'll have, what do you ladies call it?"

"A pity party," she suggested.

"Damn straight. A pity party. You can tell me all about getting kicked out of school and I can tell you how hard it is to dress myself, to say nothing of taking a piss or tying my own damn shoes."

He sat on the couch with both legs propped on the coffee table. His feet were bare.

He caught her staring. "That's right, Jones, I'm not wearing anything on my feet. I'm lucky if I can step into flip-flops."

Finn found herself laughing for the first time since she'd stood outside the school building watching black smoke billow out a side window.

Exactly forty-eight hours ago.

Tommy plucked his cell phone off the table. Finn, measuring and pouring tequila into the blender, saw his face light up as she flipped it on. She couldn't hear him but managed to catch the last of his conversation once she'd turned off the blender.

"So Finn and I are getting drunk and maybe we'll have hot monkey sex later on." He winked at Finn before she could stop him from saying anything else. "Thanks, Gert. Don't give Debbie any naughty ideas." Whatever Gert said in reply made him laugh.

When Finn came into the room carrying two frosted glasses, a bowl of salsa and a bag of chips, Tommy explained, "You're good for the night. Gert's taking Debbie to the movies, out for pizza and then they're having a girls' sleepover at her house."

"God. I forgot all about Debbie. I'm a terrible mother."

"You had other things on your mind."

"I did but I shouldn't have forgotten her."

"True." He reached for his Margarita, then patted the seat beside him. He waited until Finn picked up her glass. Holding his aloft, he said, "Here's to better days."

Finn nudged her drink against his. "Hear, hear. Better days."

They each took a healthy swallow, not always a good idea with an ice cold drink. Brain freeze was a possibility.

"To having more sex," Tommy said, setting his glass down and reaching for a chip, then dipping it into the salsa.

"More money," Finn said.

"More paying customers," he said, chewing loudly.

"More tourists."

"More sex," he said again, grinning.

Finn laughed. Tommy always knew how to cheer her up.

Two hours later, two pitchers of Margaritas later and Tommy knew all the revolting details of her culinary school denouement. He knew she'd been suspended and had to do community service before she could even apply for admission again. And, she'd do whatever it took.

Finn dropped her head against the back of the couch to the sound of Tommy's soothing voice and fell asleep.

She woke to semi-darkness, the only illumination coming from the kitchen stove light. A light blanket covered her but Tommy was nowhere to be seen. She squinted at the stove's clock. Past midnight. She sat up and was immediately sorry. She eased back down. Her head pounded, her stomach revolted. Fully sober and completely wretched, she lay still a moment, waiting for her body to settle and her vision to clear.

A knock pounded at the door. Finn couldn't imagine who would be coming to see Tommy in the middle of the night. She prayed it wasn't one of his many female friends looking for benefits.

Tommy shuffled into the room dressed in only a pair of plaid flannel boxers, his chest and feet bare, his bed hair tousled and his eyes half open. He turned on the table lamp beside her. "Go back to sleep. I'll get it."

"Sleep? With this headache?"

"You shouldn't drink tequila. It'll give you a monster hangover."

"Now you tell me."

Tommy looked through the eyehole in the door. "Damn."

"Who is it?" Finn whispered. "Jack."

"He's out of the hospital?"

His mouth fell open. "He was in the hospital?"

"Oops. My bad. Forgot to tell you. I kind of put him there." She hiccupped. "Excuse me."

Tommy opened the door and Jack stepped inside. He was pale, his face and hands covered in calamine-covered scabs.

"Wow," Tommy muttered as he closed the door

behind Jack. "You look awful."

Jack stared at Finn where she lay on the couch, then at Tommy dressed in nothing but his boxers. He fixed his eyes on her. His mouth tightened. She knew how she looked. Crazy hair stuck up in several places, her cheeks pink from the drinking, her eyes at half-mast. She knew how she looked, all right. She giggled.

"What's going on here?"

"Nothing, bro." Tommy patted his shoulder. "Want a Margarita?"

"No."

"Sit down."

"No."

"D'you want anything?"

"No."

"Can you say anything but no?"

"Not without hollering."

Finn brought her hand up to her mouth to keep from bursting out laughing.

"What's so funny?" Jack stood over her with his hands on his hips.

"You," she managed to say. "You look like an escapee from the pink clown circus. Sorry."

Tommy threw back his head and exploded with laughter.

Jack's face darkened, if possible. It was a bit hard to see through the cracked seams of calamine lotion and over-all scabbing. He gave Finn another black look, then drew back his fist and punched Tommy in the stomach.

Tommy reeled back, then bent over and vomited all over Jack's feet. The stench of re-cycled Margaritas and hot bile permeated the room.

"What the hell?" Jack muttered, jerking away.

Tommy hobbled to the bathroom. For a man with a broken leg, he surprised Finn with his speedy, though clumsy exit.

She jumped to her feet and was immediately sorry. Her head spun, her stomach threatened to follow Tommy's and spill onto the floor. "What're you doing?"

"What're *you* doing?" Jack barked. "How long have you and Tommy been getting it on?"

"We're not. We haven't. We, we don't, what are you saying?"

"You mean to tell me you're not." He waved his hand around the darkened room, the blanket wrapped around her bare feet. "Look at you. Your hair's a mess, your eyes are all soft and gooey, your clothes half on. What else would I think?"

"I don't really care what you think." In a feeble attempt to tone down her strident tone and calm her headache, she lowered her voice. "I'm a grown woman and if I want to have wild, hot sex with Tommy, I will."

"Are you?"

"Am I what?" she asked, becoming peeved with Jack's holier-than-thou attitude.

"Having wild, hot sex with Tommy?"

"That's none of your business." Sorry for the intrusion into her throbbing head, she placed her cool palms against her forehead. "Where are my shoes?"

"Who cares?"

"You hit Tommy, you jerk."

"Now that's uncalled for."

"That's what I'm saying." She found her flip-flops and stepped into them. "Go see Tommy. Make sure he's okay. Talk to him. Then kiss and make up."

"I'll talk to him all right. Maybe I'll blacken his other eye while I'm at it."

"Grow up, Jack."

He gave her one last angry stare and walked away. Once he was out of the room, she heard the two of them yelling again, the sound escalating with each passing second. She shook her head and eased out the front door, pulling the door shut behind her as she hefted her backpack into place.

Finn wobbled down the steps into the shadowed parking lot with its one meager pole giving off little light to see by. She hoped she still had that bottle of aspirin stashed in the glove box. She couldn't believe those two. How could two brothers be so confrontational? It boggled her mind. And, in its current muddled, inebriated state, it wasn't too hard to boggle.

CHAPTER SIXTEEN

Finn stuck her key in the lock of her Bug. An arm came around behind her and caught her around the neck. She screeched.

"You, devil woman, take it back, you."

Finn struggled and managed to duck beneath the arm. She shuffled away to the front of her car, breathing hard. She yanked her backpack off and rummaged through it. "How do you people keep finding me?"

"What you mean? You people?"

"Who are you and what the hell do you want?" She astounded herself with her calm. Maybe being hungover had its advantages.

"I'm Peter La Fontaine. You killed my brother, and put de spell on my personals, me. Take it back, you."

He started for her, his eyes wild, his clothes disarrayed. He smelled as if he hadn't bathed in weeks and his breath, quite possibly worse than her own, could knock down a Clydesdale in mid-gallop.

When he reached for her again, she stepped into him and wrestled him to the ground. She found the pepper spray in her pack and liberally sprayed him. For good measure, she kneed him in the groin. Panting she sat back on the asphalt. His eyes watered, his nose ran. He started howling like a baby as he clutched his groin. "You is crazy."

Finn hadn't thought she could feel worse. This idiot managed it. She leaned over him and patted her backpack. "I have a knife in here. You think things are bad now, but I promise I'll castrate you if you don't leave me alone. There are worse things than not getting it up."

She pushed herself to her feet, brushed off the seat of her pants and held the pepper spray above him. "And, for the record, I didn't kill your brother."

She leaned into her Bug. She pressed the stupid little horn for a solid minute which brought Jack running and Tommy, still dressed in nothing but plaid boxers, hobbling behind him.

La Fontaine pointed at Finn. "I say she's evil, her. She's a evil voodoo priestess who done stole away my manhood."

Jack pulled his cell phone from his pocket. He called for backup while managing a slight grin.

Tommy chuckled. "What's he talking about?"

"I don't care." Finn got in her car and slammed the door behind her. "I'm drunk and annoyed. I'm outta here."

"What'll we tell the cops?" Tommy asked.

"Tell them," she said as she stared at the two brothers, "that an evil voodoo priestess put a spell on him that made him impotent and if she stayed around any longer, she threatened to do the same to any man within ten feet of her."

"Whoa," Jack said, pocketing his phone and backing away. "I promise to be good from now on."

Finn started her car and backed out of her parking space. She rolled down her window. "Like I believe that."

"Are you good to drive?"

"Good enough."

Finn was as hungover as she'd ever been in her life.

She felt sorry for herself and didn't mind admitting it. She sat on a park bench outside Jackson Square watching the tourists walk by and listening to a jazz band that had set up on the steps in front of the Cathedral.

Franco was in jail. No, he was in the hospital with an armed guard who was probably unnecessary. She didn't care but thought it was some kind of crazy karma that he was as violently allergic to poison ivy as Jack was. At least he was no longer able to harass anyone. That anyone being Finn.

Margaret Jane Barron was gone, according to her sister whom Jack was able to track down and talk to. Barron didn't tell her sister all the details, but what she did know was that she'd bought an illegal passport with a fake name and left for an unknown island in the Caribbean that didn't have an extradition treaty with the U.S. government.

That crazy loon, Peter La Fontaine, was either in jail or in a mental hospital. Either way, he was out of her hair.

Debbie was going home to Florida tomorrow to start her junior year of high school. Benjy Arnaud was devastated but his mother thought he would live.

Since Finn had finished her morning walking tour, she had nowhere to go, no classes to attend. Neither a nagging headache nor wallowing in feeling sorry for herself took much energy.

The beautiful, sunny day only added to her irritation. It should at least be overcast and gloomy to match her mood. Rain, no, thunderstorms would be better.

Getting kicked out of culinary school had crushed the life right out of her.

She'd spent one day crying. She then kicked herself in the butt and told herself to get over it. Life would go on, not that she cared all that much. She felt hollow inside. Her dream, for the moment, seemed unattainable.

Finn looked up. She shook her head as the one and only Margaret Jane Barron sashayed toward her with a big smile on her face. "Not you again. I thought you were gone. Where's the fake gun? Gonna try and kidnap me again right here?" She waved her hand around at the crowds of people. "In front of all these tourists?"

"No," she said. Dressed in a fawn-colored skirt and jacket, she looked as out of place in Jackson Square as a pirate at a tea party. "I came to apologize. In person."

Finn eyed her as she sat down next to her, casually crossed her legs and tugged at her skirt. "Oh? I thought you did that already."

"Honestly. I didn't feel like it was fair to you to apologize over the phone or while you were working." She studied Finn a moment, and then gazed across the plaza at two children hop-scotching up and down the Cathedral steps. "I lost my head here in New Orleans. It must be the heat. I'm so not used to it." She wiped a bead of sweat coursing down her brow.

"Uh-huh. The heat." Finn was skeptical. She'd been abused by this woman and didn't much appreciate it. "A phone apology was fine."

"I used to work at a bank."

"That's where you stole the money?" Was she actually having a calm, normal conversation with a woman on the FBI's Most Wanted list? She eyed a pair of New Orleans' finest as they strolled past.

Margaret saw Finn watching the police. "You could turn me in, but I promise you will never see or hear from me again after today."

"Oh-kay." Finn wondered if she was agreeing to something illegal.

"I'm a nice person or at least I used to be. Taking the

money was the easy part. I told myself I deserved it after all the years I gave to them. I worked my way up from teller to loan officer. I was a good girl, did what I was told, worked long hours. My job was my life. I never married, hell, I hardly even dated. I never had kids even though I would have loved to. Instead the bank was it, my whole existence. So after twenty years, what do they do? They promoted Poindexter Adams over me. That was my job as a vice-president and they gave it to that little dweeb."

"Poindexter?"

"No kidding, his real name. His so-called friends called him Dex. I never called him anything but Poindexter, the moron. He only worked there five years but he sucked up to the bosses like a Hoover. He had the nerve to tell me he thought I deserved the job, but, hey, better luck next time."

"So, that's when you took the money?"

"Oh, no, I'd been doing that for years. That was the thing that pushed me over the edge."

"Over the edge?"

"Yep. I took everything I could get my hands on and walked out."

"Don't they audit banks periodically?"

Her eyes gleamed with cunning. "Oh, there are ways around all that if you know what you're doing. I'm pretty smart ordinarily. And I was not a happy camper. It's amazing what a woman can do when she's really motivated."

"Wow."

"Thank you."

"I mean, don't you have any remorse? The money's not yours."

"Grow up. The money is mine now. It's in an offshore account and unless I get picked up here in this hellhole, it's all mine."

"What do you want with me?"

"I want to say I'm sorry is all. I'm sorry I scared you. I'm sorry I scared your sister but she scared me almost as much. She's a wildcat."

"She is," Finn agreed.

"I'm sorry I kidnapped you. I don't know what I was thinking. I'm sorry I chased you through the streets of this God-forsaken town."

"We're hardly God-forsaken."

She continued as if she hadn't heard Finn. "I'm sorry I ever got involved with Johnny Franco. I thought he was harmless, a fun guy who'd give me a good time and then I'd be on my way once I said good-bye to my sister. I'm really sorry I told him about the money."

"Not exactly the way you wanted it to turn out."

"Not exactly." She got to her feet. "I never thought he'd murder anyone because of me, or even for the money. I don't think he cared about me at all, I think it was always the money. Money is the root of all evil."

"I think the quote is, 'love of money is the root of all evil.'"

"Makes more sense when you think about it."

"You would know," Finn said.

"Good-bye. Have a nice life."

"Yeah."

Finn was still contemplating Margaret Barron when a shadow crossed before her.

"I heard."

Finn looked up, shading her eyes from the sun's glare. Emmy, looking as gorgeous and cool as a runway model, stared down at her. She sat beside her, leaned over and gave her a tight hug. She seemed not to care that she might mess the silk scarf knotted around her neck or wrinkle her creamy linen shirt and pants. She held on to Finn, disregarding the tears leaking from Finn's eyes.

"You're back from the south of France." Finn didn't know if she was more surprised that she had any tears left or that Emmy was beside her trying to make her feel better. "How'd you find out?"

She laughed, a deep, sexy sound that made heads turn. "I knew you were going to cooking school already. Tommy let it slip one day over lunch. He was so bedazzled by my looks he let it drop. He called me about what happened at the school."

"I should have known," Finn said in a muffled voice against Emmy's narrow shoulder. "You can let me go now."

She released her hold, then held her by the shoulders and took in her reddened eyes, pink tee, denim shorts and out-of-control curls. "South of France? I wish. I was in Cleveland, Ohio working."

"What?" Finn asked.

"I love you," she said, tears gleaming in her eyes.

"I know."

"I know I don't act like it. I never say it. I'm way cool and act like I know what I'm doing all the time."

"You do. You are."

"It's all a big act. I honestly don't have a clue."

"You're a terrible sister."

"True. But I do keep track of you through Tommy and Jack."

Finn sighed. "Why didn't you call Debbie? She waited and waited for you. You broke her heart."

One lone tear rolled down her flawless cheek. "I was afraid."

"Afraid? You? Afraid of what? She's just a kid. She doesn't understand."

"I don't understand either. I'm seeing a therapist because I don't know why I do the things I do. I alienate the people who love me the most. I'm such a bitch."

Finn nodded. "It's true. You are."

Emmy gave a shaky laugh. "I keep busy so I don't have to deal with my feelings. According to my therapist, the reason I have three jobs and work eighty hours a week is avoidance. If I work and wear myself out, I don't have to deal with messy emotional relationships like family. It's why I date so many men, so I won't get attached to any one of them. People, especially family, know me, know my history and if I don't talk to them, I don't have to worry anyone will delve beyond the outer shell."

"Wow, you got all that from a therapist? I could have told you that for free."

"Not if I didn't talk to you, you couldn't. That's my point." A watery smile lifted her lips. "See, I'd rather pay a fortune to a stranger than have to deal with you guys."

"But Debbie, she doesn't understand."

"I'll call her. I promise."

"How did you find me here anyway?"

"I knew you had a tour this afternoon so I waited until you'd finished, and then followed you here."

"Damn, you could have saved yourself the trouble. I'm not good company."

"It doesn't matter. I'm not either. You can rant and rave about it or about me being a first class bitch. Either way, I'm here for you."

"Who are you and what have you done with my sister?"

"Very funny."

"Better late than never."

"So they say. Whoever they is." She wrapped her arm around Finn. "I've missed you."

"I've cried my eyes out. I'm sick of feeling sorry for myself. I'm sick of myself. The head chef instructor said I could come back, maybe, in the next term."

"That's good. Isn't it? Isn't this what you want? Tommy says your cooking's fantastic. Jack says so, too."

"Even though I poisoned him?"

"You didn't know he was allergic to that spice. Even he didn't know. It could have happened to anyone."

"Yeah, it could have but it happened to me. To me. I've never had the confidence you do. You've always been perfect. Except for the bitchy part, I mean."

"Have you been listening to a word I've been saying? It's all a great big fat act."

"But look at you." She gestured from Emmy's Jimmy Choo-clad feet to her trendy hundred-dollar haircut.

"Come on. It's only the shell. It's not who I am. On the inside I'm insecure, thoughtless, and mean-spirited."

"It all comes out now."

Emmy laughed, then punched Finn in the shoulder. She got to her feet, reaching for her hand. "Come on. Let's get your fortune told. My treat."

Finn stood up, slinging her backpack over her shoulder. "Oh, joy. Even more good news."

"You never know."

They strolled over to the nearest fortune-teller, one of many set up around the square.

She watched as they approached, her Tarot cards and crystal gazing ball spread out before her on a small folding table covered by an orange-fringed tablecloth and shaded by the trees overhead.

She had long black, straggly hair and wore the de rigueur costume of fortune-tellers everywhere—multi-colored broomstick skirt, colored tank, and tons of rings, bangles and necklaces.

"Can I help you?" she asked.

"You can," Emmy assured her with a bright smile.

She pushed Finn into the folding chair opposite the fortune-teller. "My sister needs her fortune told. She's had a really bad week. Maybe some good news will help cheer her up."

"There are no guarantees in the spirit world," she warned in an ominous tone.

"Do your best." Emmy glared at her until her eyes widened. She visibly shivered as if a ghost had walked over her grave. "What do you call yourself?"

"Jane."

Okay. Finn thought they all were Madame this or Madame whatever.

Jane ignored the Tarot cards and crystal ball. She took Finn's hand and turned it palm up. "You have heartache."

"Got that right." Finn nodded in agreement.

"But it will clear up soon. Your love life..."

"What love life?" Finn asked, rolling her eyes.

"Shut up, Finn, and let the woman work."

"You will meet a tall, dark stranger."

"Ha. I work as a tour guide. I meet tall, dark strangers every day."

The woman stared at Finn, her darkly shadowed eyes penetrating through Finn's sarcastic thoughts.

"Okay, all right, I'll shut up."

"Good idea," Emmy said.

"No, no." She shook her head, her lips pursed. "I'm reading it wrong. You aren't going to meet a tall, dark stranger. You already know a tall, dark man who will change your life."

"How?" Finn wondered. "Who?"

"You are on the cusp of change."

"Do you see food in my future? A restaurant?"

"That would be your financial line. I'm looking at your love line."

Finn rolled her eyes again. This was the generic

fortune she was getting? "Do you have specifics?"

"I see a Pisces in your future. I also see death." Jane stole an apprehensive look at Emmy, then shrugged her shoulders. "I can only read what's there."

"At least I'm not a Pisces. Go on." Emmy placed her hands on her hips and tapped the toe of her expensive shoe.

"Not your death," she said, "or the death of a loved one, but someone you know."

Oh, no. No, no, no, no. Enough death already!

Jane turned Finn's hand, so that she held it cupped in the two of hers. "I see love."

"Is this Pisces the love you see?" Finn wanted to know.

"Only the Fates know that."

"Who do we know who's a Pisces?"

Emmy shook her head, then handed over a wad of bills and thanked the strange woman. Finn got to her feet and they walked away.

"I know what you're thinking," Emmy said taking Finn's hand.

"I doubt it. Even I don't know what I'm thinking."

"Things look bleak right now. But you've still got your tour guide job and your job with Tommy. You've got me and Debbie and you've always got Dorie and Dan. And Aunt Gert. And Uncle Finis and Uncle Neville. You have family who loves you. Jack and Tommy, too. Even though they're men and clueless, they'll always have your back."

"I know."

"You'll get back in school and someday you'll have your own place and all of this will be behind you. You'll be rich and famous and you'll have a waiting list of six months to get a table at your very own spectacular restaurant."

"Now you're the fortune-teller?"

"You wait and see if I'm not right."

"From your mouth to God's ear." Finn smiled. She squeezed her hand. "Thanks, Emmy."

It sounded wonderful.

Some day.

First she had to get back into culinary school.

OTHER BOOKS BY AUTHOR

Bad Company
Family Man
Fortune's Treasure

ABOUT THE AUTHOR

Multi-published author Carol Carson was born and raised in central Iowa. She is a former finalist in the Romance Writers of America's Golden Heart contest. An avid bookworm who actually enjoys doing research, her other passions include travel, history, the Kansas City Chiefs, the St. Louis Cardinals and dark chocolate. She has lived in Colorado and Kansas, and currently lives with her husband in a log home on the outskirts of St. Louis, Missouri.

Write to her at **carol.carson@centurytel.net** or check out her website at **www.carolcarsonbooks.com**

Made in the USA
Middletown, DE
06 July 2022